Schott
1921.

THE DOUBLE TRAITOR

"Dear lady," he assured her, "you repay me in one moment for all the weariness of my exile." FRONTISPIECE. *See page 63.*

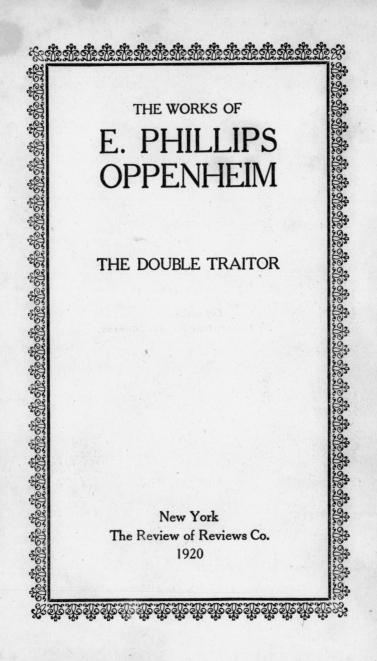

THE WORKS OF

E. PHILLIPS OPPENHEIM

THE DOUBLE TRAITOR

New York
The Review of Reviews Co.
1920

THE DOUBLE TRAITOR

THE DOUBLE TRAITOR

CHAPTER I

The woman leaned across the table towards her companion.

"My friend," she said, "when we first met — I am ashamed, considering that I dine alone with you to-night, to reflect how short a time ago — you spoke of your removal here from Paris very much as though it were a veritable exile. I told you then that there might be surprises in store for you. This restaurant, for instance! We both know our Paris, yet do we lack anything here which you find at the Ritz or Ciro's?"

The young man looked around him appraisingly. The two were dining at one of the newest and most fashionable restaurants in Berlin. The room itself, although a little sombre by reason of its oak panelling, was relieved from absolute gloom by the lightness and elegance of its furniture and appointments, the profusion of flowers, and the soft grey carpet, so thickly piled that every sound was deadened. The delicate strains of music came from an invisible orchestra concealed behind a canopy of palms. The head-waiters had the correct clerical air, half com-

placent, half dignified.   Among the other diners were
many beautiful women in marvellous toilettes.   A
variety of uniforms, worn by the officers at different
tables, gave colour and distinction to a *tout ensemble*
with which even Norgate could find no fault.

"Germany has changed very much since I was
here as a boy," he confessed.   "One has heard of
the growing wealth of Berlin, but I must say that I
scarcely expected —"

He hesitated.   His companion laughed softly at
his embarrassment.

"Do not forget," she interrupted, "that I am
Austrian — Austrian, that is to say, with much English in my blood.   What you say about Germans
does not greatly concern me."

"Of course," Norgate resumed, as he watched the
champagne poured into his glass, "one is too much
inclined to form one's conclusions about a nation
from the types one meets travelling, and you know
what the Germans have done for Monte Carlo and
the Riviera — even, to a lesser extent, for Paris and
Rome.   Wherever they have been, for the last few
years, they seem to have left the trail of the *nouveaux
riches*.   It is not only their clothes but their manners
and bearing which affront."

The woman leaned her head for a moment against
the tips of her slim and beautifully cared for fingers.
She looked steadfastly across the table at her vis-à-
vis.

"Now that you are here," she said softly, "you
must forget those things.   You are a diplomatist,
and it is for you, is it not, outwardly, at any rate, to

see only the good of the country in which your work lies."

Norgate flushed very slightly. His companion's words had savoured almost of a reproof.

"You are quite right," he admitted. "I have been here for a month, though, and you are the first person to whom I have spoken like this. And you yourself," he pointed out, "encouraged me, did you not, when you insisted upon your Austro-English nationality?"

"You must not take me too seriously," she begged, smiling. "I spoke foolishly, perhaps, but only for your good. You see, Mr. Francis Norgate, I am just a little interested in you and your career."

"And I, dear Baroness," he replied, smiling across at her, "am more than a little interested in — you."

She unfurled her fan.

"I believe," she sighed, "that you are going to flirt with me."

"I should enter into an unequal contest," Norgate asserted. "My methods would seem too clumsy, because I should be too much in earnest."

"Whatever the truth may be about your methods," she declared, "I rather like them, or else I should not be risking my reputation in this still prudish city by dining with you alone and without a chaperon. Tell me a little about yourself. We have met three times, is it not — once at the Embassy, once at the Palace, and once when you paid me that call. How old are you? Tell me about your people in England, and where else you have served besides Paris?"

"I am thirty years old," he replied. "I started

at Bukarest. From there I went to Rome. Then I was second attaché at Paris, and finally, as you see, here."

"And your people — they are English, of course?"

"Naturally," he answered. "My mother died when I was quite young, and my father when I was at Eton. I have an estate in Hampshire which seems to get on very well without me."

"And you really care about your profession? You have the real feeling for diplomacy?"

"I think there is nothing else like it in the world," he assured her.

"You may well say that," she agreed enthusiastically. "I think you might almost add that there has been no time in the history of Europe so fraught with possibilities, so fascinating to study, as the present."

He looked at her keenly. It is the first instinct of a young diplomatist to draw in his horns when a beautiful young woman confesses herself interested in his profession.

"You, too, think of these things, then?" he remarked.

She shrugged her shoulders.

"But naturally! What is there to do for a woman but think? We cannot act, or rather, if we do, it is in a very insignificant way. We are lookers-on at most of the things in life worth doing."

"I will spare you all the obvious retorts," he said, "if you will tell me why you are gazing into that mirror so earnestly?"

" I was thinking," she confessed, " what a remarkably good-looking couple we were."

He followed the direction of her eyes. He himself was of a recognised type. His complexion was fair, his face clean-shaven and strong almost to ruggedness. His mouth was firm, his nose thin and straight, his grey eyes well-set. He was over six feet and rather slim for his height. But if his type, though attractive enough, was in its way ordinary, hers was entirely unusual. She, too, was slim, but so far from being tall, her figure was almost petite. Her dark brown hair was arranged in perfectly plain braids behind and with a slight fringe in front. Her complexion was pale. Her features were almost cameo-like in their delicacy and perfection, but any suggestion of coldness was dissipated at once by the extraordinary expressiveness of her mouth and the softness of her deep blue eyes. Norgate looked from the mirror into her face. There was a little smile upon his lips, but he said nothing.

" Some day," she said, " not in the restaurant here but when we are alone and have time, I should so much like to talk with you on really serious matters."

" There is one serious matter," he assured her, " which I should like to discuss with you now or at any time."

She made a little grimace at him.

" Let it be now, then," she suggested, leaning across the table. " We will leave my sort of serious things for another time. I am quite certain that I know where your sort is going to lead us. You are going to make love to me."

"Do you mind?" he asked earnestly.

She became suddenly grave.

"Not yet," she begged. "Let us talk and live nonsense for a few more weeks. You see, I really have not known you very long, have I, and this is a very dangerous city for flirtations. At Court one has to be so careful, and you know I am already considered far too much of a Bohemian here. I was even given to understand, a little time ago, by a very great lady, that my position was quite precarious."

"Does that — does anything matter if —"

"It is not of myself alone that I am thinking. Everything matters to one in your profession," she reminded him pointedly.

"I believe," he exclaimed, "that you think more of my profession than you do of me!"

"Quite impossible," she retorted mockingly. "And yet, as I dare say you have already realised, it is not only the things you say to our statesmen here, and the reports you make, which count. It is your daily life among the people of the nation to which you are attached, the friends you make among them, the hospitality you accept and offer, which has all the time its subtle significance. Now I am not sure, even, that I am a very good companion for you, Mr. Francis Norgate."

"You are a very bad one for my peace of mind," he assured her.

She shook her head. "You say those things much too glibly," she declared. "I am afraid that you have served a very long apprenticeship."

" If I have," he replied, leaning a little across the table, " it has been an apprenticeship only, a probationary period during which one struggles towards the real thing."

" You think you will know when you have found it? " she murmured.

He drew a little breath. His voice even trembled as he answered her. " I know now," he said softly.

Their heads were almost touching. Suddenly she drew apart. He glanced at her in some surprise, conscious of an extraordinary change in her face, of the half-uttered exclamation strangled upon her lips. He turned his head and followed the direction of her eyes. Three young men in the uniform of officers had entered the room, and stood there as though looking about for a table. Before them the little company of head-waiters had almost prostrated themselves. The manager, summoned in breathless haste, had made a reverential approach.

" Who are these young men? " Norgate enquired.

His companion made no reply. Her fine, silky eyebrows were drawn a little closer together. At that moment the tallest of the three newcomers seemed to recognise her. He strode at once towards their table. Norgate, glancing up at his approach, was simply conscious of the coming of a fair young man of ordinary German type, who seemed to be in a remarkably bad temper.

" So I find you here, Anna! "

The Baroness rose as though unwillingly to her feet. She dropped the slightest of curtseys and resumed her place.

" Your visit is a little unexpected, is it not, Karl? " she remarked.

" Apparently! " the young man answered, with an unpleasant laugh.

He turned and stared at Norgate, who returned his regard with half-amused, half-impatient indifference. The Baroness leaned forward eagerly.

" Will you permit me to present Mr. Francis Norgate to you, Karl? "

Norgate, who had suddenly recognised the newcomer, rose to his feet, bowed and remained standing. The Prince's only reply to the introduction was a frown.

" Kindly give me your seat," he said imperatively. " I will conclude your entertainment of the Baroness."

For a moment there was a dead silence. In the background several of the *maîtres d'hôtel* had gathered obsequiously around. For some reason or other, every one seemed to be looking at Norgate as though he were a criminal.

" Isn't your request a little unusual, Prince? " he remarked drily.

The colour in the young man's face became almost purple.

" Did you hear what I said, sir? " he demanded. " Do you know who I am? "

" Perfectly," Norgate replied. " A prince who apparently has not learnt how to behave himself in a public place."

The young man took a quick step forward. Norgate's fists were clenched and his eyes glittering. The Baroness stepped between them.

" Mr. Norgate," she said, " you will please give me your escort home."

The Prince's companions had seized him, one by either arm. An older man who had been dining in a distant corner of the room, and who wore the uniform of an officer of high rank, suddenly approached. He addressed the Prince, and they all talked together in excited whispers. Norgate with calm fingers arranged the cloak around his companion and placed a hundred mark note upon his plate.

" I will return for my change another evening," he said to the dumbfounded waiter. " If you are ready, Baroness."

They left the restaurant amid an intense hush. Norgate waited deliberately whilst the door was somewhat unwillingly held open for him by a *maître d'hôtel*, but outside the Baroness's automobile was summoned at once. She placed her fingers upon Norgate's arm, and he felt that she was shivering.

" Please do not take me home," she faltered. " I am so sorry — so very sorry."

He laughed. " But why? " he protested. " The young fellow behaved like a cub, but no one offered him any provocation. I should think by this time he is probably heartily ashamed of himself. May I come and see you to-morrow? "

" Telephone me," she begged, as she gave him her hand through the window. " You don't quite understand. Please telephone to me."

She suddenly clutched his hand with both of hers and then fell back out of sight among the cushions. Norgate remained upon the pavement until the car had disappeared. Then he looked back once more into the restaurant and strolled across the brilliantly-lit street towards the Embassy.

CHAPTER II

Norgate, during his month's stay in Berlin, had already adopted regular habits. On the following morning he was called at eight o'clock and rode for two hours in the fashionable precincts of the city. The latter portion of the time he spent looking in vain for a familiar figure in a green riding-habit. The Baroness, however, did not appear. At ten o'clock Norgate returned to the Embassy, bathed and breakfasted, and a little after eleven made his way round to the business quarters. One of his fellow-workers there glanced up and nodded at his arrival.

" Where's the Chief? " Norgate enquired.

" Gone down to the Palace," the other young man, whose name was Ansell, replied; " telephoned for the first thing this morning. Ghastly habit William has of getting up at seven o'clock and suddenly remembering that he wants to talk diplomacy. The Chief will be furious all day now."

Norgate lit a cigarette and began to open his letters. Ansell, however, was in a discoursive mood. He swung around from his desk and leaned back in his chair.

" How can a man," he demanded, " see a question from the same point of view at seven o'clock in the morning and seven o'clock in the evening? Absolutely impossible, you know. That's what's the matter with our versatile friend up yonder. He gets all aroused over some scheme or other which comes to him in the dead of night, hops out of bed before any one civilised is awake, and rings up for ambassadors. Then at night-time he becomes normal again and takes everything back. The consequence is that this place is a regular diplomatic see-saw. Settling down in Berlin pretty well, aren't you, Norgate? "

" Very nicely, thanks," the latter replied.

" Dining alone with the Baroness von Haase! " his junior continued. " A Court favourite, too! Never been seen alone before except with her young princeling. What honeyed words did you use, Lothario —"

" Oh, chuck it! " Norgate interrupted. " Tell me about the Baroness von Haase! She is Austrian, isn't she? "

Ansell nodded.

" Related to the Hapsburgs themselves, I believe," he said. " Very old family, anyhow. They say she came to spend a season here because she was a little too go-ahead for the ladies of Vienna. I must say that I've never seen her out without a chaperon before, except with Prince Karl. They say he'd marry her — morganatically, of course — if they'd let him, and if the lady were willing. If you want to know anything more about her, go into Gray's room."

Norgate looked up from his letters.

" Why Gray's room? How does she come into his department? "

Ansell shook his head.

" No idea. I fancy she is there, though."

Norgate left the room a few minutes later, and,

strolling across the hall of the Embassy, made his
way to an apartment at the back of the house. It
was plainly furnished, there were bars across the
window, and three immense safes let into the wall.
An elderly gentleman, with gold-rimmed spectacles
and a very benevolent expression, was busy with
several books of reference before him, seated at a
desk. He raised his head at Norgate's entrance.

"Good morning, Norgate," he said.

"Good morning, sir," Norgate replied.

"Anything in my way?"

Norgate shook his head.

"Chief's gone to the Palace — no one knows why.
I just looked in because I met a woman the other day
whom Ansell says you know something about —
Baroness von Haase."

"Well?"

"Is there anything to be told about her?" Norgate asked bluntly. "I dined with her last night."

"Then I don't think I would again, if I were you,"
the other advised. "There is nothing against her,
but she is a great friend of certain members of the
Royal Family who are not very well disposed towards
us, and she is rather a brainy little person. They
use her a good deal, I believe, as a means of confidential communication between here and Vienna. She
has been back and forth three or four times lately,
without any apparent reason."

Norgate stood with his hands in his pockets, frown-
ing slightly.

"Why, she's half an Englishwoman," he remarked.

"She may be," Mr. Gray admitted drily. "The

other half's Austrian all right, though. I can't tell you anything more about her, my dear fellow. All I can say is that she is in my book, and so long as she is there, you know it's better for you youngsters to keep away. Be off now. I am decoding a dispatch."

Norgate retraced his steps to his own room. Ansell glanced up from a mass of passports as he entered.

"How's the Secret Service Department this morning?" he enquired.

"Old Gray seems much as usual," Norgate grumbled. "One doesn't get much out of him."

"Chief wants you in his room," Ansell announced. "He's just come in from the Palace, looking like nothing on earth."

"Wants me?" Norgate muttered. "Righto!"

He went to the looking-glass, straightened his tie, and made his way towards the Ambassador's private apartments. The latter was alone when he entered, seated before his table. He was leaning back in his chair, however, and apparently deep in thought. He watched Norgate sternly as he crossed the room.

"Good morning, sir," the latter said.

The Ambassador nodded.

"What have you been up to, Norgate?" he asked abruptly.

"Nothing at all that I know of, sir," was the prompt reply.

"This afternoon," the Ambassador continued slowly, "I was to have taken you, as you know, to the Palace to be received by the Kaiser. At seven o'clock this morning I had a message. I have just come from the Palace. The Kaiser has given me to understand that your presence in Berlin is unwelcome."

" Good God! " Norgate exclaimed.

" Can you offer me any explanation? "

For a moment Norgate was speechless. Then he recovered himself. He forgot altogether his habits of restraint. There was an angry note in his tone.

" It's that miserable young cub of a Prince Karl! " he exclaimed. " Last night I was dining, sir, with the Baroness von Haase at the Café de Berlin."

" Alone? "

" Alone," Norgate admitted. " It was not for me to invite a chaperon if the lady did not choose to bring one, was it, sir? As we were finishing dinner, the Prince came in. He made a scene at our table and ordered me to leave."

" And you? " the Ambassador asked.

" I simply treated him as I would any other young ass who forgot himself," Norgate replied indignantly. " I naturally refused to go, and the Baroness left the place with me."

" And you did not expect to hear of this again? "

" I honestly didn't. I should have thought, for his own sake, that the young man would have kept his mouth shut. He was hopelessly in the wrong, and he behaved like a common young bounder."

The Ambassador shook his head slowly.

" Mr. Norgate," he said, " I am very sorry for you, but you are under a misapprehension shared by many young men. You believe that there is a universal standard of manners and deportment, and a

universal series of customs for all nations. You
have our English standard of manners in your mind,
manners which range from a ploughboy to a king,
and you seem to take it for granted that these are
also subscribed to in other countries. In my position I do not wish to say too much, but let me tell you
that in Germany they are not. If a prince here
chooses to behave like a ploughboy, he is right where
the ploughboy would be wrong."

There was a moment's silence. Norgate was looking a little dazed.

"Then you mean to defend —" he began.

"Certainly not," the Ambassador interrupted.
"I am not speaking to you as one of ourselves. I
am speaking as the representative of England in
Berlin. You are supposed to be studying diplomacy.
You have been guilty of a colossal blunder. You
have shown yourself absolutely ignorant of the ideals
and customs of the country in which you are. It is
perfectly correct for young Prince Karl to behave,
as you put it, like a bounder. The people expect it
of him. He conforms entirely to the standard accepted by the military aristocracy of Berlin. It is
you who have been in the wrong — diplomatically."

"Then you mean, sir," Norgate protested, "that
I should have taken it sitting down?"

"Most assuredly you should," the Ambassador replied, "unless you were willing to pay the price.
Your only fault — your personal fault, I mean —
that I can see is that it was a little indiscreet of you
to dine alone with a young woman for whom the
Prince is known to have a foolish passion. Diplo-

matically, however, you have committed every fault possible. I am very sorry, but I think that you had better report in Downing Street as soon as possible. The train leaves, I think, at three o'clock."

Norgate for a moment was unable to speak or move. He was struggling with a sort of blind fury.

" This is the end of me, then," he muttered at last. " I am to be disgraced because I have come to a city of boors."

" You are reprimanded and in a sense, no doubt, punished," the Ambassador explained calmly, " because you have come to — shall I accept your term? — a city of boors and fail to adapt yourself. The true diplomatist adapts himself wherever he may be. My personal sympathies remain with you. I will do what I can in my report."

Norgate had recovered himself.

" I thank you very much, sir," he said. " I shall catch the three o'clock train."

The Ambassador held out his hand. The interview had finished. He permitted himself to speak differently.

" I am very sorry indeed, Norgate, that this has happened," he declared. " We all have our trials to bear in this city, and you have run up against one of them rather before your time. I wish you good luck, whatever may happen."

Norgate clasped his Chief's hand and left the apartment. Then he made his way to his rooms, gave his orders and sent a messenger to secure his seat in the train. Last of all he went to the telephone. He rang up the number which had become already familiar to him, almost with reluctance. He waited for the reply without any pleasurable antici- pations. He was filled with a burning sense of re- sentment, a feeling which extended even to the inno- cent cause of it. Soon he heard her voice.

" That is Mr. Norgate, is it not? "

" Yes," he replied. " I rang up to wish you good-by."

" Good-by! But you are going away, then? "

" I am sent away — dismissed! "

He heard her little exclamation of grief. Its com- plete genuineness broke down a little the wall of his anger.

" And it is my fault! " she exclaimed. " If only I could do anything! Will you wait — please wait? I will go to the Palace myself."

His expostulation was almost a shock to her.

" Baroness," he replied, " if I permitted your inter- vention, I could never hold my head up in Berlin again! In any case, I could not stay here. The first thing I should do would be to quarrel with that insufferable young cad who insulted us last night. I am afraid, at the first opportunity, I should tell —"

" Hush! " she interrupted. " Oh, please hush! You must not talk like this, even over the telephone. Cannot you understand that you are not in Eng- land? "

" I am beginning to realise," he answered gruffly, " what it means not to be in a free country. I am leaving by the three o'clock train, Baroness. Fare- well! "

"But you must not go like this," she pleaded. "Come first and see me."

"No! It will only mean more disgrace for you. Besides — in any case, I have decided to go away without seeing you again."

Her voice was very soft. He found himself gripping the pages of the telephone book which hung by his side.

"But is that kind? Have I sinned, Mr. Francis Norgate?"

"Of course not," he answered, keeping his tone level, almost indifferent. "I hope that we shall meet again some day, but not in Berlin."

There was a moment's silence. He thought, even, that she had gone away. Then her reply came back.

"So be it," she murmured. "Not in Berlin. Au revoir!"

CHAPTER III

Faithful to his insular prejudices, Norgate, on finding that the other seat in his coupé was engaged, started out to find the train attendant with a view to changing his place. His errand, however, was in vain. The train, it seemed, was crowded. He returned to his compartment to find already installed there one of the most complete and absolute types of Germanism he had ever seen. A man in a light grey suit, the waistcoat of which had apparently abandoned its efforts to compass his girth, with a broad, pink, good-humoured face, beardless and bland, flaxen hair streaked here and there with grey, was seated in the vacant place. He had with him a portmanteau covered with a linen case, his boots were a bright shade of yellow, his tie was of white satin with a design of lavender flowers. A pair of black kid gloves lay by his side. He welcomed Norgate with the bland, broad smile of a fellow-passenger whose one desire it is to make a lifelong friend of his temporary companion.

"We have the compartment to ourselves, is it not so? You are English?"

Some queer chance founded upon his ill-humour, his disgust of Germany and all things in it, induced Norgate to tell a deliberate falsehood.

"Sorry," he replied in English. "I don't speak German."

The man's satisfaction was complete.

"But I — I speak the most wonderful English. It pleases me always to speak English. I like to do so. It is practice for me. We will talk English together, you and I. These comic papers, they do not amuse. And books in the train, they make one giddy. What I like best is a companion and a bottle of Rhine wine."

"Personally," Norgate confessed gruffly, "I like to sleep."

The other seemed a little taken aback but remained, apparently, full of the conviction that his overtures could be nothing but acceptable.

"It is well to sleep," he agreed, "if one has worked hard. Now I myself am a hard worker. My name is Selingman. I manufacture crockery which I sell in England. That is why I speak the English language so wonderful. For the last three nights I have been up reading reports of my English customers, going through their purchases. Now it is finished. I am well posted. I am off to sell crockery in London, in Manchester, in Leeds, in Birmingham. I have what the people want. They will receive me with open arms, some of them even welcome me at their houses. Thus it is that I look forward to my business trip as a holiday."

"Very pleasant, I'm sure," Norgate remarked, curling himself up in his corner. "Personally, I can't see why we can't make our own crockery. I get tired of seeing German goods in England."

Herr Selingman was apparently a trifle hurt, but his efforts to make himself agreeable were indomitable.

"If you will," he said, "I can explain why my crockery sells in England where your own fails. For one thing, then, I am cheaper. There is a system at my works, the like of which is not known in England. From the raw material to the finished article I can produce forty per cent. cheaper than your makers, and, mind you, that is not because I save in wages. It is because of the system in the various departments. I do not like to save in wages," he went on. "I like to see my people healthy and strong and happy. I like to see them drink beer after work is over, and on feast days and Sundays I like to see them sit in the gardens and listen to the band, and maybe change their beer for a bottle of wine. Industrially, Mr. Englishman, ours is a happy country."

"Well, I hope you won't think I am rude," Norgate observed, "but from the little I have seen of it I call it a beastly country, and if you don't mind I am going to sleep."

Herr Selingman sat for several moments with his mouth still open. Then he gave a little grunt. There was not the slightest ill-humour in the ejaculation or in his expression. He was simply pained.

"I am sorry if I have talked too much," he said. "I forgot that you, perhaps, are tired. You have met with disappointments, maybe. I am sorry. I will read now and not disturb you."

For an hour or so Norgate tried in vain to sleep. All this time the man opposite turned the pages of his

book with the utmost cautiousness, moved on tiptoe
once to reach down more papers, and held out his
finger to warn the train attendant who came with
some harmless question.

"The English gentleman," Norgate heard him
whisper, "is tired. Let him sleep."

Soon after five o'clock, Norgate gave it up. He
rose to his feet, stretched himself, and was welcomed
with a pleasant smile from his companion.

"You have had a refreshing nap," the latter remarked, "and now, is it not so, you go to take a cup
of English tea?"

"You are quite right," Norgate admitted. "Better come with me."

Herr Selingman smiled a smile of triumph. It was
the reward of geniality, this! He was forming a
new friendship!

"I come with great pleasure," he decided, "only
while you drink the tea, I drink the coffee or some
beer. I will see. I like best the beer," he explained,
turning sidewise to get out of the door, "but it is not
the best for my figure. I have a good conscience
and a good digestion, and I eat and drink much.
But it is good to be happy."

They made their way down to the restaurant car
and seated themselves at a table together.

"You let me do the ordering," Herr Selingman
insisted. "The man here, perhaps, does not speak
English. So! You will drink your tea with me,
sir. It is a great pleasure to me to entertain an
Englishman. I make many friends travelling. I
like to make friends. I remember them all, and some-

times we meet again. *Kellner*, some tea for the gentleman — English tea with what you call bread and butter. So! And for me —" Selingman paused for a moment and drew a deep sigh of resignation —" some coffee."

" Very kind of you, I'm sure," Norgate murmured.

Herr Selingman beamed.

" It is a great pleasure," he said, " but many times I wonder why you Englishmen, so clever, so world-conquering, do not take the trouble to make yourselves with the languages of other nations familiar. It means but a little study. Now you, perhaps, are in business? "

" Not exactly," Norgate replied grimly. " To tell you the truth, at the present moment I have no occupation."

" No occupation! "

Herr Selingman paused in the act of conveying a huge portion of rusk to his mouth, and regarded his companion with wonder.

" So! " he repeated. " No occupation! Well, that is what in Germany we know nothing of. Every one must work, or must take up the army as a permanent profession. You are, perhaps, one of those Englishmen of whom one reads, who give up all their time to sport? "

Norgate shook his head.

" As a matter of fact," he said, " I have worked rather hard during the last five or six years. It is only just recently that I have lost my occupation."

Herr Selingman's curiosity was almost childlike in its transparency, but Norgate found himself unable to gratify it. In any case, after his denial of any knowledge of the German language, he could scarcely lay claim to even the most indirect connection with the diplomatic service.

"Ah, well," Herr Selingman declared, "opportunities will come. You have perhaps lost some post. Well, there are others. I should not, I think, be far away from the truth, sir, if I were to surmise that you had held some sort of an official position?"

"Perhaps," Norgate assented.

"That is interesting," Herr Selingman continued. "Now with the English of commerce I talk often, and I know their views of me and my country. But sometimes I have fancied that among your official classes those who are ever so slightly employed in Government service, there is — I do not love the word, but I must use it — a distrust of Germany and her peace-loving propensities."

"I have met many people," Norgate admitted, "who do not look upon Germany as a lover of peace."

"They should come and travel here," Herr Selingman insisted eagerly. "Look out of the windows. What do you see? Factory chimneys, furnaces everywhere. And further on — what? Well-tilled lands, clean, prosperous villages, a happy, domestic people. I tell you that no man in the world is so fond of his wife and children, his simple life, his simple pleasures, as the German."

"Very likely," Norgate assented, "but if you look out of the windows continually you will also see that every station-master on the line wears a military uniform, that every few miles you see barracks. These simple peasants you speak of carry themselves with a different air from ours. I don't know much about it, but I should call it the effect of their military training. I know nothing about politics. Very likely yours is a nation of peace-loving men. As a casual observer, I should call you more a nation of soldiers."

" But that," Herr Selingman explained earnestly, " is for defence only."

" And your great standing army, your wonderful artillery, your Zeppelins and your navy," Norgate asked, " are they for defence only? "

" Absolutely and entirely," Herr Selingman declared, with a new and ponderous gravity. " There is nothing the most warlike German desires more fervently than to keep the peace. We are strong only because we desire peace, peace under which our commerce may grow, and our wealth increase."

" Well, it seems to me, then," Norgate observed, " that you've gone to a great deal of expense and taken a great deal of trouble for nothing. I don't know much about these things, as I told you before, but there is no nation in the world who wants to attack Germany."

Herr Selingman laid his finger upon his nose.

" That may be," he said. " Yet there are many who look at us with envious eyes. I am a good German. I know what it is that we want. We want peace, and to gain peace we need strength, and to be strong we arm. That is everything. It will never be Germany who clenches her fist, who draws down the black clouds of war over Europe. It will never be Germany, I tell you. Why, a war would ruin half of us. What of my crockery? I sell it all in England. Believe me, young gentleman, war exists only in the brains of your sensational novelists. It does not come into the world of real purpose."

"Well, it's very interesting to hear you say so," Norgate admitted. "I wish I could wholly agree with you."

Herr Selingman caught him by the sleeve.

"You are just a little," he confided, "just a little suspicious, my young friend, you in your little island. Perhaps it is because you live upon an island. You do not expand. You have small thoughts. You are not great like we in Germany, not broad, not deep. But we will talk later of these things. I must tell you about our Kaiser."

Norgate opened his lips and closed them again.

"Presently," he muttered. "See you later on."

He strolled to his coupé, tried in vain to read, walked up and down the length of the train, smoked a cigarette, and returned to his compartment to find Herr Selingman immersed in the study of many documents.

"Records of my customers and my transactions," the latter announced blandly. "I have a great fondness for detail. I know everything. I carry with me particulars of everything. That is where we Germans are so thorough. See, I place them now all in my bag."

He did so and locked it with great care.

"We go to dinner, is it not so?" he suggested.

" I suppose we may as well," Norgate assented indifferently.

They found places in the crowded restaurant car. The manufacturer of crockery made a highly satisfactory and important meal. Norgate, on the other hand, ate little. Herr Selingman shook his head.

" My young English friend," he declared, " all is not well with you that you turn away from good food. Come. Afterwards, over a cigar, you shall tell me what troubles you have, and I will give you sound advice. I have a very wide knowledge of life. I have a way of seeing the truth, and I like to help people."

Norgate shook his head. " I am afraid," he said, " that my case is hopeless."

" Presently we will see," Herr Selingman continued, rubbing the window with his cuff. " We are arrived, I think, at Lesel. Here will board the train one of my agents. He will travel with us to the next station. It is my way of doing business, this. It is better than alighting and wasting a day in a small town. You will not mind, perhaps," he added, " if I bring him into the carriage and talk? You do not understand German, so it will not weary you."

" Certainly not," Norgate replied. " I shall probably drop off to sleep."

" He will be in the train for less than an hour," Herr Selingman explained, " but I have many competitors, and I like to talk in private. In here some one might overhear."

" How do you know that I am not an English crockery manufacturer? " Norgate remarked.

Herr Selingman laughed heartily. His stomach shook, and tears rolled down his eyes.

" That is good!" he exclaimed. " An English crockery manufacturer! No, I do not think so! I cannot see you with your sleeves turned up, walking amongst the kilns. I cannot see you, even, studying the designs for pots and basins."

" Well, bring your man in whenever you want to," Norgate invited, as he turned away. " I can promise, at least, that I shall not understand what you are saying, and that I won't sneak your designs."

There was a queer little smile on Herr Selingman's broad face. It almost seemed as though he had discovered some hidden though unsuspected meaning in the other's words.

CHAPTER IV

Norgate dozed fitfully as the train sped on through the darkness. He woke once to find Herr Selingman in close confabulation with his agent on the opposite side of the compartment. They had a notebook before them and several papers spread out upon the seat. Norgate, who was really weary, closed his eyes again, and it seemed to him that he dreamed for a few moments. Then suddenly he found himself wide-awake. Although he remained motionless, the words which Selingman had spoken to his companion were throbbing in his ears.

"I do not doubt your industry, Meyer, but it is your discretion which is sometimes at fault. These plans of the forts of Liège — they might as well be published in a magazine. We had them when they were made. We have received copies of every alteration. We know to a metre how far the guns will carry, how many men are required to man them, what stocks of ammunition are close at hand. Understand, therefore, my friend, that the sight of these carefully traced plans, which you hint to have obtained at the risk of your life, excites me not at all."

The other man's reply was inaudible. In a moment or two Selingman spoke again.

"The information which I am lacking just at present in your sphere of operations, is civilian in character. Take Ghent, for instance. What I should like here, what our records need at present, is a list of the principal inhabitants with their approximate income, and, summarising it all, the rateable value of the city. With these bases it would be easy to fix a reasonable indemnity."

Norgate was wide-awake now. He was curled up on his seat, underneath his rug, and though his eye-lids had quivered with a momentary excitement, he was careful to remain as near as possible motionless. Again Selingman's agent spoke, this time more distinctly.

"The young man opposite," he whispered. "He is English, surely?"

"He is English indeed," Selingman admitted, "but he speaks no German. That I have ascertained. Give me your best attention, Meyer. Here is again an important commission for you. Within the next few days, hire an automobile and visit the rising country eastwards from Antwerp. At some spot between six and eight miles from the city, on a slight incline and commanding the River Scheldt, we desire to purchase an acre of land for the erection of a factory. You can say that we have purchased the concession for making an American safety razor. The land is wanted, and urgently. See to this your-self and send plans and price to me in London. On my return I shall call and inspect the sites and close the bargain."

"And the Antwerp forts?"

The other pursed his lips.

"Pooh! Was it not the glorious firm of Krupp

who fitted the guns there? Do you think the men
who undertook that task were idle? I tell you that
our plans of the Antwerp fortifications are more
carefully worked out in detail than the plans held by
the Belgians themselves. Here is good work for you
to do, friend Meyer. That and the particulars from
Brussels which you know of, will keep you busy until
we meet again."

Herr Selingman began to collect his papers, but
was suddenly thrown back into his seat by the rock-
ing of the train, which came, a few moments later, to
a standstill. The sound of the opening of windows
from the other side of the corridor was heard all down
the train. Selingman and his companion followed
the general example, opening the door of the carriage
and the window opposite. A draught blew through
the compartment. One of the small folded slips of
paper from Selingman's pocket-book fluttered along
the seat. It came within reach of Norgate. Cautiously he stretched out his fingers and gripped it.
In a moment it was in his pocket. He sat up in his
place. Selingman had turned around.

" Anything the matter? " Norgate asked sleepily.

" Not that one can gather," Selingman replied.
" You have slept well. I am glad that our conversation has not disturbed you. This is my agent from
Brussels — Mr. Meyer. He sells our crockery in
that city — not so much as he should sell, perhaps,
but still he does his best."

Mr. Meyer was a dark little man who wore gold-
rimmed spectacles, neat clothes, and a timid smile.
Norgate nodded to him good-humouredly.

" You should get Herr Selingman to come oftener and help you," he remarked, yawning. " I can imagine that he would be able to sell anything he tried to."

" It is what I often tell him, sir," Mr. Meyer replied, " but he is too fond of the English trade."

" English money is no better than Belgian," Herr Selingman declared, " but there is more of it. Let us go round to the restaurant car and drink a bottle of wine together while the beds are prepared."

" Certainly," Norgate assented, stretching himself. " By-the-by, you had better look after your papers there, Herr Selingman. Just as I woke up I saw a small slip fluttering along the seat. You made a most infernal draught by opening that door, and I almost fancy it went out of the window."

Herr Selingman's face became suddenly grave. He went through the papers one by one, and finally locked them up in his bag.

" Nothing missing, I hope? " Norgate asked.

Herr Selingman's face was troubled.

" I am not sure," he said. " It is my belief that I had with me here a list of my agents in England. I cannot find it. In a sense it is unimportant, yet if a rival firm should obtain possession of it, there might be trouble."

Norgate looked out into the night and smiled.

" Considering that it is blowing half a hurricane and commencing to rain," he remarked, " the slip of paper which I saw blowing about will be of no use to any one when it is picked up."

They called the attendant and ordered him to prepare the sleeping berths. Then they made their way down to the buffet car, and Herr Selingman ordered a bottle of wine.

" We will drink," he proposed, " to our three countries. In our way we represent, I think, the industrial forces of the world — Belgium, England, and Germany. We are the three countries who stand for commerce and peace. We will drink prosperity to ourselves and to each other."

Norgate threw off, with apparent effort, his sleepiness.

" What you have said about our three countries is very true," he remarked. " Perhaps as you, Mr. Meyer, are a Belgian, and you, Mr. Selingman, know Belgium well and have connections with it, you can tell me one thing which has always puzzled me. Why is it that Belgium, which is, as you say, a commercial and peace-loving country, whose neutrality is absolutely guaranteed by three of the greatest Powers in Europe, should find it necessary to have spent such large sums upon fortifications? "

" In which direction do you mean? " Selingman asked, his eyes narrowing a little as he looked across at Norgate.

" The forts of Liège and Namur," Norgate replied, " and Antwerp. I know nothing more about it than I gathered from an article which I read not long ago in a magazine. I had always looked upon Belgium as being outside the pale of possible warfare, yet according to this article it seems to be bristling to the teeth with armaments."

Herr Selingman cleared his throat.

" I will tell you the reason," he said. " You have come to the right man to know. I am a civilian, but there are few things in connection with my country which I do not understand. Mr. Meyer here, who is a citizen of Brussels, will bear me out. It is the book of a clever, intelligent, but misguided German writer which has been responsible for Belgium's unrest — Bernhardi's *Germany and the Next War* — that and articles of a similar tenor which preceded it."

" Never read any of them," Norgate remarked.

" It was erroneously supposed," Selingman continued, " that Bernhardi represented the dominant military opinion of Germany when he wrote that if Germany ever again invaded France, it would be, notwithstanding her guarantees of neutrality, through Belgium. Bernhardi was a clever writer, but he was a soldier, and soldiers do not understand the world policy of a great nation such as Germany. Germany will make no war upon any one, save commercially. She will never again invade France except under the bitterest provocation, and if ever she should be driven to defend herself, it will assuredly not be at the expense of her broken pledges. The forts of Belgium might just as well be converted into apple-orchards. They stand there to-day as the proof of a certain lack of faith in Germany on the part of Belgium, ministered to by that King of the Jingoes, as you would say in English, Bernhardi. How often it is that a nation suffers most from her own patriots ! "

" Herr Selingman has expressed the situation admirably," Mr. Meyer declared approvingly.

" Very interesting, I'm sure," Norgate murmured. " There is one thing about you foreigners," he added, with an envious sigh. " The way you all speak the languages of other countries is wonderful. Are you a Belgian, Mr. Meyer?"

" Half Belgian and half French."

" But you speak English almost without accent," Norgate remarked.

" In commerce," Herr Selingman insisted, " that is necessary. All my agents speak four languages."

" You deserve to capture our trade," Norgate sighed.

" To a certain extent, my young friend," Selingman declared, " we mean to do it. We are doing it. And yet there is enough for us both. There is trade enough for your millions and for mine. So long as Germany and England remain friends, they can divide the commerce of the world between them. It is our greatest happiness, we who have a business rely-ing upon the good-will of the two nations, to think that year by year the clouds of discord are rolling away from between us. Young sir, as a German citizen, I will drink a toast with you, an English one. I drink to everlasting peace between my country and yours!"

Norgate drained his glass. Selingman threw back his head as he followed suit, and smacked his lips appreciatively.

" And now," the former remarked, rising to his feet, " I think I'll go and turn in. I dare say you two still have some business to talk about, especially if Mr. Meyer is leaving us shortly."

Norgate made his way back to his compartment, undressed leisurely and climbed into the upper bunk. For an hour or two he indulged in the fitful slumber usually engendered by night travelling. At the frontier he sat up and answered the stereotyped questions. Herr Selingman, in sky-blue pyjamas, and with face looking more beaming and florid than ever, poked his head cheerfully out of the lower bunk.

" Awake? " he enquired.

" Very much so," Norgate yawned.

" I have a surprise," Herr Selingman announced. " Wait."

Almost as he spoke, an attendant arrived from the buffet car with some soda-water. Herr Selingman's head vanished for a moment or two. When he re-appeared, he held two glasses in his hand.

" A whisky soda made in real English fashion," he proclaimed triumphantly. " A good nightcap, is it not? Now we are off again."

Norgate held out his hand for the tumbler.

" Awfully good of you," he murmured.

" I myself," Selingman continued, seated on the edge of the bunk, with his legs far apart to steady himself, " I myself enjoy a whisky soda. It will be indeed a nightcap, so here goes."

He drained his glass and set it down. Norgate followed suit. Selingman's hand came up for the tumbler and Norgate was conscious of a curious mixture of sensations which he had once experienced before in the dentist's chair. He could see Selingman distinctly, and he fancied that he was watching him closely, but the rest of the carriage had become chaos.

The sound of the locomotive was beating hard upon the drums of his ears. His head fell back.

It was broad daylight when he awoke. Selingman, fully dressed and looking more beaming than ever, was seated upon a ridiculously inadequate camp-stool upon the floor, smoking a cigarette. Norgate stared at him stupidly.

" My young friend," Herr Selingman declared impressively, " if there is one thing in the world I envy you, it is that capacity for sleep. You all have it, you English. Your heads touch the pillow, and off you go. Do you know that the man is waiting for you to take your coffee? "

Norgate lay quite still for several moments. Beyond a slight headache, he was feeling as usual. He leaned over the side of the bunk.

" How many whiskies and soda did I have last night? " he asked.

Herr Selingman smiled.

" But one only," he announced. " There was only one to be had. I found a little whisky in my flask. I remembered that I had an English travelling companion, and I sent for some soda-water. You drank yours, and you did sleep. I go now and sit in the corridor while you dress."

Norgate swung round in his bunk and slipped to the floor.

" Jolly good of you," he muttered sleepily, " but it was very strong whisky."

CHAPTER V

There was a babel of voices as the long train came to a stand-still in the harbour station at Ostend. Selingman, with characteristic forcefulness, pushed his way down the narrow corridor, driving before him passengers of less weight and pertinacity, until finally he descended on to the platform itself. Norgate, who had followed meekly in his wake, stood listening for a moment to the confused stream of explanations. He understood well enough what had happened, but with Selingman at his elbow he assumed an air of non-comprehension.

"It is extraordinary!" the latter exclaimed. "Never do I choose this route but I am visited with some mishap. You hear what has happened?"

"Fellow's trying to tell me," Norgate replied, "but his Flemish is worse to understand than German."

"The steamer," Selingman announced, "has met with an accident entering the harbour. There will be a delay of at least six hours — possibly more. It is most annoying. My appointments in London have been fixed for days."

"Bad luck!" Norgate murmured.

"You do not seem much distressed."

"Why should I be? I really came this way because I was not sure whether I would not stay here for a few days."

"That is all very well for you," Selingman declared, as they followed their porters into the shed. "For me, I am a man of affairs. It is different. My business goes by clockwork. All is regulated by rule, with precision, with punctuality. Now I shall be many hours behind my schedule. I shall be compelled to alter my appointments — I, who pride myself always upon altering nothing. But behold! One must make the best of things. What a sunshine! What a sea! We shall meet, without a doubt, upon the Plage. I have friends here. I must seek them. Au revoir, my young travelling companion. To the good fortune!"

They drifted apart, and Norgate, having made arrangements about his luggage, strolled through the town and on to the promenade. It was early for the full season at Ostend, but the sands were already crowded with an immense throng of children and holiday-makers. The hotels were all open, and streams of people were passing back and forth along the front. Norgate, who had no wish to meet acquaintances, passed the first period of his enforced wait a little wearily. He took a taxicab and drove as far as Knocke. Here he strolled across the links and threw himself down finally amongst a little wave of sandy hillocks close to the sea. The silence, and some remains of the sleepiness of the previous night, soon began to have their natural effect. He closed his eyes and began to doze. When he awoke, curiously enough, it was a familiar voice which first fell upon his ears. He turned his head cautiously. Seated not a dozen yards away from him was a tall, thin man with a bag of golf clubs by his side. He was listening with an air of engrossed attention to his companion's impressive remarks. Norgate, raising himself upon his elbow, no longer had any doubts. The man stretched upon his back on the sand, partly hidden from sight by a little grass-grown undulation, was his late travelling companion.

"You do well, my dear Marquis, believe me!" the latter exclaimed. "Property in Belgium is valuable to-day. Take my advice. Sell. There are so many places where one may live, where the climate is better for a man of your constitution."

"That is all very well," his companion replied querulously, "but remember that Belgium, after all, is my country. My château and estates came to me by inheritance. Notwithstanding the frequent intermarriages of my family with the aristocracy of your country, I am still a Belgian."

"Ah! but, my dear friend," Selingman protested, "you are more than a Belgian, more than a man of local nationality. You are a citizen of the world of intelligence. You are able to see the truth. The days are coming when small states may exist no longer without the all-protecting arm of a more powerful country. I say no more than this. The position of Belgium is artificial. Of her own will, or of necessity, she must soon become merged in the onward flow of mightier nations."

"What about Holland, then?"

"Holland, too," Selingman continued, "knows the

truth. She knows very well that the limit of her days as an independent kingdom is almost reached. The Power which has absorbed the states of Prussia into one mighty empire, pauses only to take breath. There are many signs —"

" But, my worthy friend," the other man interrupted irritably, " you must take into consideration the fact that Belgium is in a different position. Our existence as a separate kingdom might certainly be threatened by Germany, but all that has been foreseen. Our neutrality is guaranteed. Your country has pledged its honour to maintain it, side by side with France and England. What have we to fear, then? "

" You have to fear, Marquis," Selingman replied ponderously, " the inevitable laws which direct the progress of nations. Treaties solemnly subscribed to in one generation become worthless as time passes and conditions change."

" But I do not understand you there! " the other man exclaimed. " What you say sounds to me like a reflection upon the honour of your country. Do you mean to insinuate that she would possibly — that she would ever for a moment contemplate breaking her pledged and sealed word? "

" My friend," Selingman pronounced drily, " the path of honour and glory, the onward progress of a mighty, struggling nation, carrying in its hand culture and civilisation, might demand even such a sacrifice. Germany recognises, is profoundly imbued with the splendour of her own ideals, the matchlessness of her own culture. She feels justified in spreading herself out wherever she can find an outlet — at any cost, mind, because the end must be good."

There was a moment's silence. Then the tall man stood upright.

" If you came out to find me, my friend Selingman, to bring me this warning, I suppose I should consider myself your debtor. As a matter of fact, I do not. You have inspired me with nameless misgivings. Your voice sounds in my ears like the voice of an ugly fate. I am, as you have often reminded me, half German, and I have shown my friendship for Germany many times. Unlike most of the aristocracy of my country, I look more often northwards than towards the south. But I tell you frankly that there are limits to my Germanism. I will play no more golf. I will walk with you to the club-house."

" All that I have to say," Selingman went on, " is not yet said. This opportunity of meeting you is too precious to be wasted. Come. As we walk there are certain questions I wish to put to you."

They passed within a few feet of where Norgate was lying. He closed his eyes and held his breath. It was not until their figures were almost specks in the distance that he rose cautiously to his feet. He made his way back to the club-house by another angle, gained his taxicab unobserved, and drove back to Ostend.

Towards evening Norgate strolled into one of the cosmopolitan bars at the back of the Casino. The first person he saw as he handed over his hat to a waiter, was Selingman, spread out upon a cushioned seat with a young lady upon either side of him. He at once summoned Norgate to his table.

" An *apéritif*," he insisted. " Come, you must not refuse me. In two hours we start. We tear ourselves away from this wonderful atmosphere. In atmosphere, mademoiselle," he added, bowing to the right and the left, " all is included."

" It is not," Norgate admitted, " an invitation to be disregarded. On the other hand, I have already an appetite."

Selingman thundered out an order.

" Here," he remarked, " we dwell for a few brief moments in Bohemia. I do not introduce you. You sit down and join us. You are one of us. That you speak only English counts for nothing. Mademoiselle Alice here is American. Now tell us at once, how have you spent this afternoon? You have bathed, perhaps, or walked upon the sands? "

Norgate was on the point of speaking of his excursion to Knocke but was conscious of Selingman's curiously intent gaze. The spirit of duplicity seemed to grow upon him.

" I walked for a little way," he said. " Afterwards I lay upon the sands and slept. When I found that the steamer was still further delayed, I had a bath. That was half an hour ago. I asked a man whom I met on the promenade where one might dine in travelling clothes, lightly but well, and he sent me here — the Bar de Londres — and here, for my good fortune, I am."

" It is a pity that monsieur does not speak French," one of Selingman's companions murmured.

" But, mademoiselle," Norgate protested, " I have spoken French all my life. Herr Selingman here has misunderstood me. It is German of which I am ignorant."

The young lady, who immediately introduced herself as Mademoiselle Henriette, passed her arm through Selingman's.

" We dine here all together, my friend, is it not so? " she begged. " He will not be in the way, and for myself, I am *triste*. You talk all the time to Mademoiselle l'Américaine, perhaps because she is the friend of some one in whom you are interested. But for me, it is dull. Monsieur l'Anglais shall talk with me, and you may hear all the secrets that Alice has to tell. We," she murmured, looking up at Norgate, " will speak of other things, is it not so? "

For a moment Selingman hesitated. Norgate would have moved on with a little farewell nod, but Selingman's companions were insistent.

" It shall be a *partie carrée*," they both declared, almost in unison.

" You need have no fear," Mademoiselle Henriette continued. " I will talk all the time to monsieur. He shall tell me his name, and we shall be very great friends. I am not interested in the things of which they talk, those others. You shall tell me of London, monsieur, and how you live there."

" Join us, by all means," Selingman invited.

" On condition that you dine with me," Norgate insisted, as he took up the menu.

" Impossible! " Selingman declared firmly.

" Oh! it matters nothing," Mademoiselle Henriette exclaimed, " so long as we dine."

" So long," Mademoiselle Alice intervened, " as we have this brief glimpse of Mr. Selingman, let us make the best of it. We see him only because of a *contretemps*. I think we must be very nice to him and persuade him to take us to London to-night."

Selingman's shake of the head was final.

" Dear young ladies," he said, " it was delightful to find you here. I came upon the chance, I admit, but who in Ostend would not be here between six and eight? We dine, we walk down to the quay, and if you will, you shall wave your hands and wish us *bon voyage*, but London just now is *triste*. It is here you may live the life the *bon Dieu* sends, where the sun shines all the time and the sea laps the sands like a great blue lake, and you, mademoiselle, can wear those wonderful costumes and charm all hearts. There is nothing like that for you in London."

They ordered dinner and walked afterwards down to the quay. Mademoiselle Henriette lingered behind with Norgate.

" Let them go on," she whispered. " They have much to talk about. It is but a short distance, and your steamer will not start before ten. We can walk slowly and listen to the music. You are not in a hurry, monsieur, to depart? Your stay here is too short already."

Norgate's reply, although gallant enough, was a little vague. He was watching Selingman with his companion. They were talking together with undoubted seriousness.

" Who is Mr. Selingman? " he enquired. " I know him only as a travelling companion."

Mademoiselle Henriette extended her hands. She shrugged her little shoulders and looked with wide-open eyes up into her companion's grave face.

" But who, indeed, can answer that question? " she exclaimed. " Twice he has been here for flying visits. Once Alice has been to see him in Berlin. He is, I believe, a very wealthy manufacturer there. He crosses often to England. He has money, and he is always gay."

" And Mademoiselle Alice? "

" Who knows? " was the somewhat pointless reply. " She came from America. She arrived here this season with Monsieur le Général."

" What General? " Norgate asked. " A Belgian? "

" But no," his companion corrected. " All the world knows that Alice is the friend of General le Foys, chief of the staff in Paris. He is a very great soldier. He spends eleven months working and one month here."

" And she is also," Norgate observed meditatively, " the friend of Herr Selingman. Tell me, mademoiselle, what do you suppose those two are talking of now? See how close their heads are together. I don't think that Herr Selingman is a Don Juan."

" They speak, perhaps, of serious matters," his companion surmised, " but who can tell? Besides, is it for us to waste our few moments wondering? You will come back to Ostend, monsieur? "

Norgate looked back at the streaming curve of lights flashing across the dark waters.

" One never knows," he answered.

" That is what Monsieur Selingman himself says," she remarked, with a little sigh. " ' Enjoy your Ostend to-day, my little ones,' he said, when he first met us this evening. ' One never knows how long these days will last.' So, monsieur, we must indeed part here? "

They had all come to a standstill at the gangway of the steamer. Selingman had apparently finished his conversation with his companion. He hurried Norgate off, and they waved their hands from the deck as a few minutes later the steamer glided away.

" A most delightful interlude," Selingman declared. " I have thoroughly enjoyed these few hours. I trust that every time this steamer meets with a little accident, it will be at this time of the year and when I am on my way to England."

" You seem to have friends everywhere," Norgate observed, as he lit a cigar.

" Young ladies, yes," Selingman admitted. " It chanced that they were both well-known to me. But who else? "

Norgate made no reply. He felt that his companion was watching him.

" It is something," he remarked, " to find charming young ladies in a strange place to dine with one."

Selingman smiled broadly.

" If we travelled together often, my young friend," he said, " you would discover that I have friends everywhere. If I have nothing else to do, I go out and make a friend. Then, when I revisit that place, it loses its coldness. There is some one there to welcome me, some one who is glad to see me again. Look steadily in that direction, a few points to the left of the bows. In two hours' time you will see the lights of your country. I have friends there, too, who will welcome me. Meantime, I go below to sleep. You have a cabin?"

Norgate shook his head.

"I shall doze on deck for a little time," he said. "It is too wonderful a night to go below."

"It is well for me that it is calm," Selingman acknowledged. "I do not love the sea. Shall we part for a little time? If we meet not at Dover, then in London, my young friend. London is the greatest city in the world, but it is the smallest place in Europe. One cannot move in the places one knows of without meeting one's friends."

"Until we meet in London, then," Norgate observed, as he settled himself down in his chair.

CHAPTER VI

Norgate spent an utterly fruitless morning on the day after his arrival in London. After a lengthy but entirely unsatisfactory visit to the Foreign Office, he presented himself soon after midday at Scotland Yard.

" I should like," he announced, " to see the Chief Commissioner of the Police."

The official to whom he addressed his enquiry eyed him tolerantly.

" Have you, by any chance, an appointment? " he asked.

" None," Norgate admitted. " I only arrived from the Continent this morning."

The policeman shook his head slowly.

" It is quite impossible, sir," he said, " to see Sir Philip without an appointment. Your best course would be to write and state your business, and his secretary will then fix a time for you to call."

" Very much obliged to you, I'm sure," Norgate replied. " However, my business is urgent, and if I can't see Sir Philip Morse, I will see some one else in authority."

Norgate was regaled with a copy of *The Times* and a seat in a barely-furnished waiting-room. In about twenty minutes he was told that a Mr. Tyritt would see him, and was promptly shown into the presence of that gentleman. Mr. Tyritt was a burly and black-bearded person of something more than middle-age. He glanced down at Norgate's card in a somewhat puzzled manner and motioned him to a seat.

" What can I do for you, sir? " he enquired. " Sir Philip is very much engaged for the next few days, but perhaps you can tell me your business? "

" I have just arrived from Berlin," Norgate explained. " Would you care to possess a complete list of German spies in this country? "

Mr. Tyritt's face was not one capable of showing the most profound emotion. Nevertheless, he seemed a little taken aback.

" A list of German spies? " he repeated. " Dear me, that sounds very interesting! "

He took up Norgate's card and glanced at it. The action was, in its way, significant.

" You probably don't know who I am," Norgate continued. " I have been in the Diplomatic Service for eight years. Until a few days ago, I was attached to the Embassy in Berlin."

Mr. Tyritt was somewhat impressed by the statement.

" Have you any objection to telling me how you became possessed of this information? "

" None whatever," was the prompt reply. " You shall hear the whole story."

Norgate told him, as briefly as possible, of his meeting with Selingman, their conversation, and the subsequent happenings, including the interview which he had overheard on the golf links at Knocke. When he had finished, there was a brief silence.

" Sounds rather like a page out of a novel, doesn't it, Mr. Norgate? " the police official remarked at last.

" It may," Norgate assented drily. " I can't help what it sounds like. It happens to be the exact truth."

" I do not for a moment doubt it," the other declared politely. " I believe, indeed, that there are a large number of Germans working in this country who are continually collecting and forwarding to Berlin commercial and political reports. Speaking on behalf of my department, however, Mr. Norgate," he went on, " this is briefly our position. In the neighbourhood of our naval bases, our dockyards, our military aëroplane sheds, and in other directions which I need not specify, we keep the most scrupulous and exacting watch. We even, as of course you are aware, employ decoy spies ourselves, who work in conjunction with our friends at Whitehall. Our system is a rigorous one and our supervision of it unceasing. But — and this is a big ' but,' Mr. Norgate — in other directions — so far as regards the country generally, that is to say — we do not take the subject of German spies seriously. I may almost say that we have no anxiety concerning their capacity for mischief."

" Those are the views of your department? " Norgate asked.

" So far as I may be said to represent it, they are," Mr. Tyritt assented. " I will venture to say that there are many thousands of letters a year which leave this country, addressed to Germany, purporting to contain information of the most important nature, which might just as well be published in the newspapers. We ought to know, because at different times we have opened a good many of them."

"Forgive me if I press this point," Norgate begged. "Do you consider that because a vast amount of useless information is naturally sent, that fact lessens the danger as a whole? If only one letter in a thousand contains vital information, isn't that sufficient to raise the subject to a more serious level?"

Mr. Tyritt crossed his legs. His tone still indicated the slight tolerance of the man convinced beforehand of the soundness of his position.

"For the last twelve years," he announced,— "ever since I came into office, in fact,— this bogey of German spies has been costing the nation something like fifty thousand a year. It is only lately that we have come to take that broader view of the situation which I am endeavouring to — to — may I say enunciate? Germans over in this country, especially those in comparatively menial positions, such as barbers and waiters, are necessary to us industrially. So long as they earn their living reputably, conform to our laws, and pay our taxes, they are welcome here. We do not wish to unnecessarily disturb them. We wish instead to offer them the full protection of the country in which they have chosen to do productive work."

"Very interesting," Norgate remarked. "I have heard this point of view before. Once I thought it common sense. To-day I think it academic piffle.

If we leave the Germans engaged in the inland towns alone for a moment, do you realise, I wonder, that there isn't any seaport in England that hasn't its sprinkling of Germans engaged in the occupations of which you speak? "

"And in a general way," Mr. Tyritt assented, smiling, " they are perfectly welcome to write home to their friends and relations each week and tell them everything they see happening about them, everything they know about us."

Norgate rose reluctantly to his feet.

"I won't trouble you any longer," he decided. "I presume that if I make a few investigations on my own account, and bring you absolute proof that any one of these people whose names are upon my list are in traitorous communication with Germany, you will view the matter differently? "

"Without a doubt," Mr. Tyritt promised. "Is that your list? Will you allow me to glance through it? "

"I brought it here to leave in your hands," Norgate replied, passing it over. "Your attitude, however, seems to render that course useless."

Mr. Tyritt adjusted his eyeglasses and glanced benevolently at the document. A sharp ejaculation broke from his lips. As his eyes wandered downwards, his first expression of incredulity gave way to one of suppressed amusement.

"Why, Mr. Norgate," he exclaimed, as he laid it down, " do you mean to seriously accuse these people of being engaged in any sort of league against us? "

"Most certainly I do," Norgate insisted.

"But the thing is ridiculous!" Mr. Tyritt declared. "There are names here of princes, of bankers, of society women, many of them wholly and entirely English, some of them household names. You expect me to believe that these people are all linked together in what amounts to a conspiracy to further the cause of Germany at the expense of the country in which they live, to which they belong?"

Norgate picked up his hat.

"I expect you to believe nothing, Mr. Tyritt," he said drily. "Sorry I troubled you."

"Not at all," Mr. Tyritt protested, the slight irritation passing from his manner. "Such a visit as yours is an agreeable break in my routine work. I feel as though I might be a character in a great modern romance. The names of your amateur criminals are still tingling in my memory."

Norgate turned back from the door.

"Remember them, if you can, Mr. Tyritt," he advised. "You may have cause to, some day."

CHAPTER VII

Norgate sat, the following afternoon, upon the leather-stuffed fender of a fashionable mixed bridge club in the neighbourhood of Berkeley Square, exchanging greetings with such of the members as were disposed to find time for social amenities. A smartly-dressed woman of dark complexion and slightly foreign appearance, who had just cut out of a rubber, came over and seated herself by his side. She took a cigarette from her case and accepted a match from Norgate.

"So you are really back again!" she murmured. "It scarcely seems possible."

"I am just beginning to realise it myself," he replied. "You haven't altered, Bertha."

"My dear man," she protested, "you did not expect me to age in a month, did you? It can scarcely be more than that since you left for Berlin. Are you not back again sooner than you expected?"

Norgate nodded.

"Very much sooner," he admitted. "I came in for some unexpected leave, which I haven't the slightest intention of spending abroad, so here I am."

"Not, apparently, in love with Berlin," the lady, whose name was Mrs. Paston Benedek, remarked.

Norgate's air of complete candour was very well assumed.

"I shall never be a success as a diplomatist," he confessed. "When I dislike a place or a person, every one knows it. I hated Berlin. I hate the thought of going back again."

The woman by his side smiled enigmatically.

"Perhaps," she murmured, "you may get an exchange."

"Perhaps," Norgate assented. "Meanwhile, even a month away from London seems to have brought a fresh set of people here. Who is the tall, thin young man with the sunburnt face? He seems familiar, somehow, but I can't place him."

"He is a sailor," she told him. "Captain Baring his name is."

"Friend of yours?"

She looked at him sidewise.

"Why do you ask?"

"Jealousy," Norgate sighed, "makes one observant. You were lunching with him in the Carlton Grill. You came in with him to the club this afternoon."

"Sherlock Holmes!" she murmured. "There are other men in the club with whom I lunch — even dine."

Norgate glanced across the room. Baring was playing bridge at a table close at hand, but his attention seemed to be abstracted. He looked often towards where Mrs. Benedek sat. There was a restlessness about his manner scarcely in keeping with the rest of his appearance.

"One misses a great deal," Norgate regretted, "through being only an occasional visitor here."

" As, for instance? "

" The privilege of being one of those fortunate few."

She laughed at him. Her eyes were full of challenge. She leaned a little closer and whispered in his ear: " There is still a vacant place."

" For to-night or to-morrow? " he asked eagerly.

" For to-morrow," she replied. " You may telephone — 3702 Mayfair — at ten o'clock."

He scribbled down the number. Then he put his pocket-book away with a sigh.

" I'm afraid you are treating that poor sailor-man badly," he declared.

" Sometimes," she confided, " he bores me. He is so very much in earnest. Tell me about Berlin and your work there? "

" I didn't take to Germany," Norgate confessed, " and Germany didn't take to me. Between ourselves — I shouldn't like another soul in the club to know it — I think it is very doubtful if I go back there."

" That little *contretemps* with the Prince," she murmured under her breath.

He stiffened at once.

" But how do you know of it? "

She bit her lip. For a moment a frown of annoyance clouded her face. She had said more than she intended.

" I have correspondents in Berlin," she explained. " They tell me of everything. I have a friend, in fact, who was in the restaurant that night."

" What a coincidence! " he exclaimed.

She nodded and selected a fresh cigarette.

" Isn't it! But that table is up. I promised to cut in there. Captain Baring likes me to play at the same table, and he is here for such a short time that one tries to be kind. It is indeed kindness," she added, taking up her gold purse and belongings, " for he plays so badly."

She moved towards the table. It happened to be Baring who cut out, and he and Norgate drifted together. They exchanged a few remarks.

" I met you at Marseilles once," Norgate reminded him. " You were with the Mediterranean Squadron, commanding the *Leicester*, I believe."

" Thought I'd seen you somewhere before," was the prompt acknowledgment. " You're in the Diplomatic Service, aren't you? "

Norgate admitted the fact and suggested a drink. The two men settled down to exchange confidences over a whisky and soda. Baring looked around him with some disapprobation.

" I can't really stick this place," he asserted. " If it weren't for — for some of the people here, I'd never come inside the doors. It's a rotten way of spending one's time. You play, I suppose? "

" Oh, yes, I play," Norgate admitted, " but I rather agree with you. How wonderfully well Mrs. Benedek is looking, isn't she! "

Baring withdrew his admiring eyes from her vicinity.

" Prettiest and smartest woman in London," he declared.

" By-the-by, is she English? " Norgate asked.

" A mixture of French, Italian, and German, I

believe," Baring replied. "Her husband is Benedek the painter, you know."

"I've heard of him," Norgate assented. "What are you doing now?"

"I've had a job up in town for a week or so, at the Admiralty," Baring explained. "We are examining the plans of a new — but you wouldn't be interested in that."

"I'm interested in anything naval," Norgate assured him.

"In any case, it isn't my job to talk about it," Baring continued apologetically. "We've just got a lot of fresh regulations out. Any one would think we were going to war to-morrow."

"I suppose war isn't such an impossible event," Norgate remarked. "They all say that the Germans are dying to have a go at you fellows."

Baring grinned.

"They wouldn't have a dog's chance," he declared. "That's the only drawback of having so strong a navy. We don't stand any chance of getting a fight."

"You'll have all you can do to keep up, judging by the way they talk in Germany," Norgate observed.

"Are you just home from there?"

Norgate nodded. "I am at the Embassy in Berlin, or rather I have been," he replied. "I am just home on six months' leave."

"And that's your real impression?" Baring enquired eagerly. "You really think that they mean to have a go at us?"

"I think there'll be a war soon," Norgate confessed. " It probably won't commence at sea, but you'll have to do your little lot, without a doubt."

Baring gazed across the room. There was a hard light in his eyes.

" Sounds beastly, I suppose," he muttered, " but I wish to God it would come! A war would give us all a shaking up — put us in our right places. We all seem to go on drifting any way now. The Services are all right when there's a bit of a scrap going sometimes, but there's a nasty sort of feeling of dry rot about them, when year after year all your preparations end in the smoke of a sham fight. Now I am on this beastly land job — but there, I mustn't bother you with my grumblings."

" I am interested," Norgate assured him. " Did you say you were considering something new? "

Baring nodded.

" Plans of a new submarine," he confided. " There's no harm in telling you as much as that."

Mrs. Benedek, who was dummy for the moment, strolled over to them.

" I am not sure," she murmured, " whether I like the expression you have brought back from Germany with you, Mr. Norgate."

Norgate smiled. " Have I really acquired the correct diplomatic air? " he asked. " I can assure you that it is an accident — or perhaps I am imitative."

" You have acquired," she complained, " an air of unnatural reserve. You seem as though you had found some problem in life so weighty that you could not lose sight of it even for a moment. Ah ! "

The glass-topped door had been flung wide open

with an unusual flourish.   A barely perceptible start
escaped Norgate.   It was indeed an unexpected appearance, this!   Dressed with a perfect regard to the
latest London fashion, with his hair smoothly brushed
and a pearl pin in his black satin tie, Herr Selingman
stood upon the threshold, beaming upon them.

CHAPTER VIII

Selingman had the air of a man who returns after a long absence to some familiar spot where he expects to find friends and where his welcome is assured. Mrs. Paston Benedek slipped from her place upon the cushioned fender and held out both her hands.

" Ah, it is really you! " she exclaimed. " Welcome, dear friend! For days I have wondered what it was in this place which one missed all the time. Now I know."

Selingman took the little outstretched hands and raised them to his lips.

" Dear lady," he assured her, " you repay me in one moment for all the weariness of my exile."

She turned towards her companion.

" Captain Baring," she begged, " please ring the bell. Mr. Selingman and I always drink a toast together the moment he first arrives to pay us one of his too rare visits. Thank you! You know Captain Baring, don't you, Mr. Selingman? This is another friend of mine whom I think that you have not met — Mr. Francis Norgate, Mr. Selingman. Mr. Norgate has just arrived from Berlin, too."

For a single moment the newcomer seemed to lose his Cheeryble-like expression. The glance which he flashed upon Norgate contained other elements besides those of polite pleasure. He was himself again, however, almost instantly. He grasped his new acquaintance by the hand.

" Mr. Norgate and I are already old friends," he insisted. " We occupied the same coupé coming from Berlin and drank a bottle of wine together in the buffet."

Mrs. Benedek threw back her head and laughed, a familiar gesture which her enemies declared was in some way associated with the dazzling whiteness of her teeth.

" And now," she exclaimed, " you find that you belong to the same bridge club. What a coincidence!"

" It is rather surprising, I must admit," Norgate assented. " Mr. Selingman and I discussed many things last night, but we did not speak of bridge. In fact, from the tone of our conversation, I should have imagined that cards were an amusement which scarcely entered into Mr. Selingman's scheme of life."

" One must have one's distractions," Selingman protested. " I confess that auction bridge, as it is played over here, is the one game in the world which attracts me."

" But how about the crockery? " Norgate asked. " Doesn't that come first? "

" First, beyond a doubt," Selingman agreed heartily. " Always, though, my plan of campaign is the same. On the day of my arrival here, I take things easily. I spend an hour or so at the office in the morning, and the afternoon I take holiday. After that I settle down for one week's hard work. London — your great London — takes always first place with me. In the mornings I see my agents and my customers. Perhaps I lunch with one of them. At four o'clock I close my desk, and crockery does not exist for me any longer. I get into a taxi, and I come here. My first game of bridge is a treat to which I look forward eagerly. See, there are three of us and several sitting out. Let us make another table. So!"

They found a fourth without difficulty and took possession of a table at the far end of the room. Selingman, with a huge cigar in his mouth, played well and had every appearance of thoroughly enjoying the game. Towards the end of their third rubber, Mrs. Benedek, who was dummy, leaned across towards Norgate.

"After all, perhaps you are better off here," she murmured in German. "There is nothing like this in Berlin."

"One is at least nearer the things one cherishes," Norgate quoted in the same language.

Selingman was playing the hand and held between his fingers a card already drawn to play. For a moment, it was suspended in the air. He looked towards Norgate, and there was a new quality in his piercing gaze, an instant return in his expression of the shadow which had swept the broad good-humour from his face on his first appearance. The change came and went like a flash. He finished playing the hand and scored his points before he spoke. Then he turned to Norgate.

"Your gift of acquiring languages in a short space of time is most extraordinary, my young friend!

Since yesterday you have become able to speak German, eh? Prodigious!"

Norgate smiled without embarrassment. The moment was a critical one, portentous to an extent which no one at that table could possibly have realised.

" I am afraid," he confessed, " that when I found that I had a fellow traveller in my coupé I felt most ungracious and unsociable. I was in a thoroughly bad temper and indisposed for conversation. The simplest way to escape from it seemed to be to plead ignorance of any language save my own."

Selingman chuckled audibly. The cloud had passed from his face. To all appearance that momentary suspicion had been strangled.

" So you found me a bore!" he observed. " Then I must admit that your manners were good, for when you found that I spoke English and that you could not escape conversation, you allowed me to talk on about my business, and you showed few signs of weariness. You should be a diplomatist, Mr. Norgate."

" Mr. Norgate is, or rather he was," Mrs. Paston Benedek remarked. " He has just left the Embassy at Berlin."

Selingman leaned back in his chair and thrust both hands into his trousers pockets. He indulged in a few German expletives, bombastic and thunderous, which relieved him so much that he was able to conclude his speech in English.

" I am the densest blockhead in all Europe!" he announced emphatically. " If I had realised your identity, I would willingly have left you alone. No wonder you were feeling indisposed for idle conversation! Mr. Francis Norgate, eh? A little affair at the Café de Berlin with a lady and a hot-headed young princeling. Well, well! Young sir, you have become more to me than an ordinary acquaintance. If I had known the cause of your ill-humour, I would certainly have left you alone, but I would have shaken you first by the hand."

The fourth at the table, who was an elderly lady of somewhat austere appearance, produced a small black cigar from what seemed to be a harmless-looking reticule which she was carrying, and lit it. Selingman stared at her with his mouth open.

" Is this a bridge-table or is it not? " she enquired severely. " These little personal reminiscences are very interesting among yourselves, I dare say, but I cut in here with the idea of playing bridge."

Selingman was the first to recover his manners, although his eyes seemed still fascinated by the cigar.

" We owe you apologies, madam," he acknowledged. " Permit me to cut."

The rubber progressed and finished in comparative silence. At its conclusion, Selingman glanced at the clock. It was half-past seven.

" I am hungry," he announced.

Mrs. Benedek laughed at him. " Hungry at half-past seven! Barbarian! "

" I lunched at half-past twelve," he protested. " I ate less than usual, too. I did not even leave my office, I was so anxious to finish what was necessary and to find myself here."

Mrs. Benedek played with the cards a moment and then rose to her feet with a little grimace.

" Well, I suppose I shall have to give in," she sighed. " I am taking it for granted, you see, that you are expecting me to dine with you."

" My dear lady," Selingman declared emphatically, " if you were to break through our time-honoured custom and deny me the joy of your company on my first evening in London, I think that I should send another to look after my business in this country, and retire myself to the seclusion of my little country home near Potsdam. The inducements of managing one's own affairs in this country, Mr. Norgate," he added, " are, as you may imagine, manifold and magnetic."

" We will not grudge them to you so long as you don't come too often," Norgate remarked, as he bade them good night. " The man who monopolised Mrs. Benedek would soon make himself unpopular here."

CHAPTER IX

Norgate had chosen, for many reasons, to return to London as a visitor. His somewhat luxurious rooms in Albemarle Street were still locked up. He had taken a small flat in the Milan Court, solely for the purpose of avoiding immediate association with his friends and relatives. His whole outlook upon lifs was confused and disturbed. Until he received a definite pronouncement from the head-quarters of officialdom, he felt himself unable to settle down to any of the ordinary functions of life. And behind all this, another and a more powerful sentiment possessed him. He had left Berlin without seeing or hearing anything further from Anna von Haase. No word had come from her, nor any message. And now that it was too late, he began to feel that he had made a mistake. It seemed to him that he had visited upon her, in some indirect way, the misfortune which had befallen him. It was scarcely her fault that she had been the object of attentions which nearly every one agreed were unwelcome, from this young princeling. Norgate told himself, as he changed his clothes that evening, that his behaviour had been the behaviour of a jealous school-boy. Then an inspiration seized him. Half dressed as he was, he sat down at the writing-table and wrote to her. He wrote rapidly, and when he had finished, he sealed and addressed the envelope without glancing once more at its contents. The letter was stamped and posted within a few minutes, but somehow or other it seemed to have made a difference. His depression was no longer so complete. He looked forward to his lonely dinner, at one of the smaller clubs to which he belonged, with less aversion.

"Do you know where any of my people are, Hardy?" he asked his servant.

"In Scotland, I believe, sir," the man replied. "I called round this afternoon, although I was careful not to mention the fact that you were in town. The house is practically in the hands of caretakers."

"Try to keep out of the way as much as you can, Hardy," Norgate enjoined. "For a few days, at any rate, I should like no one to know that I am in town."

"Very good, sir," the man replied. "Might I venture to enquire, sir, if you are likely to be returning to Berlin?"

"I think it is very doubtful, Hardy," Norgate observed grimly. "We are more likely to remain here for a time."

Hardy brushed his master's hat for a moment or two in silence.

"You will pardon my mentioning it, sir," he said —"I imagine it is of no importance — but one of the German waiters on this floor has been going out of his way to enter into conversation with me this evening. He seemed to know your name and to know that you had just come from Germany. He hinted at some slight trouble there, sir."

" The dickens he did!" Norgate exclaimed.
" That's rather quick work, Hardy."

" So I thought, sir," the man continued.   " A very
inquisitive individual indeed I found him.   He wanted
to know whether you had had any news yet as to any
further appointment.   He seemed to know quite well
that you had been at the Foreign Office this morning."

" What did you tell him? "

" I told him that I knew nothing, sir.   I explained
that you had not been back to lunch, and that I had
not seen you since the morning.   He tried to make
an appointment with me to give me some dinner and
take me to a music-hall to-night."

" What did you say to that? " Norgate enquired.

" I left the matter open, sir," the man replied.   " I
thought I would enquire what your wishes might be?
The person evidently desires to gain some information about your movements.   I thought that possibly
it might be advantageous for me to tell him just what
you desired."

Norgate lit a cigarette.   For the moment he was
puzzled.   It was true that during their journey he
had mentioned to Selingman his intention of taking
a flat at the Milan Court, but if this espionage were
the direct outcome of that information, it was indeed
a wonderful organisation which Selingman controlled.

" You have acted very discreetly, Hardy," he said.
" I think you had better tell your friend that I am
expecting to leave for somewhere at a moment's
notice.   For your own information," he added, " I
rather think that I shall stay here.   It seems to me

quite possible that we may find London, for a few weeks, just as interesting as any city in the world."

" I am very glad to hear you say so, sir," the man murmured. " Shall I fetch your overcoat? "

The telephone bell suddenly interrupted them. Hardy took up the receiver and listened for a moment.

" Mr. Hebblethwaite would like to speak to you, sir," he announced.

Norgate hurried to the telephone. A cheery voice greeted him.

" Hullo! That you, Norgate? This is Hebblethwaite. I'm just back from a few days in the country — found your note here. I want to hear all about this little matter at once. When can I see you? "

" Any time you like," Norgate replied promptly.

" Let me see," the voice continued, " what are you doing to-night? "

" Nothing! "

" Come straight round to the House of Commons and dine. Or no — wait a moment — we'll go somewhere quieter. Say the club in a quarter of an hour — the Reform Club. How will that suit you? "

" I'll be there, with pleasure," Norgate promised.

" Righto! We'll hear what you've been doing to these peppery Germans. I had a line from Leveson himself this morning. A lady in the case, I hear? Well, well! Never mind explanations now. See you in a few minutes."

Norgate laid down the receiver. His manner, as he accepted his well-brushed hat, had lost all its depression. There was no one in the Cabinet with more influence than Hebblethwaite. He would have his chance, at any rate, and his chance at other things.

"Look here, Hardy," he ordered, as he drew on his gloves, "spend as much time as you like with that fellow and let me know what sort of questions he asks you. Be careful not to mention the fact that I am dining with Mr. Hebblethwaite. For the rest, fence with him. I am not quite sure what it all means. If by any chance he mentions a man named Selingman, let me know. Good night!"

"Good night, sir!" the man replied.

Norgate descended into the Strand and walked briskly towards Pall Mall. The last few minutes seemed to him to be fraught with promise of a new interest in life. Yet it was not of any of these things that he was thinking as he made his way towards his destination. He was occupied most of the time in wondering how long it would be before he could hope to receive a reply from Berlin to his letter.

CHAPTER X

The Right Honourable John Hebblethwaite, M.P., since he had become a Cabinet Minister and had even been mentioned as the possible candidate for supreme office, had lost a great deal of that breezy, almost boisterous effusion of manner which in his younger days had first endeared him to his constituents. He received Norgate, however, with marked and hearty cordiality, and took his arm as he led him to the little table which he had reserved in a corner of the dining-room. The friendship between the entirely self-made politician and Norgate, who was the nephew of a duke, and whose aristocratic connections were multifarious and far-reaching, was in its way a genuine one. There were times when Hebblethwaite had made use of his younger friend to further his own undoubted social ambitions. On the other hand, since he had become a power in politics, he had always been ready to return in kind such offices. The note which he had received from Norgate that day was, however, the first appeal which had ever been made to him.

" I have been away for a week-end's golf," Hebblethwaite explained, as they took their places at the table. " There comes a time when figures pall, and snapping away in debate seems to stick in one's throat. I telephoned directly I got your note. Fortunately, I wasn't doing anything this evening. We won't play about. I know you don't want to see me to talk about the weather, and I know something's up, or Leveson wouldn't have written to me, and you wouldn't be back from Berlin. Let's have the whole story with the soup and fish, and we'll try and hit upon a way to put things right before we reach the liqueurs."

" I've lots to say to you," Norgate admitted simply. " I'll begin with the personal side of it. Here's just a brief narration of exactly what happened to me in the most fashionable restaurant of Berlin last Thursday night."

Norgate told his story. His friend listened with the absorbed attention of a man who possesses complete powers of concentration.

" Rotten business," he remarked, when it was finished. " I suppose you've told old — I mean you've told them the story at the Foreign Office? "

" Had it all out this morning," Norgate replied.

" I know exactly what our friend told you," Mr. Hebblethwaite continued, with a gleam of humour in his eyes. " He reminded you that the first duty of a diplomat — of a young diplomat especially — is to keep on friendly terms with the governing members of the country to which he is accredited. How's that, eh? "

" Pretty nearly word for word," Norgate admitted. " It's the sort of platitude I could watch framing in his mind before I was half-way through what I had to say. What they don't seem to take sufficient account of in that museum of mummied brains and parchment tongues — forgive me, Hebblethwaite, but it isn't your department — is that the Prince's behaviour to me is such as no Englishman, subscribing to any code of honour, could possibly tolerate. I will admit, if you like, that the Kaiser's attitude may render it advisable for me to be transferred from Berlin. I do not admit that I am not at once eligible for a position of similar importance in another capital."

"No one would doubt it," John Hebblethwaite grumbled, "except those particular fools we have to deal with. I suppose they didn't see it in the same light."

"They did not," Norgate admitted.

"We've a tough proposition to tackle," Hebblethwaite confessed cheerfully, "but I am with you, Norgate, and to my mind one of the pleasures of being possessed of a certain amount of power is to help one's friends when you believe in the justice of their cause. If you leave things with me, I'll tackle them to-morrow morning."

"That's awfully good of you, Hebblethwaite," Norgate declared gratefully, "and just what I expected. We'll leave that matter altogether just now, if we may. My own little grievance is there, and I wanted to explain exactly how it came about. Apart from that altogether, there is something far more important which I have to say to you."

Hebblethwaite knitted his brows. He was clearly puzzled.

"Still personal, eh?" he enquired.

Norgate shook his head.

" It is something of vastly more importance," he said, " than any question affecting my welfare. I am almost afraid to begin for fear I shall miss any chance, for fear I may not seem convincing enough."

" We'll have the champagne opened at once, then," Mr. Hebblethwaite declared. " Perhaps that will loosen your tongue. I can see that this is going to be a busy meal. Charles, if that bottle of Pommery 1904 is iced just to the degree I like it, let it be served, if you please, in the large sized glasses. Now, Norgate."

" What I am going to relate to you," Norgate began, leaning across the table and speaking very earnestly, " is a little incident which happened to me on my way back from Berlin. I had as a fellow passenger a person whom I am convinced is high up in the German Secret Service Intelligence Department."

" All that ! " Mr. Hebblethwaite murmured. " Go ahead, Norgate. I like the commencement of your story. I almost feel that I am moving through the pages of a diplomatic romance. All that I am praying is that your fellow passenger was a foreign lady — a princess, if possible — with wonderful eyes, fascinating manners, and of a generous disposition."

" Then I am afraid you will be disappointed," Norgate continued drily. " The personage in question was a man whose name was Selingman. He told me that he was a manufacturer of crockery and that he came often to England to see his customers. He called himself a peace-loving German, and he professed the utmost good-will towards our country and our national policy. At the commencement of our conversation, I managed to impress him with the idea that I spoke no German. At one of the stations on the line he was joined by a Belgian, his agent, as he told me, in Brussels for the sale of his crockery. I overheard this agent, whose name was Meyer, recount to his principal his recent operations. He offered him an exact plan of the forts of Liège. I heard him instructed to procure a list of the wealthy inhabitants of Ghent and the rateable value of the city, and I heard him commissioned to purchase land in the neighbourhood of Antwerp for a secret purpose."

Mr. Hebblethwaite's eyebrows became slowly upraised. The twinkle in his eyes remained, however.

" My! " he exclaimed softly. " We're getting on with the romance all right! "

" During the momentary absence of this fellow and his agent from the carriage," Norgate proceeded, " I possessed myself of a slip of paper which had become detached from the packet of documents they had been examining. It consisted of a list of names mostly of people resident in the United Kingdom, purporting to be Selingman's agents. I venture to believe that this list is a precise record of the principal German spies in this country."

" German spies! " Mr. Hebblethwaite murmured. " Whew! "

He sipped his champagne.

" That list," Norgate went on, " is in my pocket. I may add that although I was careful to keep up the fiction of not understanding German, and although

I informed Herr Selingman that I had seen the paper in question blow out of the window, he nevertheless gave me that night a drugged whisky and soda, and during the time I slept he must have been through every one of my possessions. I found my few letters and papers turned upside down, and even my pockets had been ransacked."

" Where was the paper, then? " Mr. Hebblethwaite enquired.

" In an inner pocket of my pyjamas," Norgate explained. " I had them made with a sort of belt inside, at the time I was a king's messenger."

Mr. Hebblethwaite played with his tie for a moment and drank a little more champagne.

" Could I have a look at the list? " he asked, as though with a sudden inspiration.

Norgate passed it across the table to him. Mr. Hebblethwaite adjusted his pince-nez, gave a little start as he read the first name, leaned back in his chair as he came to another, stared at Norgate about half-way down the list, as though to make sure that he was in earnest, and finally finished it in silence. He folded it up and handed it back.

" Well, well! " he exclaimed, a little pointlessly. " Now tell me, Norgate, you showed this list down there? "— jerking his head towards the street.

" I did," Norgate admitted.

" And what did they say? "

" Just what you might expect men whose lives are spent within the four walls of a room in Downing Street to say," Norgate replied. " You are half inclined to make fun of me yourself, Hebblethwaite, but at any rate I know you have a different outlook from theirs. Old Carew was frantically polite. He even declared the list to be most interesting! He rambled on for about a quarter of an hour on the general subject of the spy mania. German espionage, he told me, was one of the shadowy evils from which England had suffered for generations. So far as regards London and the provincial towns, he went on, whether for good or evil, we have a large German population, and if they choose to make reports to any one in Germany as to events happening here which come under their observation, we cannot stop it, and it would not even be worth while to try. As regards matters of military and naval importance, there was a special branch, he assured me, for looking after these, and it was a branch of the Service which was remarkably well-served and remarkably successful. Having said this, he folded the list up and returned it to me, rang the bell, gave me a frozen hand to shake, a mumbled promise about another appointment as soon as there should be a vacancy, and that was the end of it."

"About that other appointment," Mr. Hebblethwaite began, with some animation —

"Damn the other appointment!" Norgate interrupted testily. "I didn't come here to cadge, Hebblethwaite. I am never likely to make use of my friends in that way. I came for a bigger thing. I came to try and make you see a danger, the reality of which I have just begun to appreciate myself for the first time in my life."

Mr. Hebblethwaite's manner slowly changed. He

pulled down his waistcoat, finished off a glass of wine, and leaned forward.

"Norgate," he said, "I am sorry that this is the frame of mind in which you have come to me. I tell you frankly that you couldn't have appealed to a man in the Cabinet less in sympathy with your fears than I myself."

"I am sorry to hear that," Norgate replied grimly, "but go on."

"Before I entered the Cabinet," Mr. Hebble-thwaite continued, "our relations with Foreign Powers were just the myth to me that they are to most people who read the *Morning Post* one day and the *Daily Mail* the next. However, I made the best part of half a million in business through knowing the top and the bottom and every corner of my job, and I started in to do the same when I began to have a share in the government of the country. The *entente* with France is all right in its way, but I came to the conclusion that the greatest and broadest stroke of diplomacy possible to Englishmen to-day was to cultivate more benevolent and more confidential relations with Germany. That same feeling has been spreading through the Cabinet during the last two years. I am ready to take my share of the blame or praise, whichever in the future shall be allotted to the inspirer of that idea. It is our hope that when the present Government goes out of office, one of its chief claims to public approval and to historical praise will be the improvement of our relations with Germany. We certainly do not wish to disturb the growing confidence which exists between the two

countries by any maladroit or unnecessary investigations. We believe, in short, that Germany's attitude
towards us is friendly, and we intend to treat her in
the same spirit."

" Tell me," Norgate asked, " is that the reason
why every scheme for the expansion of the army has
been shelved? Is that the reason for all the troubles
with the Army Council? "

" It is," Hebblethwaite admitted. ",I trust you,
Norgate, and I look upon you as a friend. I tell you
what the whole world of responsible men and women
might as well know, but which we naturally don't
care about shouting from the housetops. We have
come to the conclusion that there is no possible
chance of the peace of Europe being disturbed. We
have come to the conclusion that civilisation has
reached that pitch when the last resource of arms is
absolutely unnecessary. I do not mind telling you
that the Balkan crisis presented opportunities to
any one of the Powers to plunge into warfare, had
they been so disposed. No one bade more boldly for
peace then than Germany. No one wants war.
Germany has nothing to gain by it, no animosity
against France, none towards Russia. Neither of
these countries has the slightest intention, now or at
any time, of invading Germany. Why should they?
The matter of Alsace and Lorraine is finished. If
these provinces ever come back to France, it will be
by political means and not by any mad-headed attempt to wrest them away."

" Incidentally," Norgate asked, " what about the
enormous armaments of Germany? What about her

navy? What about the military spirit which practically rules the country?"

"I have spent three months in Germany during the last year," Hebblethwaite replied. "It is my firm belief that those armaments and that fleet are necessary to Germany to preserve her place of dignity among the nations. She has Russia on one side and France on the other, allies, watching her all the time, and of late years England has been chipping at her whenever she got a chance, and flirting with France. What can a nation do but make herself strong enough to defend herself against unprovoked attack? Germany, of course, is full of the military spirit, but it is my opinion, Norgate, that it is a great deal fuller of the great commercial spirit. It isn't war with Germany that we have to fear. It's the ruin of our commerce by their great assiduity and more up-to-date methods. Now you've had a statement of policy from me for which the halfpenny Press would give me a thousand guineas if I'd sign it."

"I've had it," Norgate admitted, "and I tell you frankly that I hate it. I am an unfledged young diplomat in disgrace, and I haven't your experience or your brains, but I have a hateful idea that I can see the truth and you can't. You're too big and too broad in this matter, Hebblethwaite. Your head's lifted too high. You see the horrors and the needlessness, the logical side of war, and you brush the thought away from you."

Mr. Hebblethwaite sighed.

"Perhaps so," he admitted. "One can only act according to one's convictions. You must remember, though, Norgate, that we don't carry our pacificism to extremes. Our navy is and always will be an irresistible defence."

"Even with hostile naval and aeroplane bases at — say — Calais, Boulogne, Dieppe, Ostend?"

Mr. Hebblethwaite pushed a box of cigars towards his guest, glanced at the clock, and rose.

"Young fellow," he said, "I have engaged a box at the Empire. Let us move on."

CHAPTER XI

"My position as a Cabinet Minister," Mr. Hebblethwaite declared, with a sigh, "renders my presence in the Promenade undesirable. If you want to stroll around, Norgate, don't bother about me."

Norgate picked up his hat. "Jolly good show," he remarked. "I'll be back before it begins again."

He descended to the lower Promenade and sauntered along towards the refreshment bar. Mrs. Paston Benedek, who was seated in the stalls, leaned over and touched his arm.

"My friend," she exclaimed, "you are *distrait!* You walk as though you looked for everything and saw nothing. And behold, you have found me!"

Norgate shook hands and nodded to Baring, who was her escort.

"What have you done with our expansive friend?" he asked. "I thought you were dining with him."

"I compromised," she laughed. "You see what it is to be so popular. I should have dined and have come here with Captain Baring — that was our plan for to-night. Captain Baring, however, was generous when he saw my predicament. He suffered me to dine with Mr. Selingman, and he fetched me afterwards. Even then we could not quite get rid of the dear man. He came on here with us, and he is now,

I believe, greeting acquaintances everywhere in the Promenade. I am perfectly convinced that I shall have to look the other way when we go out."

" I think I'll see whether I can rescue him," Norgate remarked. " Good show, isn't it? " he added, turning to her companion.

" Capital," replied Baring, without enthusiasm. " Too many people here, though."

Norgate strolled on, and Mrs. Benedek tapped her companion on the knuckles with her fan.

" How dared you be so rude! " she exclaimed. " You are in a very bad humour this evening. I can see that I shall have to punish you."

" That's all very well," Baring grumbled, " but it gets more difficult to see you alone every day. This evening was to have been mine. Now this fat German turns up and lays claim to you, and then, about the first moment we've had a chance to talk, Norgate comes gassing along. You're not nearly as nice to me, Bertha, as you used to be."

" My dear man," she protested, " in the first place I deny it. In the second, I ask myself whether you are quite as devoted to me as you were when you first came."

" In what way? " he demanded.

She turned her wonderful eyes upon him.

" At first when you came," she declared, " you told me everything. You spoke of your long mornings and afternoons at the Admiralty. You told me of the room in which you worked, the men who worked there with you. You told me of the building of that little model, and how you were all allowed to try your own pet ideas with regard to it. And then, all of a sudden, nothing — not a word about what you have been doing. I am an intelligent woman. I love to have men friends who do things, and if they are really friends of mine, I like to enter into their life, to know of their work, to sympathise, to take an interest in it. It was like that with you at first. Now it has all gone. You have drawn down a curtain. I do not believe that you go to the Admiralty at all. I do not believe that you have any wonderful invention there over which you spend your time."

" Bertha, dear," he remonstrated, " do be reasonable."

She shrugged her shoulders.

" But am I not? See how reasonably I have spoken to you. I have told you the exact truth. I have told you why I do not take quite that same pleasure in your company as when you first came."

" Do consider," he begged. " I spoke to you freely at first because we had not reached the stage in the work when secrecy was absolutely necessary. At present we are all upon our honour. From the moment we pass inside that little room, we are, to all effects and purposes, dead men. Nothing that happens there is to be spoken of or hinted at, even to our wives or our dearest friends. It is the etiquette of my profession, Bertha. Be reasonable."

" Pooh! " she exclaimed. " Fancy asking a woman to be reasonable! Don't you realise, you stupid man, that if you were at liberty to tell everybody what it is that you do there, well, then I should have no more interest in it? It is just because you say that you will not and you may not tell, that, womanlike, I am curious."

"But whatever good could it be to you to know?" he protested. "I should simply addle your head with a mass of technical detail, not a quarter of which you would be able to understand. Besides, I have told you, Bertha, it is a matter of honour."

She looked intently at her programme.

"There are men," she murmured, "who love so much that even honour counts for little by the side of —"

"Of what?" he whispered hoarsely.

"Of success."

For a moment they sat in silence. The place was not particularly hot, yet there were little beads of perspiration upon Baring's forehead. The fingers which held his programme twitched. He rose suddenly to his feet.

"May I go out and have a drink?" he asked. "I won't go if you don't want to be alone."

"My dear friend, I do not mind in the least," she assured him. "If you find Mr. Norgate, send him here."

In one of the smaller refreshment rooms sat Mr. Selingman, a bottle of champagne before him and a wondrously attired lady on either side. The heads of all three were close together. The lady on the left was talking in a low tone but with many gesticulations.

"Dear friend," she exclaimed, "for one single moment you must not think that I am ungrateful! But consider. Success costs money always, and I have been successful — you admit that. My rooms are frequented entirely by the class of young men you have wished me to encourage. Pauline and I here, and Rose, whom you have met, seek our friends in no other direction. We are never alone, and, as you very well know, not a day has passed that I have not sent you some little word of gossip or information — the gossip of the navy and the gossip of the army — and there is always some truth underneath what these young men say. It is what you desire, is it not?"

"Without a doubt," Selingman assented. "Your work, my dear Helda, has been excellent. I commend you. I think with fervour of the day when first we talked together, and the scheme presented itself to me. Continue to play Aspasia in such a fashion to the young soldiers and sailors of this country, and your villa at Monte Carlo next year is assured."

The woman shrugged her shoulders.

"I will not say that you are not generous," she declared, "for that would be untrue, but sometimes you forget that these young men have very little money, and the chief profit from their friendship, therefore, must come to us in other ways."

"You want a larger allowance?" Selingman asked slowly.

"Not at present, but I want to warn you that the time may come when I shall need more. A salon in Pimlico, dear friend, is an expensive thing to maintain. These young men tell their friends of our hospitality, the music, our entertainment. We become almost too much the fashion, and it costs money."

Selingman held up his champagne glass, gazed at the wine for a moment, and slowly drank it.

"I am not of those," he announced, "who expect service for nothing, especially good service such as yours. Watch for the postman, dear lady. Any morning this week there may come for you a pleasant little surprise."

She leaned over and patted his arm.

"You are a prince," she murmured. "But tell me, who is the grave-looking young man?"

Selingman glanced up. Norgate, who had been standing at the bar with Baring, was passing a few feet away.

"The rake's progress," the former quoted solemnly.

Selingman raised his glass.

"Come and join us," he invited.

Norgate shook his head slightly and passed on. Selingman leaned a little forward, watching his departing figure. The buoyant good-nature seemed to have faded out of his face.

"If you could get that young man to talk, now, Helda," he muttered, "it would be an achievement."

She glanced after him. "To me," she declared, "he looks one of the difficult sort."

"He is an Englishman with a grievance," Selingman continued. "If the grievance cuts deep enough, he may — But we gossip."

"The other was a navy man," the girl remarked. "His name is Baring."

Selingman nodded.

" You need not bother about him," he said. " If it is possible for him to be of use, that is arranged for in another quarter. So! Let us finish our wine and separate. That letter shall surely come. Have no fear."

Selingman strolled away, a few minutes later. Baring had returned to Mrs. Paston Benedek, and Norgate had resumed his place in the box. Selingman, with a gold-topped cane under his arm, a fresh cigar between his lips, and a broad smile of good-fellowship upon his face, strolled down one of the wings of the Promenade. Suddenly he came to a standstill. In the box opposite to him, Norgate and Hebblethwaite were seated side by side. Selingman regarded them for a moment steadfastly.

" A friend of Hebblethwaite's!" he muttered. " Hebblethwaite — the one man whom Berlin doubts!"

He withdrew a little into the shadows, his eyes fixed upon the box. A little way off, in the stalls, Mrs. Paston Benedek was whispering to Baring. Further back in the Promenade, Helda was entertaining a little party of friends. Selingman's eyes remained fixed upon Norgate.

CHAPTER XII

Mrs. Paston Benedek, on the following afternoon, sat in one corner of the very comfortable lounge set with its back to the light in her charming drawing-room. Norgate sat in the other.

"I think it is perfectly sweet of you to come," she declared. "I do not care how many enemies I make — I will certainly dine with you to-night. How I shall manage it I do not yet know. You shall call for me here at eight o'clock — or say a quarter past, then we need not hurry away too early from the club. If Captain Baring is there, perhaps it would be better if you did not speak of our engagement."

Norgate sighed.

"What is the wonderful attraction about Baring?" he asked discontentedly.

"Really, there isn't any," she replied. "I like to be kind, that is all. I do not like to hurt anybody's feelings, and I know that Captain Baring would like very much to dine with me to-night himself. I was obliged to throw him over last night because of Mr. Selingman's arrival."

"You have not always been so considerate," he persisted. "Why this especial care for Baring's feelings?"

She turned her head a little towards him. She was

leaning back in her corner of the lounge, her hands clasped behind her head. There was an elaborate carelessness about her pose which she numbered among her best effects.

" Perhaps," she retorted, " I, too, find your sudden attraction for me a little remarkable. On those few occasions when you did honour us at the club before you left for Berlin, you were agreeable enough, but I do not remember that you once asked me to dine with you. There was no Captain Baring then."

" The truth is," Norgate confessed, " since I returned, I have felt rather like hiding myself. I don't care about going to my own club or visiting my own friends. I came to the St. James's as a sort of compromise."

" You are not very flattering," she complained.

" Wouldn't you rather I were truthful? " asked Norgate. " One's friends, one's real friends, are scarcely likely to be found at a mixed bridge club."

"After that," she sighed, " I am going to telephone to Captain Baring. He, at any rate, is in love with me, and I need something to restore my self-respect."

" In love with you, perhaps, but are you in love with him? "

She laughed, softly at first, but with an ever more insistent note of satire underlying her mirth.

" The woman," she said, " who expects to get anything out of life worth having, doesn't fall in love. She may give a good deal, she may seem to give everything, but if she is wise, she keeps her heart."

" Poor Baring! "

" Are you sure," she asked, fixing her brilliant eyes

upon him, " that he needs your sympathy? He is very much in love with me, and there are times when I could almost persuade myself that I am in love with him. At any rate, he attracts me."

Norgate was momentarily sententious. " The psychology of love," he murmured, looking into the fire, " is a queer study."

Once more she laughed at him.

" Before you went to Berlin," she said, " you used not to talk of the psychology of love. Your methods, so far as I remember them, were a little different. Confess now — you fell in love in Berlin."

Norgate stifled a sudden desire to confide in his companion.

" At my age! " he exclaimed.

" It is true that it is not a susceptible age," Mrs. Benedek admitted. " You are in what I call your mid-youth. Mid-youth, as a rule, is an age of cynicism. As you grow older, you will appreciate more the luxury of emotion. But tell me, was it the little Baroness who fascinated you? She is a great beauty, is she not? "

" I took her out to dinner," Norgate observed. " Therefore I suppose it was my duty to be in love with her."

" Fancy sharing the same sofa," she laughed, " with a rival of princes! Do you know that the Baroness is a friend of mine? She comes sometimes to London."

" I am much more interested in your love affair," he protested.

" And I find far more interest in your future,"

she insisted. " Let us talk sensibly, like good friends
and companions. What are you going to do?
They will not treat this affair seriously at the Foreign
Office? They cannot think that you were to blame? "

" In a sense, no," he replied. " Diplomatically,
however, I am, from their point of view, a heinous
offender. I rather think I am going to be shelved for
six months."

" Just what one would expect from this horrible
Government!" Mrs. Benedek exclaimed indignantly.

" What do you know about the Government? " he
asked. " Are you taking up politics as well as the
study of the higher auction? "

She sighed, and her eyes were fixed upon him very
earnestly, as she declared: " You do not understand
me, my friend. You never did. I am not altogether
frivolous; I am not altogether an artist. I have my
serious moments."

" Is this going to be one of them? "

" Don't make fun of me, please," she begged.
" You are like so many Englishmen. Directly a
woman tries to talk seriously, you will push her back
into her place. You like to treat her as something to
frivol with and make love to. Is it your *amour
propre* which is wounded, when you feel sometimes
forced to admit that she has as clear an insight into
the more important things of life as you yourself? "

" Do you talk like that with Baring? " he asked.

For several seconds she was silent. Her eyes had
contracted a little. She seemed to be seeking for
some double meaning in his words.

" Captain Baring is an intelligent man," she said,

"and he is a man, too, who understands his own particular subject. Of course it is a pleasure to talk to him about it."

"I thought navy men, as a rule," he remarked, "were not communicative."

"Do you call it communicative," she enquired, "to discuss the subject you love best with your greatest friend? But let us not talk any more of Captain Baring. It is in you just now that I am interested, you and your future. You seem to think that your friends at the Foreign Office are not going to find you another position — for some time, at any rate. You are not one of those men who think of nothing but sport and amusing themselves. What are you going to do during the next few months?"

"At present," he confessed thoughtfully, "I have only the vaguest ideas. Perhaps you could help me."

"Perhaps I could," she admitted. "We will talk of that another time, if you like."

It was obvious that she was speaking under a certain tension. The silence which ensued was significant.

"Why not now?" he asked.

"It is too soon," she answered, "and you would not understand. I might say things to you which would perhaps end our friendship, which would give you a wrong impression. No, let us stay just as we are for a little time."

"This is most tantalising," grumbled Norgate.

She leaned over and patted his hand.

"Have patience, my friend," she whispered. "The great things come to those who wait."

An interruption, commonplace enough, yet in its way startling, checked the words which were already upon his lips. The telephone bell from the little instrument on the table within a few feet of them, rang insistently. For a moment Mrs. Benedek herself appeared taken by surprise. Then she raised the receiver to her ear.

"My friend," she said to Norgate, "you must excuse me. I told them distinctly to disconnect the instrument so that it rang only in my bedroom. I am disobeyed, but no matter. Who is that?"

Norgate leaned back in his place. His companion's little interjection, however, was irresistible. He glanced towards her. There was a slight flush of colour in her cheeks, her head was moving slowly as though keeping pace to the words spoken at the other end. Suddenly she laughed.

"Do not be so foolish," she said. "Yes, of course. You keep your share of the bargain and I mine. At eight o'clock, then. I will say no more now, as I am engaged with a visitor. *Au revoir!*"

She set down the receiver and turned towards Norgate, who was turning the pages of an illustrated paper. She made a little grimace.

"Oh, but life is very queer!" she declared. "How I love it! Now I am going to make you look glum, if indeed you do care just that little bit which is all you know of caring. Perhaps you will be a little disappointed. Tell me that you are, or my vanity will be hurt. Listen and prepare. To-night I cannot dine with you."

He turned deliberately around. "You are going to throw me over?" he demanded, looking at her steadfastly.

"To throw you over, dear friend," she repeated cheerfully. "You would do just the same, if you were in my position."

"It is an affair of duty," he persisted, "or the triumph of a rival?"

She made a grimace at him. "It is an affair of duty," she admitted, "but it is certainly with a rival that I must dine."

He moved a little nearer to her on the lounge.

"Tell me on your honour," he said, "that you are not dining with Baring, and I will forgive!"

For a moment she seemed as though she were summoning all her courage to tell the lie which he half expected. Instead she changed her mind.

"Do not be unkind," she begged. "I am dining with Captain Baring. The poor man is distracted. You know that I cannot bear to hurt people. Be kind this once. You may take my engagement book, you may fill it up as you will, but to-night I must dine with him. Consider, my friend. You may have many months before you in London. Captain Baring finishes his work at the Admiralty to-day, and leaves for Portsmouth to-morrow morning. He may not be in London again for some time. I promised him long ago that I would dine with him to-night on one condition. That condition he is keeping. I cannot break my word."

Norgate rose gloomily to his feet.

"Of course," he said, "I don't want to be un-

reasonable, and any one can see the poor fellow is
head over ears in love with you."

She took his arm as she led him towards the door.

"Listen," she promised, laughing into his face,
"when you are as much in love with me as he is, I
will put off every other engagement I have in the
world, and I will dine with you. You understand?
We shall meet later at the club, I hope. Until then,
au revoir!"

Norgate hailed a taxi outside and was driven at
once to the nearest telephone call office. There,
after some search in the directory, he rang up a number and enquired for Captain Baring. There was a
delay of about five minutes. Then Baring spoke
from the other end of the telephone.

"Who is it wants me?" he enquired, rather impatiently.

"Are you Baring?" Norgate asked, deepening
his voice a little.

"Yes! Who are you?"

"I am a friend," Norgate answered slowly.

"What the devil do you mean by 'a friend'?"
was the irritated reply. "I am engaged here most
particularly."

"There can be nothing so important," Norgate
declared, "as the warning I am charged to give to
you. Remember that it is a friend who speaks.
There is a train about five o'clock to Portsmouth.
Your work is finished. Take that train and stay
away from London."

Norgate set down the receiver without listening to
the tangle of exclamations from the other end, and

walked quickly out of the shop.   He re-entered his taxi.

"The St. James's Club," he ordered.

CHAPTER XIII

Norgate found Selingman in the little drawing-room of the club, reclining in an easy-chair, a small cup of black coffee by his side. He appeared to be exceedingly irate at the performance of his partner in a recent rubber, and he seized upon Norgate as a possibly sympathetic confidant.

"Listen to me for one moment," he begged, " and tell me whether I have not the right to be aggrieved. I go in on my own hand, no trump. I am a careful declarer. I play here every day when I am in London, and they know me well to be a careful declarer. My partner — I do not know his name; I hope I shall never know his name; I hope I shall never see him again — he takes me out. 'Into what?' you ask. Into diamonds! I am regretful, but I recognise, as I believe, a necessity. I ask you, of what do you suppose his hand consists? Down goes my no trump on the table — a good, a very good no trump. He has in his hand the ace, king, queen and five diamonds, the king of clubs guarded, the ace and two little hearts, and he takes me out into diamonds from no trumps with a score at love all. Two pences they had persuaded me to play, too, and it was the rubber game. Afterwards he said to me: 'You seem annoyed'; and I replied 'I am annoyed,' and I am. I come in here to drink coffee and cool myself. Pres-

ently I will cut into another rubber, where that young
man is not. Perhaps our friend Mrs. Benedek will
be here. You and I and Mrs. Benedek, but not, if
we can help it, the lady who smokes the small black
cigars. She is very amiable, but I cannot attend to
the game while she sits there opposite to me. She
fascinates me. In Germany sometimes our women
smoke cigarettes, but cigars, and in public, never!"

"We'll get a rubber presently, I dare say," Norgate remarked, settling himself in an easy-chair.
"How's business?"

"Business is very good," Selingman declared.
"It is so good that I must be in London for another
week or so before I set off to the provinces. It grows
and grows all the time. Soon I must find a manager
to take over some of my work here. At my time of
life one likes to enjoy. I love to be in London; I do
not like these journeys to Newcastle and Liverpool
and places a long way off. In London I am happy.
You should go into business, young man. It is not
well for you to do nothing."

"Do you think I should be useful in the crockery
trade?" Norgate asked.

Herr Selingman appeared to take the enquiry quite
seriously.

"Why not?" he demanded. "You are well-edu-
cated, you have address, you have intelligence. Mrs.
Benedek has spoken very highly of you. But you —
oh, no! It would not suit you at all to plunge yourself into commerce, nor would it suit you, I think,
to push the affairs of a prosperous German concern.
You are very English, Mr. Norgate, is that not so?"

"Not aggressively," Norgate replied. "As a matter of fact, I am rather fed up with my own country just now."

Mr. Selingman sat quite still in his chair. Some signs of a change which came to him occasionally were visible in his face. He was for that moment no longer the huge, overgrown schoolboy bubbling over with the joy and appetite of life. His face seemed to have resolved itself into sterner lines. It was the face of a thinker.

"There are other Englishmen besides you," Selingman said, "who are a little — what you call ' fed up ' with your country. You have much common sense. You do not believe that yours is the only country in the world. You like sometimes to hear plain speech from one who knows?"

"Without a doubt," Norgate assented.

Mr. Selingman stroked his knee with his fat hand.

"You in England," he continued, "you are too prosperous. Very, very slowly the country is drifting into the hands of the people. A country that is governed entirely by the people goes down, down, down. Your classes are losing their hold and their influence. You have gone from Tory to Whig, from Whig to Liberal, from Liberal to Radical, and soon it will be the Socialists who govern. You know what will come then? Colonies! What do your radicals care about colonies? Institutions! What do they care about institutions? All you who have inherited money, they will bleed. You will become worse than a nation of shop-keepers. You will be an illustration to all the world of the dangers of democracy.

So! I go on. I tell you why that comes about. You are in the continent of Europe, and you will not do as Europe does. You are a nation outside. You have believed in yourselves and believed in yourselves, till you think that you are infallible. Before long will come the revolution. It will be a worse revolution than the French Revolution."

Norgate smiled. "Too much common sense about us, I think, Mr. Selingman, for such happenings," he declared. "I grant you that the classes are getting the worst of it so far as regards the government of the country, but I can't quite see the future that you depict."

"Good Englishman!" Herr Selingman murmured approvingly. "That is your proper attitude. You do not see because you will not see. I tell you that the best thing in all the world would be a little blood-letting. You do not like your Government. Would it not please you to see them humiliated just a little?"

"In what way?"

"Oh! there are ways," Selingman declared. "A little gentle smack like this,"— his two hands came together with a crash which echoed through the room —"a little smack from Germany would do the business. People would open their eyes and begin to understand. A Radical Government may fill your factories with orders and rob the rich to increase the prosperity of the poor, but it will not keep you a great nation amongst the others."

Norgate nodded.

"You seem to have studied the question pretty closely," he remarked.

"I study the subject closely," Selingman went on, "because my interests are yours. My profits are made in England. I am German born, but I am English, too, in feeling. To me the two nations are one. We are of the same race. That is why I am sorrowful when I see England slipping back. That is why I would like to see her have just a little lesson."

Selingman paused. Norgate rose to his feet and stood on the hearthrug, with his elbow upon the mantelpiece.

"Twice we have come as far as that, Mr. Selingman," he pointed out. "England requires a little lesson. You have something in your mind behind that, something which you are half inclined to say to me. Isn't that so? Why not go on?"

"Because I am not sure of you," Selingman confessed frankly. "Because you might misunderstand what I say, and we should be friends no longer, and you would say silly things about me and my views. Therefore, I like to keep you for a friend, and I go no further at present. You say that you are a little angry with your country, but you Englishmen are so very prejudiced, so very quick to take offence, so very insular, if I may use the word. I do not know how angry you are with your country. I do not know if your mind is so big and broad that you would be willing to see her suffer a little for her greater good. Ah, but the lady comes at last!"

Mrs. Benedek was accompanied by a tall, middle-aged man, of fair complexion, whom Selingman greeted with marked respect. She turned to Norgate.

"Let me present you," she said, "to Prince Edward of Lenemaur — Mr. Francis Norgate."

The two men shook hands.

"I played golf with you once at Woking," Norgate reminded his new acquaintance.

"I not only remember it," Prince Edward answered, "but I remember the result. You beat me three up, and we were to have had a return, but you had to leave for Paris on the next day."

"You will be able to have your return match now," Mrs. Benedek observed. "Mr. Norgate is going to be in England for some time. Let us play bridge. I have to leave early to-night — I am dining out — and I should like to make a little money."

They strolled into the bridge-room. Selingman hung behind with Norgate.

"Soon," he suggested, "we must finish our talk, is it not so? Dine with me to-night. Mrs. Benedek has deserted me. We will eat at the Milan Grill. The cooking there is tolerable, and they have some Rhine wine — but you shall taste it."

"Thank you," Norgate assented, "I shall be very pleased."

They played three or four rubbers. Then Mrs. Benedek glanced at the clock.

"I must go," she announced. "I am dining at eight o'clock."

"Stay but for one moment," Selingman begged. "We will all take a little mixed vermouth together. I shall tell the excellent Horton how to prepare it. Plenty of lemon-peel, and just a dash — but I will not give my secret away."

He called the steward and whispered some instructions in his ear. While they were waiting for the result, a man came in with an evening paper in his hand. He looked across the room to a table beyond that at which Norgate and his friends were playing.

" Heard the news, Monty? " he asked.

" No! What is it? " was the prompt enquiry.

" Poor old Baring —"

The newcomer stopped short. For the first time he noticed Mrs. Benedek. She half rose from her chair, however, and her eyes were fixed upon him.

" What is it? " she exclaimed. " What has happened? "

There was a moment's awkward silence. Mrs. Benedek snatched the paper away from the man's fingers and read the little paragraph out aloud. For a moment she was deathly white.

" What is it? " Selingman demanded.

" Freddy Baring," she whispered —" Captain Baring — shot himself in his room at the Admiralty this afternoon! Some one telephoned to him. Five minutes later he was found — dead — a bullet wound through his temple! . . . Give me my chair, please. I think that I am going to faint."

CHAPTER XIV

Selingman and Norgate dined together that evening in a corner of a large, popular grill-room near the Strand. They were still suffering from the shock of the recent tragedy. They both rather avoided the topic of Baring's sudden death. Selingman made but one direct allusion to it.

"Only yesterday," he remarked, "I said to little Bertha — I have known her so long that I call her always Bertha — that this bureau work was bad for Baring. When I was over last, a few months ago, he was the picture of health. Yesterday he looked wild and worried. He was at work with others, they say, at the Admiralty upon some new invention. Poor fellow!"

Norgate, conscious of a curious callousness which even he himself found inexplicable, made some conventional reply only. Selingman began to talk of other matters.

"Truly," he observed, "a visit to your country is good for the patriotic German. Behold! here in London, we are welcomed by a German *maître d'hôtel;* we are waited on by a German waiter; we drink German wine; we eat off what I very well know is German crockery."

"And some day, I suppose," Norgate put in, "we are to be German subjects. Isn't that so?"

Selingman's denial was almost unduly emphatic.

"Never!" he exclaimed. "There is nothing so foolish as the way many of you English seem to regard us Germans as though we were wild beasts of prey. Now it gives me pleasure to talk with a man like yourself, Mr. Norgate. I like to look a little into the future and speculate as to our two countries. Above all things, this thing I do truly know. The German nation stands for peace. Yet in order that peace shall everywhere prevail, a small war, a humanely-conducted war, may sometime within the future, one must believe, take place. It would last but a short time, but it might lead to great changes. I have sometimes thought, my young friend Norgate, that such a war might be the greatest blessing which England could ever experience."

"As a discipline, you mean?" Norgate murmured.

"As a cleansing tonic," Selingman declared. "It would sweep out your Radical Government. It would bring the classes back to power. It would kindle in the spirits of your coming generation the spark of that patriotism which is, alas! just now a very feeble flame. What do you think? You agree with me, eh?"

"It is going a long way," Norgate said cautiously, "to approve of a form of discipline so stringent."

"But not too far — oh, believe me, not too far!" Selingman insisted. "If that war should come, it would come solely with the idea of sweeping away this Government, which is most distasteful to all German politicians. It would come solely with the idea that with a new form of government here, more solid and lasting terms of friendship could be arranged between Germany and England."

"A very interesting theory," Norgate remarked. "Do you believe in it yourself?"

Selingman paused to give an order to a waiter. His tone suddenly became more serious. He pointed to the menu.

"They have dared," he exclaimed, "to bring us *Hollandaise* sauce with the asparagus! A gastronomic indignity! It is such things as this which would endanger the *entente* between our countries."

"I don't mind *Hollandaise*," Norgate ventured.

"Then of eating you know very little," Herr Selingman pronounced. "There is only one sauce to be served with asparagus, and that is finely drawn butter. I have explained to the *maître d'hôtel*. He must bring us what I desire. Meanwhile, we spoke, I think, of our two countries. You asked me a question. I do indeed believe in the theories which I have been advancing."

"But wouldn't a war smash up your crockery business?" Norgate asked.

"For six months, yes! And after that six months, fortunes for all of us, trade such as the world has never known, a settled peace, a real union between two great and friendly countries. I wish England well. I love England. I love my holidays over here, my business trips which are holidays in themselves, and for their sake and for my own sake, I say that just a little wrestle, a slap on the cheek from one and a punch on the nose from the other, and we should find ourselves."

"War is a very dangerous conflagration," Norgate remarked. "I cannot think of any experiment more hazardous."

"It is no experiment," Selingman declared. "It is a certainty. All that we do in my country, we do by what we call previously ascertained methods. We test the ground in front of us before we plant our feet upon it. We not only look into the future, but we stretch out our hands. We make the doubtful places sure. Our turn of mind is scientific. Our road-making and our bridge-building, our empire-making and our diplomacy, they are all fashioned in the same manner. If you could trust us, Mr. Norgate, if you could trust yourself to work for the good of both countries, we could make very good and profitable use of you during the next six months. Would you like to hear more?"

"But I know nothing about crockery!"

"Would you like to hear more?" Selingman repeated.

"I think I should."

"Very well, then," Selingman proceeded. "To-morrow we will talk of it. There are some ways in which you might be very useful, useful at the same time to your country and to ours. Your position might be somewhat peculiar, but that you would be prepared for a short time to tolerate."

"Peculiar in what respect?" Norgate asked.

Selingman held his glass of yellow wine up to the light and criticised it for a moment. He set it down empty.

"Peculiar," he explained, "inasmuch as you might

seem to be working with Germany, whereas you were really England's best friend. But let us leave these details until to-morrow. We have talked enough of serious matters. I have a box at the Gaiety, and we must not be late — also a supper party afterwards. This is indeed a country for enjoyment. To-morrow we speak of these things again. You have seen our little German lady at the Gaiety? You have heard her sing and watch her dance? Well, to-night you shall meet her."

" Rosa Morgen? " Norgate exclaimed.

Selingman nodded complacently.

" She sups with us," he announced, " she and others. That is why, when they spoke to me of going back for bridge to-night, I pretended that I did not hear. Bridge is very good, but there are other things. To-night I am in a frivolous vein. I have many friends amongst the young ladies of the Gaiety. You shall see how they will welcome me."

" You seem to have found your way about over here," Norgate remarked, as he lit a cigar and waited while his companion paid the bill.

" I am a citizen of the world," Selingman admitted. " I enjoy myself as I go, but I have my eyes always fixed upon the future. I make many friends, and I do not lose them. I set my face towards the pleasant places, and I keep it in that direction. It is the cult of some to be miserable; it is mine to be happy. The person who does most good in the world is the person who reflects the greatest amount of happiness. Therefore, I am a philanthropist. You shall learn from me, my young friend, how to banish some of that gloom from your face. You shall learn how to find happiness."

They made their way across to the Gaiety, where Selingman was a very conspicuous figure in the largest and most conspicuous box. He watched with complacency the delivery of enormous bouquets to the principal artistes, and received their little bow of thanks with spontaneous and unaffected graciousness. Afterwards he dragged Norgate round to the stage-door, installed him in a taxi, and handed over to his escort two or three of his guests.

"I entrust you, Mr. Norgate," he declared, "with our one German export more wonderful, even, than my crockery — Miss Rosa Morgen. Take good care of her and bring her to the Milan. The other young ladies are my honoured guests, but they are also Miss Morgen's. She will tell you their names. I have others to look after."

Norgate's last glimpse of Selingman was on the pavement outside the theatre, surrounded by a little group of light-hearted girls and a few young men.

"He is perfectly wonderful, our Mr. Selingman," Miss Morgen murmured, as they started off. "Tell me how long you have known him, Mr. Norgate?"

"Four days," Norgate replied.

She screamed with laughter.

"It is so like him," she declared. "He makes friends everywhere. A day is sufficient. He gives such wonderful parties. I do not know why we all like to come, but we do. I suppose that we all get half-a-dozen invitations to supper most nights, but there is not one of us who does not put off everything to sup with Mr. Selingman. He sits in the middle — oh, you shall watch him to-night! — and what he says I do not know, but we laugh, and then we laugh again, and every one is happy."

" I think he is the most irresistible person," Norgate agreed. " I met him two or three nights ago, coming over from Berlin, and he spoke of nothing but crockery and politics. To-night I dine with him, and I find a different person."

" He is a perfect dear," one of the other girls exclaimed, " but so curiously inquisitive! I have a great friend, a gunner, whom I brought with me to one of his parties, and he is always asking me questions about him and his work. I had to absolutely worry Dick so as to be able to answer all his questions, didn't I, Rosa? "

Miss Morgen nodded a little guardedly.

" I should not call him really inquisitive," she said. " It is because he likes to seem interested in the subject which interests you."

" I am not at all sure whether that is true," the other young lady objected. " You remember when Ellison Gray was always around with us? Why, I know that Mr. Selingman simply worried Maud's life out of her to get a little model of his aëroplane from him. There were no end of things he wanted to know about cubic feet and dimensions. He is a dear, all the same."

" A perfect dear! " the others echoed.

They drew up outside the Milan. Rosa Morgen turned to their escort.

"We will meet you in the hall in five minutes," she said. "Then we can all go together and find Mr. Selingman."

CHAPTER XV

Selingman's supper party was in some respects both distinctive and unusual. Norgate, looking around him, thought that he had never in his life been among such a motley assemblage of people. There were eight or nine musical comedy young ladies; a couple of young soldiers, one of whom he knew slightly, who had arrived as escorts to two of the young ladies; Prince Edward of Lenemaur; a youthful peer, who by various misdemeanours had placed himself outside the pale of any save the most Bohemian society, and several other men whose faces were unfamiliar. They occupied a round table just inside the door of the restaurant, and they sat there till long after the lights were lowered. The conversation all the time was of the most general and frivolous description, and Selingman, as the hour grew later, seemed to grow larger and redder and more joyous. The only hint at any serious conversation came from the musical comedy star who sat at Norgate's left.

" Do you know our host very well? " she asked Norgate once.

" I am afraid I can't say that I know him well at all," Norgate replied. " I met him in the train coming from Berlin, a few nights ago."

" He is the most original person," she declared.

" He entertains whenever he has a chance ; he makes new friends every hour ; he eats and drinks and seems always to be enjoying himself like an overgrown baby. And yet, all the time there is such a very serious side to him. One feels that he has a purpose in it all."

" Perhaps he has," Norgate ventured.

" Perhaps he has," she agreed, lowering her voice a little. " At least, I believe one thing. I believe that he is a good German and yet a great friend of England."

" You don't find the two incompatible, then ? "

" I do not," the young lady replied firmly. " I do not understand everything, of course, but I am half German and half English, so I can appreciate both sides, and I do believe that Mr. Selingman, if he had not been so immersed in his business, might have been a great politician."

The conversation drifted into other channels. Norgate was obliged to give some attention to the more frivolous young lady on his right. The general exodus to the bar smoking-room only took place long after midnight. Every one was speaking of going on to a supper club to dance, and Norgate quietly slipped away. He took a hurried leave of his host.

" You will excuse me, won't you ? " he begged. " Enjoyed my evening tremendously. I'd like you to come and dine with me one night."

" We will meet at the club to-morrow afternoon," Selingman declared. " But why not come on with us now ? You are not weary ? They are taking me to a supper club, these young people. I have engaged myself to dance with Miss Morgen — I, who weigh nineteen stone! It will be a thing to see. Come with us."

Norgate excused himself and left the place a moment later. It was a fine night, and he walked slowly towards Pall Mall, deep in thought. Outside one of the big clubs on the right-hand side, a man descended from a taxicab just as Norgate was passing. They almost ran into one another.

" Norgate, you reprobate! "

" Hebblethwaite! "

The latter passed his arm through the young man's and led him towards the club steps.

" Come in and have a drink," he invited. " I am just up from the House. I do wish you could get some of your military friends to stop worrying us, Norgate. Two hours to-night have been absolutely wasted because they would talk National Service and heckle us about the territorials."

" I'll have the drink, although heaven knows I don't need any! " Norgate replied. " As for the rest, I am all on the side of the hecklers. You ought to know that."

They drew two easy-chairs together in a corner of the great, deserted smoking-room, and Hebblethwaite ordered the whiskies and sodas.

" Yes," he remarked, " I forgot. You are on the other side, aren't you? I haven't a word to say against the navy. We spend more money than is necessary upon it, and I stick out for economy whenever I can. But as regards the army, my theory is that it is useless. It's only a temptation to us to meddle in things that don't concern us. The navy is sufficient to defend these shores, if any one were foolish enough to wish to attack us. If we need an army at all, we should need one ten times the size, but we don't. Nature has seen to that. Yet tonight, when I was particularly anxious to get on with some important domestic legislation, we had to sit and listen to hours of prosy military talk, the possibilities of this and that. They don't realise, these brain-fogged ex-military men, that we are living in days of common sense. Before many years have passed, war will belong to the days of romance."

"For a practical politician, Hebblethwaite," Norgate pronounced, "you have some of the rottenest ideas I ever knew. You know perfectly well that if Germany attacked France, we are almost committed to chip in. We couldn't sit still, could we, and see Calais and Boulogne, Dieppe and Ostend, fortified against us?"

"If Germany should attack France!" Hebblethwaite repeated. "If Prussia should send an expeditionary force to Cornwall, or the Siamese should declare themselves on the side of the Ulster men! We must keep in politics to possibilities that are reasonable."

"Take another view of the same case, then," Norgate continued. "Supposing Germany should violate Belgium's independence?"

"You silly idiot!" Hebblethwaite exclaimed, as he took a long draught of his whisky and soda, lit a cigar, and leaned back in his chair, "the neutrality of Belgium is guaranteed by a treaty, actually signed by Germany!"

"Supposing she should break her treaty?" Norgate persisted. "I told you what I heard in the train the other night. It isn't for nothing that that sort of work is going on."

Hebblethwaite shook his head.

"You are incorrigible, Norgate! Germany is one of the Powers of Europe undoubtedly possessing a high sense of honour and rectitude of conduct. If any nation possesses a national conscience, and an appreciation of national ethics, they do. Germany would be less likely than any nation in the world to break a treaty."

"Hebblethwaite," Norgate declared solemnly, "if you didn't understand the temperament and character of your constituents better than you do the German temperament and character, you would never have set your foot across the threshold of Westminster. The fact of it is you're a domestic politician of the very highest order, but as regards foreign affairs and the greater side of international politics, well, all I can say is you've as little grasp of them as a local mayor might have."

"Look here, young fellow," Hebblethwaite protested, "do you know that you are talking to a Cabinet Minister?"

"To a very possible Prime Minister," Norgate replied, "but I am going to tell you what I think, all the same. I'm fed up with you all. I bring you some certain and sure information, proving conclusively that Germany is maintaining an extraordinary system of espionage over here, and you tell me to mind my own business. I tell you, Hebblethwaite, you and your Party are thundering good legislators, but you'll ruin the country before you've finished. I've had enough. It seems to me we thoroughly deserve the shaking up we're going to get. I am going to turn German spy myself and work for the other side."

"You do, if there's anything in it," Hebblethwaite retorted, with a grin. "I promise we won't arrest you. You shall hop around the country at your own sweet will, preach Teutonic doctrines, and pave the way for the coming of the conquerors. You'll have to keep away from our arsenals and our flying places, because our Service men are so prejudiced. Short of that you can do what you like."

Norgate finished his cigar in silence. Then he threw the end into the fireplace, finished his whisky and soda, and rose.

"Hebblethwaite," he said, "this is the second time you've treated me like this. I shall give you another chance. There's just one way I may be of use, and I am going to take it on. If I get into trouble about it, it will be your fault, but next time I come and talk with you, you'll have to listen to me if I shove the words down your throat. Good night!"

"Good night, Norgate," Hebblethwaite replied pleasantly. "What you want is a week or two's change somewhere, to get this anti-Teuton fever out of your veins. I think we'll send you to Tokyo and let you have a turn with the geishas in the cherry groves."

"I wouldn't go out for your Government, any-way," Norgate declared. "I've given you fair warning. I am going in on the other side. I'm fed up with the England you fellows represent."

"Nice breezy sort of chap you are for a pal!" Hebblethwaite grumbled. "Well, get along with you, then. Come and look me up when you're in a better humour."

"I shall probably find you in a worse one," Norgate retorted. "Good night!"

It was one o'clock when Norgate let himself into his rooms. To his surprise, the electric lights were burning in his sitting-room. He entered a little abruptly and stopped short upon the threshold. A slim figure in dark travelling clothes, with veil pushed back, was lying curled up on his sofa. She stirred a little at his coming, opened her eyes, and looked at him.

CHAPTER XVI

Throughout those weeks and months of tangled, lurid sensations, of amazing happenings which were yet to come, Norgate never once forgot that illuminative rush of fierce yet sweet feelings which suddenly thrilled his pulses. He understood in that moment the intolerable depression of the last few days. He realised the absolute advent of the one experience hitherto missing from his life. The very intensity of his feelings kept him silent, kept him unresponsive to her impetuous but unspoken welcome. Her arms dropped to her side, her lips for a moment quivered. Her voice, notwithstanding her efforts to control it, shook a little. She was no longer the brilliant young Court beauty of Vienna. She was a tired and disappointed girl.

"You are surprised — I should not have come here! It was such a foolish impulse."

She caught up her gloves feverishly, but Norgate's moment of stupefaction had passed. He clasped her hands.

"Forgive me," he begged. "It is really you — Anna!"

His words were almost incoherent, but his tone was convincing. Her fears passed away.

"You don't wonder that I was a little surprised, do you?" he exclaimed. "You were not only the last person whom I was thinking of, but you were certainly the last person whom I expected to see in London or to welcome here."

"But why?" she asked. "I told you that I came often to this country."

"I remember," Norgate admitted. "Yet I never ventured to hope —"

"Of course I should not have come here," she interrupted. "It was absurd of me, and at such an hour! And yet I am staying only a few hundred yards away. The temptation to-night was irresistible. I felt as one sometimes does in this queer, enormous city — lonely. I telephoned, and your servant, who answered me, said that you were expected back at any moment. Then I came myself."

"You cannot imagine that I am not glad to see you," he said earnestly.

"I want to believe that you are glad," she answered. "I have been restless ever since you left. Tell me at once, what did they say to you here?"

"I am practically shelved," he told her bitterly. "In twelve months' time, perhaps, I may be offered something in America or Asia — countries where diplomacy languishes. In a word, your mighty autocrat has spoken the word, and I am sacrificed."

She moved towards the window.

"I am stifled!" she exclaimed. "Open it wide, please."

He threw it open. They looked out eastwards. The roar of the night was passing. Here and there were great black spaces. On the Thames a sky-sign or two remained. The blue, opalescent glare from the Gaiety dome still shone. The curving lights which spanned the bridges and fringed the Embankment still glittered. The air, even here, high up as they were on the seventh story of the building, seemed heavy and lifeless.

" There is a storm coming," she said. " I have felt it for days."

She stood looking out, pale, her large eyes strained as though seeking to read something which eluded her in the clouds or the shadows which hung over the city. She had rather the air of a frightened but eager child. She rested her fingers upon his arm, not exactly affectionately, but as though she felt the need of some protection.

" Do you know," she whispered, " the feeling of this storm has been in my heart for days. I am afraid — afraid for all of us! "

" Afraid of what? " he asked gently.

" Afraid," she went on, " because it seems to me that I can hear, at times like this, when one is alone, the sound of what one of your writers called footsteps amongst the hills, footsteps falling upon wool, muffled yet somehow ominous. There is trouble coming. I know it. I am sure of it."

" In this country they do not think so," he reminded her. " Most of our great statesmen of to-day have come to the conclusion that there will be no more war."

" You have no great statesmen," she answered simply. " You have plenty of men who would make very fine local administrators, but you have no statesmen, or you would have provided for what is coming."

There was a curious conviction in her words, a sense of one speaking who has seen the truth.

"Tell me," he asked, "is there anything that you know of —"

"Ah! but that I may not tell you," she interrupted, turning away from the window. "Of myself just now I say nothing — only of you. I am here for a day or two. It is through me that you have suffered this humiliation. I wanted to know just how far it went. Is there anything I can do?"

"What could any one do?" he asked. "I am the victim of circumstances."

"But for a whole year!" she exclaimed. "You are not like so many young Englishmen. You do not wish to spend your time playing polo and golf, and shooting. You must do something. What are you going to do with that year?"

He moved across the room and took a cigarette from a box.

"Give me something to drink, please," she begged.

He opened a cupboard in his sideboard and gave her some soda-water. She had still the air of waiting for his reply.

"What am I going to do?" he repeated. "Well, here I am with an idle twelve months. It makes no difference to anybody what time I get up, what time I go to bed, with whom or how I spend the day. I suppose to some people it would sound like Paradise. To me it is hateful. Shall I be your secretary?"

"How do you know that I need a secretary?" she asked.

" How should I ? " he replied. " Yet you are not altogether an idler in life, are you? "

For a moment she did not answer. The silence in the room was almost impressive. He looked at her over the top of the soda-water syphon whose handle he was manipulating.

" What do you imagine might be my occupation, then? " she asked.

" I have heard it suggested," he said slowly, " that you have been a useful intermediary in carrying messages of the utmost importance between the Kaiser and the Emperor of Austria."

" Your Intelligence Department is not so bad," she remarked. " It is true. Why not? At the German Court I count for little, perhaps. In Austria my father was the Emperor's only personal friend. My mother was scarcely popular there — she was too completely English — but since my father died the Emperor will scarcely let me stay a week away. Yes, your information is perhaps true. I will supplement it, if you like. Since our little affair in the Café de Berlin, the Kaiser, who went out of his way to insist upon your removal from Berlin, has notified the Emperor that he would prefer to receive his most private dispatches either through the regular diplomatic channels or by some other messenger."

Norgate's emphatic expletive was only half-stifled as she continued.

" For myself," she said with a shrug, " I am not sorry. I found it very interesting, but of late those feelings of which I have told you have taken hold of me. I have felt as though a terrible shadow were brooding over the world."

"Let me ask you once more," he begged. "Why are you in London?"

"I received a wire from the Emperor," she explained, "instructing me to return at once to Vienna. If I go there, I know very well that I shall not be allowed to leave the city. I have been trusted implicitly, and they will keep me practically a prisoner. They will think that I may feel a resentment against the Kaiser, and they will be afraid. Therefore, I came here. I have every excuse for coming. It is according to my original plans. You will find that by to-morrow morning I shall have a second message from Vienna. All the same, I am not sure that I shall go."

There was a ring at the bell. Norgate started, and Anna looked at the clock.

"Who is that?" she asked. "Do you see the time?"

Norgate moved to the door and threw it open. A waiter stood there.

"What do you want?" demanded Norgate.

The man pointed to the indicator.

"The bell rang, sir," he replied. "Is there anything I can get for you?"

"I rang no bell," Norgate asserted. "Your indicator must be out of order."

Norgate would have closed the door, but Anna intervened.

"Tell the waiter I wish to speak to him," she begged.

The man advanced at once into the room and glanced interrogatively at Anna. She addressed him suddenly in Austrian, and he replied without hesitation. She nodded. Then she turned to Norgate and laughed softly.

"You see how perfect the system is," she said. "I was followed here, passed on to your floor-waiter. You are a spy, are you not?" she added, turning to the man. "But of course you are!"

"Madame!" the man protested. "I do not understand."

"You can go away," she replied. "You can tell Herr Selingman in your morning's report that I came to Mr. Norgate's rooms at an early hour in the morning and spent an hour talking with him. You can go now."

The man withdrew without remark. He was a quiet, inoffensive-looking person, with sallow complexion, suave but silent manners. Norgate closed the door behind him.

"A victim of the system which all Europe knows of except you people," she remarked lightly. "Well, after this I must be careful. Walk with me to my hotel."

"Of course," he assented.

They made their way along the silent corridors to the lift, out into the streets, empty of traffic now save for the watering-carts and street scavengers.

"Will there be trouble for you," Norgate asked at last, "because of this?"

"There is more trouble in my own heart," she told him quietly. "I feel strangely disturbed, uncertain which way to move. Let me take your arm — so. I like to walk like that. Somehow I think, Mr. Francis Norgate, that that little fracas in the Café de Berlin is going to make a great difference in both our lives. I know now what I had begun to believe. Like all the trusted agents of sovereigns, I have become an object of suspicion. Well, we shall see. At least I am glad to know that there is some one whom I can trust. Perhaps to-morrow I will tell you all that is in my heart. We might even, if you wished it, if you were willing to face a few risks, we might even work together to hold back the thunder. So! Good night, my friend," she added, turning suddenly around.

He held her hand for a moment as they stood together on the pavement outside her hotel. For a single moment he fancied that there was a change in that curious personal aloofness which seemed so distinctive of her. It passed, however, as she turned from him with her usual half-insolent, half gracious little nod.

" To-morrow," she directed, " you must ring me up. Let it be at eleven o'clock."

CHAPTER XVII

The Ambassador glanced at the clock as he entered his library to greet his early morning visitor. It was barely nine o'clock.

"Dear friend," he exclaimed, as he held out his hands, "I am distressed to keep you waiting! Such zeal in our affairs must, however, not remain unnoticed. I will remember it in my reports."

Anna smiled as he stooped to kiss her fingers.

"I had special reasons," she explained, "for my haste. I was disappointed, indeed, that I could not see you last night."

"I was at Windsor," her host remarked. "Now come, sit there in the easy-chair by the side of my table. My secretaries have not yet arrived. We shall be entirely undisturbed. I have ordered coffee here, of which we will partake together. A compromising meal to share, dear Baroness, but in the library of my own house it may be excused. The Princess sends her love. She will be glad if you will go to her apartments after we have finished our talk."

A servant entered with a tray, spread a cloth on a small round table, upon which he set out coffee, with rolls and butter and preserves. For a few moments they talked lightly of the weather, of her crossing, of mutual friends in Berlin and Vienna.

Then Anna, as soon as they were alone, leaned a little forward in her chair.

"You know that I have a sort of mission to you," she said. "I should not call it that, perhaps, but it comes to very nearly the same thing. The Emperor has charged me to express to you and to Count Lanyoki his most earnest desire that if the things should come which we know of, you both maintain your position here at any cost. The Emperor's last words to me were: 'If war is to come, it may be the will of God. We are ready, but there is one country which must be kept from the ranks of our enemies. That country is England. England must be dealt with diplomatically.' He looks across the continent to you, Prince. This is the friendly message which I have brought from his own lips."

The Prince stirred his coffee thoughtfully. He was a man just passing middle-age, with grey hair, thin in places but carefully trimmed, brushed sedulously back from his high forehead. His moustache, too, was grey, and his face was heavily lined, but his eyes, clear and bright, were almost the eyes of a young man.

"You can reassure the Emperor," he declared. "As you may imagine, my supply of information here is plentiful. If those things should come that we know of, it is my firm belief that with some reasonable yet nominal considerations, this Government will never lend itself to war."

"You really believe that?" she asked earnestly.

"I do," her companion assured her. "I try to be fair in my judgments. London is a pleasant city to live in, and English people are agreeable and well-bred, but they are a people absolutely without vital impulses. Patriotism belongs to their poetry books. Indolence has stagnated their blood. They are like a nation under a spell, with their faces turned towards the pleasant and desirable things. Only a few months ago, they even further reduced the size of their ridiculous army and threw cold water upon a scheme for raising untrained help in case of emergency. Even their navy estimates are passed with difficulty. The Government which is conducting the destinies of a people like this, which believes that war belongs to a past age, is never likely to become a menace to us."

Anna drew a little sigh and lit the cigarette which the Prince passed her. She threw herself back in her chair with an air of contentment.

" It is so pleasant once more to be among the big things," she declared. " In Berlin I think they are not fond of me, and they are so pompous and secretive. Tell me, dear Prince, will you not be kinder to me? Tell me what is really going to happen? "

He moved his chair a little closer to hers.

" I see no reason," he said cautiously, " why you should not be told. Events, then, will probably move in this direction. Provocation will be given by Servia. That is easily arranged. Tension will be caused, Austria will make enormous demands, Russia will remonstrate, and, before any one has time to breathe, the clouds will part to let the lightnings through. If anything, we are over-ready, straining with over-readiness."

"And the plan of campaign?"

"Austria and Italy," the Prince continued slowly, "will easily keep Russia in check. Germany will seize Belgium and rush through to Paris. She will either impose her terms there or leave a second-class army to conclude the campaign. There will be plenty of time for her then to turn back and fall in with her allies against Russia."

"And England?" Anna asked. "Supposing?"

The Prince tapped the table with his forefinger.

"Here," he announced, "we conquer with diplomacy. We have imbued the present Cabinet, even the Minister who is responsible for the army, with the idea that we stand for peace. We shall seem to be the attacked party in this war. We shall say to England —'Remain neutral. It is not your quarrel, and we will be capable of a great act of self-sacrifice. We will withhold our fleet from bombarding the French towns. England could do no more than deal with our fleet if she were at war. She shall do the same without raising a finger.' No country could refuse so sane and businesslike an offer, especially a country which will at once count upon its fingers how much it will save by not going to war."

"And afterwards?"

The Prince shrugged his shoulders. "Afterwards is inevitable."

"Please go on," she insisted.

"We shall occupy the whole of the coast from Antwerp to Havre. The indemnity which France and Russia will pay us will make us the mightiest nation on earth. We shall play with England as a

cat with a mouse, and when the time comes. . . .
Well, perhaps that will do," the Prince concluded,
smiling.

Anna was silent for several moments.

" I am a woman, you know," she said simply, " and
this sounds, in a way, terrible. Yet for months I
have felt it coming."

" There is nothing terrible about it," the Prince
replied, " if you keep the great principles of progress always before you. If a million or so of lives
are sacrificed, the great Germany of the future, gathering under her wings the peoples of the world, will
raise them to a pitch of culture and contentment and
happiness which will more than atone for the sacri-
fices of to-day. It is, after all, the future to which
we must look."

A telephone bell rang at the Prince's elbow. He
listened for a moment and nodded.

" An urgent visitor demands a moment of my
time," he said, rising.

" I have taken already too much," Anna declared,
" but I felt it was time that I heard the truth. They
fence with me so in Berlin, and, believe me, Prince
Herschfeld, in Vienna the Emperor is almost wholly
ignorant of what is planned."

The door was opened behind them. The Prince
turned around. A young man had ushered in Herr
Selingman. For a moment the latter looked steadily
at Anna. Then he glanced at the Ambassador as
though questioningly.

" You two must have met," the Prince murmured.

" We have met," Anna declared, smiling, as she

made her way towards the door, " but we do not know one another. It is best like that. Herr Selingman and I work in the same army —"

" But I, madame, am the sergeant," Selingman interrupted, with a low bow, " whilst you are upon the staff."

She laughed as she made her adieux and departed. The door closed heavily behind her. Selingman came a little further into the room.

" You have read your dispatches this morning, Prince? " he asked.

" Not yet," the latter replied. " Is there news, then? "

Selingman pointed to the closed door. " You have spoken for long with her? "

" Naturally," the Prince assented. " She is a confidential friend of the Emperor. She has been entrusted for the last two years with all the private dispatches between Vienna and Berlin."

" In your letters you will find news," Selingman declared. " She is pronounced suspect. She is under my care at this moment. A report was brought to me half an hour ago that she was here. I came on at once myself. I trust that I am in time? "

The Prince stood quite silent for a moment.

" Fortunately," he answered coolly, " I have told her nothing."

CHAPTER XVIII

As Norgate entered the premises of Selingman, Horsfal and Company a little later on the same morning he looked around him in some surprise. He had expected to find a deserted warehouse — probably only an office. He saw instead all the evidences of a thriving and prosperous business. Drays were coming and going from the busy door. Crates were piled up to the ceiling, clerks with notebooks in their hands passed continually back and forth. A small boy in a crowded office accepted his card and disappeared. In a few minutes he led Norgate into a waiting-room and handed him a paper.

"Mr. Selingman is engaged with a buyer for a few moments, sir," he reported. "He will see you presently."

Norgate looked through the windows out into the warehouse. There was no doubt whatever that this was a genuine and considerable trading concern. Presently the door of the inner office opened, and he heard Mr. Selingman's hearty tones.

"You have done well for yourself and well for your firm, sir," he was saying. "There is no one in Germany or in the world who can produce crockery at the price we do. They will give you a confirmation of the order in the office. Ah! my young friend," he went on, turning to Norgate, " you have kept your word, then. You are not a customer, but you may walk in. I shall make no money out of you, but we will talk together."

Norgate passed on into a comfortably furnished office, a little redolent of cigar smoke. Selingman bit off the end of a cigar and pushed the box towards his visitor.

" Try one of these," he invited. " German made, but Havana tobacco — mild as milk."

" Thank you," Norgate answered. " I don't smoke cigars in the morning. I'll have a cigarette, if I may."

" As you will. What do you think of us now that you have found your way here? "

" Your business seems to be genuine enough, at all events," Norgate observed.

" Genuine? Of course it is! " Selingman declared emphatically. " Do you think I should be fool enough to be connected with a bogus affair? My father and my grandfather before me were manufacturers of crockery. I can assure you that I am a very energetic and a very successful business man. If I have interests in greater things, those interests have developed naturally, side by side with my commercial success. When I say that I am a German, that to me means more, much more, than if I were to declare myself a native of any other country in the world. Sit opposite to me there. I have a quarter of an hour to spare. I can show you, if you will, over a thousand designs of various articles. I can show you orders — genuine orders, mind — from some of your big wholesale houses, which would astonish you. Or, if you prefer it, we can talk of affairs from another point of view. What do you say?"

"My interest in your crockery," Norgate announced, "is non-existent. I have come to hear your offer. I have decided to retire — temporarily, at any rate — from the Diplomatic Service. I understand that I am in disgrace, and I resent it. I resent having had to leave Berlin except at my own choice. I am looking for a job in some other walk of life."

Selingman nodded approvingly.

"Forgive me," he said, "but it is true, then, that you are in some way dependent upon your profession?"

"I am not a pauper outside it," Norgate replied, "but that is not the sole question. I need work, an interest in life, something to think about. I must either find something to do, or I shall go to Abyssinia. I should prefer an occupation here."

"I can help you," Selingman said slowly, "if you are a young man of common sense. I can put you in the way of earning, if you will, a thousand pounds a year and your travelling expenses, without interfering very much with your present mode of life."

"Selling crockery?"

Selingman flicked the ash from the end of his cigar. He shook his head good-naturedly.

"I am a judge of character, young man," he declared. "I pride myself upon that accomplishment. I know very well that in you we have one with brains.

Nevertheless, I do not believe that you would sell my crockery."

"It seems easy enough," Norgate observed.

"It may seem easy," Selingman objected, "but it is not. You have not, I am convinced, the gifts of a salesman. You would not reason and argue with these obstinate British shopkeepers. No! Your value to me would lie in other directions — in your social position, your opportunities of meeting with a class above the commercial one in which I have made my few English friends, and in your own intelligence."

"I scarcely see of what value these things would be to a vendor of crockery."

"They would be of no value at all," Selingman admitted. "It is not in the crockery business that I propose to make use of you. I believe that we both know that. We may dismiss it from our minds. It is only fencing with words. I will take you a little further. You have heard, by chance, of the Anglo-German Peace Society?"

"The name sounds familiar," Norgate confessed. "I can't say that I know anything about it."

"It was I who inaugurated that body," Selingman announced. "It is I who direct its interests."

"Congratulate you, I'm sure. You must find it uphill work sometimes."

"It is uphill work all the time," the German agreed. "Our great object is, as you can guess from the title, to promote good-feeling between the two countries, to heal up all possible breaches, to soothe and dispel that pitiful jealousy, of which, alas! too

much exists. It is not easy, Mr. Norgate. It is
not easy, my young friend. I meet with many disappointments. Yet it is a great and worthy under-
taking."

"It sounds all right," Norgate observed.
"Where do I come in?"

"I will explain. To carry out the aims of our
society, there is much information which we are continually needing. People in Germany are often
misled by the Press here. Facts and opinions are
presented to them often from an unpalatable point
of view. Furthermore, there is a section of the
Press which, so far from being on our side, seems
deliberately to try to stir up ill-feeling between the
two countries. We want to get behind the Press.
For that purpose we need to know the truth about
many matters; and as the truth is a somewhat rare
commodity, we are willing to pay for it. Now we
come face to face. It will be your business, if you
accept my offer, to collect such facts as may be useful to us."

"I see," Norgate remarked dubiously, "or rather
I don't see at all. Give me an example of the sort
of facts you require."

Mr. Selingman leaned a little forward in his chair.
He was warming to his subject.

"By all means. There is the Irish question,
then."

"The Irish question," Norgate repeated. "But
of what interest can that be to you in Germany?"

"Listen," Selingman continued. "Just as you
in London have great newspapers which seem to de-

vote themselves to stirring up bitter feeling between
our two countries, so we, alas! in Germany, have
newspapers and journals which seem to devote all
their energies to the same object. Now in this Irish
question the action of your Government has been
very much misrepresented in that section of our
Press and much condemned. I should like to get at
the truth from an authoritative source. I should
like to get it in such a form that I can present it
fairly and honestly to the public of Germany."

"That sounds reasonable enough," Norgate admitted. "There are several pamphlets —"

"I do not want pamphlets," Selingman interrupted. "I want an actual report from Ulster and
Dublin of the state of feeling in the country, and,
if possible, interviews with prominent people. For
this the society would pay a bonus over and above
the travelling expenses and your salary. If you accept my offer, this is probably one of the first tasks
I should commit to you."

"Give me a few more examples," Norgate
begged.

"Another subject," Selingman continued, "upon
which there is wide divergence of opinions in Germany, and a great deal of misrepresentation, is the
attitude of certain of your Cabinet Ministers towards
the French *entente:* how far they would support it,
at what they would stop short."

"Isn't that rather a large order? " Norgate ventured. "I don't number many Cabinet Ministers
among my personal friends."

Selingman puffed away at his cigar for a moment.

Then he withdrew it from his mouth and expelled large volumes of smoke.

" You are, I believe, intimately acquainted with Mr. Hebblethwaite? "

" How the mischief did you know that? " Norgate demanded.

" Our society," Selingman announced, smiling ponderously, " has ramifications in every direction. It is our business to know much. We are collectors of information of every sort and nature."

" Seems to have been part of your business to follow me about," observed Norgate.

" Perhaps so. If we thought it good for us to have you followed about, we certainly should," Selingman admitted. " You see, in Germany," he added, leaning back in his chair, " we lay great stress upon detail and intelligence. We get to know things: not the smattering of things, like you over here are too often content with, but to know them thoroughly and understand them. Nothing ever takes us by surprise. We are always forewarned. So far as any one can, we read the future."

" You are a very great nation, without a doubt," Norgate acknowledged, " but my quarter of an hour is coming to an end. Tell me what else you would expect from me if I accepted this post? "

" For the moment, I can think of nothing," Selingman replied. " There are many ways in which we might make use of you, but to name them now would be to look a little too far into the future."

" By whom should I really be employed? "

" By the Anglo-German Peace Society," Selingman answered promptly. "Let me say a word more about that society. I am proud of it. I am one of those prominent business men who are responsible for its initiation. I have given years of time and thought to it. All our efforts are directed towards promoting a better understanding with England, towards teaching the two countries to appreciate one another. But in the background there is always something else. It is useless to deny that the mistrust existing between the two countries has brought them more than once almost to the verge of war. What we want is to be able, at critical times, to throw oil upon the troubled waters, and if the worst should come, if a war really should break out, then we want to be able to act as peacemakers, to heal as soon as possible any little sores that there may be, and to enter afterwards upon a greater friendship with a purified England."

"It sounds very interesting," Norgate confessed. "I had an idea that you were proposing something quite different."

"Please explain."

"To be perfectly frank with you," Norgate acknowledged, "I thought you wanted me to do the ordinary spy business — traces of fortresses, and particulars about guns and aeroplanes —"

"Rubbish, my dear fellow!" Selingman interrupted. "Rubbish! Those things we leave to our military department, and pray that the question of their use may never arise. We are concerned wholly with economic and social questions, and our great aim is not war but peace."

"Very well, then," Norgate decided, "I accept. When shall I start?"

Selingman laid his hand upon the other's shoulder as he rose to his feet.

"Young man," he said, "you have come to a wise decision. Your salary will commence from the first of this month. Continue to live as usual. Let me have the opportunity of seeing you at the club, and let me know each day where you can be found. I will give you your instructions from day to day. You will be doing a great work, and, mind you, a patriotic work. If ever your conscience should trouble you, remember that. You are working not for Germany but for England."

"I will always remember that," Norgate promised, as he turned away.

CHAPTER XIX

Norgate found Anna waiting for him in the hall of the smaller hotel, a little further westward, to which she had moved. He looked admiringly at her cool white muslin gown and the perfection of her somewhat airy toilette.

" You are five minutes late," she remonstrated.

" I had to go into the city," he apologised. " It was rather an important engagement. Soon I must tell you all about it."

She looked at him a little curiously.

" I will be patient," promised Anna, " and ask no questions."

" You are still depressed? "

" Horribly," she confessed. " I do not know why, but London is getting on my nerves. It is so hatefully, stubbornly, obstinately imperturbable. I would find another word, but it eludes me. I think you would call it smug. And it is so noisy. Can we not go somewhere for lunch where it is tranquil, where one can rest and get away from this roar? "

" We could go to Ranelagh, if you liked," suggested Norgate. " There are some polo matches on this afternoon, but it will be quiet enough for lunch."

" I should love it! " she exclaimed. " Let us go quickly."

They lunched in a shady corner of the restaurant

and sat afterwards under a great oak tree in a retired spot at the further end of the gardens. Anna was still a little thoughtful.

"Do you know," she told her companion, "that I have received a hint to present myself in Berlin as soon as possible?"

"Are you going?" Norgate demanded quickly.

"I am not sure," she answered. "I feel that I must, and yet, in a sense, I do not like to go. I have a feeling that they do not mean to let me out of Berlin again. They think that I know too much."

"But why should they suddenly lose faith in you?" Norgate asked.

"Perhaps because the end is so near," she replied. "They know that I have strong English sympathies. Perhaps they think that they would not bear the strain of the times which are coming."

"You are an even greater pessimist than I myself," Norgate observed. "Do you really believe that the position is so critical?"

"I know it," she assured him. "I will not tell you all my reasons. There is no need for me to break a trust without some definite object. It seems to me that if your Secret Service Department were worth anything at all, your country would be in a state almost of panic. What is it they are playing down there? Polo, isn't it? There are six or eight military teams, crowds of your young officers making holiday. And all the time Krupps are working overtime, working night and day, and surrounded by sentries who shoot at sight any stranger. There are parts of the country, even now, under martial law.

The streets and the plains resound to the footsteps of armed hosts."

"But there is no excuse for war," he reminded her.

"An excuse is very easily found," she sighed. "German diplomacy is clumsy enough, but I think it can manage that. Do you know that this morning I had a letter from one of the greatest nobles of our own Court at Vienna? He knew that I had intended to take a villa in Normandy for August and September. He has written purposely to warn me not to do so, to warn me not to be away from Austria or Germany after the first of August."

"So soon!" he murmured.

They listened to the band for a moment. In the distance, an unceasing stream of men and women were passing back and forth under the trees and around the polo field.

"It will come like a thunderbolt," she said, "and when I think of it, all that is English in me rises up in revolt. In my heart I know so well that it is Germany and Germany alone who will provoke this war. I am terrified for your country. I admit it, you see, frankly. The might of Germany is only half understood here. It is to be a war of conquest, almost of extermination."

"That isn't the view of your friend Selingman," Norgate reminded her. "He, too, hints at coming trouble, but he speaks of it as just a salutary little lesson."

"Selingman, more than any one else in the world, knows differently," she assured him. "But come, we talk too seriously on such a wonderful afternoon.

I have made up my mind on one point, at least. I will stay here for a few days longer. London at this time of the year is wonderful. Besides, I have promised the Princess of Thurm that I will go to Ascot with her. Why should we talk of serious things any longer? Let us have a little rest. Let us promenade there with those other people, and listen to the band, and have some tea afterwards."

Norgate rose with alacrity, and they strolled across the lawns and down towards the polo field. Very soon they found themselves meeting friends in every direction. Anna extricated herself from a little group of acquaintances who had suddenly claimed her and came over to Norgate.

" Prince Herschfeld wants to talk to me for a few minutes," she whispered. " I think I should like to hear what he has to say. The Princess is there, too, whom I have scarcely seen. Will you come and be presented? "

" Might I leave you with them for a few minutes? " Norgate suggested. " There is a man here whom I want to talk to. I will come back for you in half an hour."

" You must meet the Prince first," she insisted. " He was interested when he heard who you were."

She turned to the little group who were awaiting her return. The Ambassador moved a little forward.

" Prince," she said, " may I present to you Mr. Francis Norgate? Mr. Norgate has just come from Berlin."

" Not with the kindliest feelings towards us, I am afraid," remarked the Prince, holding out his hand.

" I hope, however, that you will not judge us, as a nation, too severely."

" On the contrary, I was quite prepared to like Germany," Norgate declared. " I was simply the victim of a rather unfortunate happening."

" There are many others besides myself who sincerely regret it," the Prince said courteously. " You are kind enough to leave the Baroness for a little time in our charge. We will take the greatest care of her, and I hope that when you return you will give me the great pleasure of presenting you to the Princess."

" You are very kind," Norgate murmured.

" We shall meet again, then," the Prince declared, as he turned away with Anna by his side.

" In half an hour," Anna whispered, smiling at him over her shoulder.

CHAPTER XX

The Right Honourable John William Hebblethwaite strolled along by the rails of the polo ground, exchanging greetings with friends, feeling very well content with himself and the world generally. A difficult session was drawing towards an end. The problem which had defeated so many governments seemed at last, under his skilful treatment, capable of solution. Furthermore, the session had been one which had added to his reputation both as an orator and a statesman. There had been an astonishingly flattering picture of him in an illustrated paper that week, and he was exceedingly pleased with the effect of the white hat which he was wearing at almost a jaunty angle. He was a great man and he knew it. Nevertheless, he greeted Norgate with ample condescension and engaged him at once in conversation.

" Delighted to see you in such company, my young friend," he declared. " I think that half an hour's conversation with Prince Herschfeld would put some of those fire-eating ideas out of your head. That's the man whom we have to thank for the everyday improvement of our relations with Germany."

" The Prince has the reputation of being a great diplomatist," Norgate remarked.

" Added to which," Hebblethwaite continued, " he

came over here charged, as you might say, almost
with a special mission. He came over here to make
friends with England. He has done it. So long as
we have him in London, there will never be any serious fear of misunderstanding between the two countries."

"What a howling optimist you are!" Norgate observed.

"My young friend," Hebblethwaite protested, "I
am nothing of the sort. I am simply a man of much
common sense, enjoying, I may add, a few hours' holiday. By-the-by, Norgate, if one might venture to
enquire without indiscretion, who was the remarkably
charming foreign lady whom you were escorting?"

"The Baroness von Haase," Norgate replied.
"She is an Austrian."

Mr. Hebblethwaite sighed. He rather posed as an
admirer of the other sex.

"You young fellows," he declared, "who travel
about the world, are much to be envied. There is an
elegance about the way these foreign women dress,
a care for detail in their clothes and jewellery, and
a carriage which one seldom finds here."

They had reached the far end of the field, having
turned their backs, in fact, upon the polo altogether.
Norgate suddenly abandoned their conversation.

"Look here," he said, in an altered tone, "do you
feel inclined to answer a few questions?"

"For publication?" Hebblethwaite asked drily.
"You haven't turned journalist, by any chance, have
you?"

Norgate shook his head. "Nevertheless," he admitted, " I have changed my profession. The fact is that I have accepted a stipend of a thousand a year and have become a German spy."

" Good luck to you ! " exclaimed Hebblethwaite, laughing softly. " Well, fire away, then. You shall pick the brains of a Cabinet Minister at your leisure, so long as you'll give me a cigarette — and present me, when we have finished, to the Baroness. The country has no secrets from you, Norgate. Where will you begin? "

" Well, you've been warned, any way," Norgate reminded him, as he offered his cigarette case. " Now tell me. It is part of my job to obtain from you a statement of your opinion as to exactly how far our *entente* with France is binding upon us."

Hebblethwaite cleared his throat.

" If this is for publication," he remarked, " could you manage a photograph of myself at the head of the interview, in these clothes and with this hat? I rather fancy myself to-day. A pocket kodak is, of course, part of the equipment of a German spy."

" Sorry," Norgate regretted, " but that's a bit out of my line. I am the disappointed diplomatist, doing the dirty work among my late friends. What we should like to know from Mr. Hebblethwaite, confidentially narrated to a personal friend, is whether, in the event of a war between Germany and Russia and France, England would feel it her duty to intervene? "

Hebblethwaite glanced around. The throng of people had cleared off to watch the concluding stages of the match.

" I have a sovereign on this," he remarked, glancing at his card.

" Which have you backed? " Norgate enquired.

" The Lancers."

" Well, it's any odds on the Hussars, so you've lost your money," Norgate told him.

Hebblethwaite sighed resignedly. " Well," he said, " the question you submit is a problem which has presented itself to us once or twice, although I may tell you that there isn't a soul in the Cabinet except one who believes in the chance of war. We are not a fire-eating lot, you know. We are all for peace, and we believe we are going to have it. However, to answer your questions more closely, our obligations depend entirely upon the provocation giving cause for the war. If France and Russia provoked it in any way, we should remain neutral. If it were a war of sheer aggression from Germany against France, we might to a certain extent intervene. There is not one of us, however, who believes for a single moment that Germany would enter upon such a war."

" When you admit that we might to a certain extent intervene," Norgate said, " exactly how should we do it, I wonder? We are not in a particular state of readiness to declare war upon anybody or anything, are we? " he added, as they turned around and strolled once more towards the polo ground.

" We have had no money to waste upon senseless armaments," Mr. Hebblethwaite declared severely, " and if you watch the social measures which we have passed during the last two years, you will see that every penny we could spare has been necessary in order to get them into working order. It is our contention that an army is absolutely unnecessary and would simply have the effect of provoking military reprisals. If we, by any chance in the future, were drawn into war, our navy would be at the service of our allies. What more could any country ask than to have assured for them the absolute control of the sea?"

"That's all very well," Norgate assented. "It might be our fair share on paper, and yet it might not be enough. What about our navy if Antwerp, Ostend, Dunkirk, Calais, Boulogne, and Havre were all German ports, as they certainly would be in an unassisted conflict between the French and the Germans?"

They were within hearing now of the music of the band. Hebblethwaite quickened his pace a little impatiently.

"Look here," he protested, "I came down here for a holiday. I tell you frankly that I believe in the possibility of war just as much as I believe in the possibility of an earthquake. My own personal feeling is that it is just as necessary to make preparations against one as the other. There you are, my German spy, that's all I have to say to you. Here are your friends. I must pay my respects to the Prince, and I should like to meet your charming companion."

Anna detached herself from a little group of men at their approach, and Norgate at once introduced his friend.

"I have only been able to induce Mr. Hebble-thwaite to talk to me for the last ten minutes," he declared, "by promising to present him to you."

"A ceremony which we will take for granted," she suggested, holding out her fingers. "Each time I have come to London, Mr. Hebblethwaite, I have hoped that I might have this good fortune. You interest us so much on the Continent."

Mr. Hebblethwaite bowed and looked as though he would have liked the interest to have been a little more personal.

"You see," Anna explained, as she stood between the two men, "both Austria and Germany, the two countries where I spend most of my time, are almost military ridden. Our great statesmen, or the men who stand behind them, are all soldiers. You represent something wholly different. Your nation is as great and as prosperous as ours, and yet you are a pacifist, are you not, Mr. Hebblethwaite? You scorn any preparations for war. You do not believe in it. You give back the money that we should spend in military or naval preparations to the people, for their betterment. It is very wonderful."

"We act according to our convictions," Mr. Hebblethwaite pronounced. "It is our earnest hope that we have risen sufficiently in the scale of civilisation to be able to devote our millions to more moral objects than the massing of armaments."

"And you have no fears?" she persisted earnestly. "You honestly believe that you are justified in letting the fighting spirit of your people lie dormant?"

"I honestly believe it, Baroness," Mr. Hebblethwaite replied. " Life is a battle for all of them, but the fighting which we recognise is the fight for moral and commercial supremacy, the lifting of the people by education and strenuous effort to a higher plane of prosperity."

" Of course," Anna murmured, " what you say sounds frightfully convincing. History only will tell us whether you are in the right."

" My thirst," Mr. Hebblethwaite observed, glancing towards the little tables set out under the trees, " suggests tea and strawberries."

" If some one hadn't offered me tea in a moment or two," Anna declared, " I should have gone back to the Prince, with whom I must confess I was very bored. Shall we discuss politics or talk nonsense? "

" Talk nonsense," Mr. Hebblethwaite decided. " This is my holiday. My brain has stopped working. I can think of nothing beyond tea and strawberries. We will take that table under the elm trees, and you shall tell us all about Vienna."

CHAPTER XXI

Norgate, after leaving Anna at her hotel, drove on to the club, where he arrived a few minutes before seven. Selingman was there with Prince Edward, and half a dozen others. Selingman, who happened not to be playing, came over at once and sat by his side on the broad fender.

"You are late, my young freind," he remarked.

"My new career," Norgate replied, "makes demands upon me. I can no longer spend the whole afternoon playing bridge. I have been attending to business."

"It is very good," Selingman declared amiably. "That is the way I like to hear you talk. To amuse oneself is good, but to work is better still. Have you, by chance, any report to make?"

"I have had a long conversation with Mr. Hebblethwaite at Ranelagh this afternoon," Norgate announced.

There was a sudden change in Selingman's expression, a glint of eagerness in his eyes.

"With Hebblethwaite! You have begun well. He is the man above all others of whose views we wish to feel absolutely certain. We know that he is a strong man and a pacifist, but a pacifist to what extent? That is what we wish to be clear about. Now tell me, you spoke to him seriously?"

" Very seriously, indeed," Norgate assented.
" The subject suggested itself naturally, and I con-
trived to get him to discuss the possibilities of a European war. I posed rather as a pessimist, but he simply jeered at me. He assured me that an earthquake
was more probable. I pressed him on the subject of
the *entente*. He spoke of it as a thing of romance
and sentiment, having no place in any possible development of the international situation. I put hy-
pothetical cases of a European war before him, but
he only scoffed at me. On one point only was he
absolutely and entirely firm — under no circumstances whatever would the present Cabinet declare
war upon anybody. If the nation found itself face
to face with a crisis, the Government would simply
choose the most dignified and advantageous solution which embraced peace. In short, there is one
thing which you may count upon as absolutely certain. If England goes to war at any time within
the next four years, it will be under some other government."

Selingman was vastly interested. He had drawn
very close to Norgate, his pudgy hands stretched
out upon his knees. He dropped his voice so that
it was audible only a few feet away.

" Let me put an extreme case," he suggested.
" Supposing Russia and Germany were at war, and
France, as Russia's ally, were compelled to mobilise. It would not be a war of Germany's provocation, but Germany, in self-defence, would be bound
to attack France. She might also be compelled by
strategic considerations to invade Belgium. What

do you think your friend Hebblethwaite would say to that?"

"I am perfectly convinced," Norgate replied, "that Hebblethwaite would work for peace at any price. The members of our present Government are pacifists, every one of them, with the possible exception of the Secretary of the Admiralty."

"Ah!" Mr. Selingman murmured. "Mr. Spencer Wyatt! He is the gentleman who clamours so hard and fights so well for his navy estimates. Last time, though, not all his eloquence could prevail. They were cut down almost a half, eh?"

"I believe that was so," Norgate admitted.

"Mr. Spencer Wyatt, eh?" Selingman continued, his eyes fixed upon the ceiling. "Well, well, one cannot wonder at his attitude. It is not his rôle to pose as an economist. He is responsible for the navy. Naturally he wants a big navy. I wonder what his influence in the Cabinet really is."

"As to that," Norgate observed, "I know no more than the man in the street."

"Naturally," Mr. Selingman agreed. "I was thinking to myself."

There was a brief silence. Norgate glanced around the room.

"I don't see Mrs. Benedek here this afternoon," he remarked.

Selingman shook his head solemnly.

"The inquest on the death of that poor fellow Baring is being held to-day," he explained. "That is why she is staying away. A sad thing that, Norgate — a very sad happening."

"It was indeed."

"And mysterious," Selingman went on. "The man apparently, an hour before, was in high spirits. The special work upon which he was engaged at the Admiralty was almost finished. He had received high praise for his share in it. Every one who had seen him that day spoke of him as in absolutely capital form. Suddenly he whips out a revolver from his desk and shoots himself, and all that any one knows is that he was rung up by some one on the telephone. There's a puzzle for you, Norgate."

Norgate made no reply. He felt Selingman's eyes upon him.

"A wonderful plot for the sensational novelist. To the ordinary human being who knew Baring, there remains a substratum almost of uneasiness. Where did that voice come from that spoke along the wires, and what was its message? Baring, by all accounts, had no secrets in his life. What was the message — a warning or a threat?"

"I did not read the account of the inquest," Norgate observed. "Wasn't it possible to trace the person who rang up, through the telephone office?"

"In an ordinary case, yes," Selingman agreed. "In this case, no! The person who rang up made use of a call office. But come, it is a gloomy subject, this. I wish I had known that you were likely to see Mr. Hebblethwaite this afternoon. Bear this in mind in case you should come across him again. It would interest me very much to know whether any breach of friendship has taken place at all between him and Mr. Spencer Wyatt. Do you know Spencer Wyatt, by-the-by? "

" Only slightly," Norgate replied. " Not well enough to talk to him intimately, as I can do to Hebblethwaite."

" Well, remember that last little commission," Selingman concluded. " Are you staying on or leaving now? If you are going, we will walk together. A little exercise is good for me sometimes. My figure requires it. It is a very short distance, but it is better than nothing at all."

" I am quite ready," Norgate assured him.

They left the room and descended the stairs together. At the entrance to the building, Selingman paused for a moment. Then he seemed suddenly to remember.

" It is habit," he declared. " I stand here for a taxi, but we have agreed to walk, is it not so? Come ! "

Norgate was looking across the street to the other side of the pavement. A man was standing there, engaged in conversation with a plainly-dressed young woman. To Norgate there was something vaguely familiar about the latter, who turned to glance at him as they strolled by on the other side of the road. It was not until they reached the corner of the street, however, that he remembered. She was the young woman at the telephone call office near Westbourne Grove !

CHAPTER XXII

Mr. Hebblethwaite was undoubtedly annoyed. He found himself regretting more than ever the good nature which had prompted him to give this visitor an audience at a most unusual hour. He had been forced into the uncomfortable position of listening to statements the knowledge of which was a serious embarrassment to him.

"Whatever made you come to me, Mr. Harrison?" he exclaimed, when at last his caller's disclosures had been made. "It isn't my department."

"I came to you, sir," the official replied, "because I have the privilege of knowing you personally, and because I was quite sure that in your hands the matter would be treated wisely."

"You are sure of your facts, I suppose?"

"Absolutely, sir."

"I do not know much about navy procedure," Mr. Hebblethwaite said thoughtfully, "but it scarcely seems to me possible for what you tell me to have been kept secret."

"It is not only possible, sir," the man assured him, "but it has been done before in Lord Charles Beresford's time. You will find, if you make enquiries, that not only are the Press excluded to-day from the shipbuilding yards in question, but the work-people are living almost in barracks. There are double

sentries at every gate, and no one is permitted under any circumstances to pass the outer line of offices."

Mr. Hebblethwaite sat, for a few moments, deep
in thought.

"Well, Mr. Harrison," he said at last, " there is
no doubt that you have done what you conceived to
be your duty, although I must tell you frankly that
I wish you had either kept what you know to yourself or taken the information somewhere else.   Since
you have brought it to me, let me ask you this question.   Are you taking any further steps in the matter at all? "

"Certainly not, sir," was the quiet reply.   " I
consider that I have done my duty and finished with
it, when I leave this room."

"You are content, then," Mr. Hebblethwaite observed, " to leave this matter entirely in my
hands? "

"Entirely, sir," the official assented.   " I am perfectly content, from this moment, to forget all that
I know.   Whatever your judgment prompts you to
do, will, I feel sure, be satisfactory."

Mr. Hebblethwaite rose to his feet and held out
his hand.

"Well, Mr. Harrison," he concluded, " you have
performed a disagreeable duty in a tactful manner.
Personally, I am not in the least grateful to you,
for, as I dare say you know, Mr. Spencer Wyatt is
a great friend of mine.   As a member of the Government, however, I think I can promise you that your
services shall not be forgotten.   Good evening! "

The official departed. Mr. Hebblethwaite thrust his hands into his pockets, glanced at the clock impatiently, and made use of an expression which seldom passed his lips. He was in evening dress, and due to dine with his wife on the other side of the Park. Furthermore, he was very hungry. The whole affair was most annoying. He rang the bell.

"Ask Mr. Bedells to come here at once," he told the servant, "and tell your mistress I am exceedingly sorry, but I shall be detained here for some time. She had better go on without me and send the car back. I will come as soon as I can. Explain that it is a matter of official business. When you have seen Mrs. Hebblethwaite, you can bring me a glass of sherry and a biscuit."

The man withdrew, and Mr. Hebblethwaite opened a telephone directory. In a few moments Mr. Bedells, who was his private secretary, appeared.

"Richard," his chief directed, "ring up Mr. Spencer Wyatt. Tell him that whatever his engagements may be, I wish to see him here for five minutes. If he is out, you must find out where he is. You can begin by ringing up at his house."

Bedells devoted himself to the telephone. Mr. Hebblethwaite munched a biscuit and sipped his sherry. Presently the latter laid down the telephone and reported success.

"Mr. Spencer Wyatt was on his way to a city dinner, sir," he announced. "They caught him in the hall and he will call here."

Mr. Hebblethwaite nodded. "See that he is sent up directly he comes."

In less than five minutes Mr. Spencer Wyatt was ushered in. He was wearing the uniform of an Admiral of the Fleet — a tall, broad-shouldered man, fair complexioned, and with the bearing of a sailor.

"Hullo, Hebblethwaite, what's wrong?" he asked. "Your message just caught me. I am dining with the worshipful tanners — turtle soup and all the rest of it. Don't let me miss more than I can help."

Mr. Hebblethwaite walked to the door to be sure that it was closed and came back again.

"Look here, Wyatt," he exclaimed, "what the devil have you been up to?"

Wyatt whistled softly. A light broke across his face.

"What do you mean?" he demanded.

"You know perfectly well what I mean," Hebblethwaite continued. "Five weeks ago we had it all out at a Cabinet meeting. You asked Parliament to lay down six battleships, four cruisers, thirty-five submarines, and twelve torpedo boats. You remember what a devil of a row there was. Eventually we compromised for half the number of battleships, two cruisers, and the full amount of small craft."

"Well?"

"I am given to understand," Hebblethwaite said slowly, "that you have absolutely disregarded the vote — that the whole number of battleships are practically commenced, and the whole number of cruisers, and rather more than the number of smaller craft."

Wyatt threw his cocked hat upon the table.

" Well, I am up against it a bit sooner than I expected," he remarked. " Who's been peaching? "

" Never mind," Hebblethwaite replied. " I am not telling you that. You've managed the whole thing very cleverly, and you know very well, Wyatt, that I am on your side. I was on your side in pressing the whole of your proposals upon the Cabinet, although honestly I think they were far larger than necessary. However, we took a fair vote, and we compromised. You had no more right to do what you have done —"

" I admit it, Hebblethwaite," Wyatt interrupted quickly. " Of course, if this comes out, my resignation's ready for you, but I tell you frankly, as man to man, I can't go on with my job, and I won't, unless I get the ships voted that I need. We are behind our standard now. I spent twenty-four hours making up my mind whether I should resign or take this risk. I came to the conclusion that I should serve my country better by taking the risk. So there you are. What are you going to do about it? "

" What the mischief can I do about it? " Hebblethwaite demanded irritably. " You are putting me in an impossible position. Let me ask you this, Wyatt. Is there anything at the back of your head that the man in the street doesn't know about? "

" Yes! "

" What is it, then? "

" I have reasons to believe," Wyatt announced deliberately, " reasons which are quite sufficient for me, although it was impossible for me to get up in Parliament and state them, that Germany is secretly making preparations for war either before the end of this year or the beginning of next."

Hebblethwaite threw himself into an easy-chair.

" Sit down, Wyatt," he said. " Your dinner can wait for a few minutes. I have had another man — only a youngster, and he doesn't know anything — talking to me like that. We are fully acquainted with everything that is going on behind the scenes. All our negotiations with Germany are at this moment upon the most friendly footing. We haven't a single matter in dispute. Old Busby, as you know, has been over in Berlin himself and has come back a confirmed pacifist. If he had his way, our army would practically cease to exist. He has been on the spot. He ought to know, and the army's his job."

" Busby," Wyatt declared, " is the silliest old ass who ever escaped petticoats by the mere accident of sex. I tell you he is just the sort of idiot the Germans have been longing to get hold of and twist round their fingers. Before twelve months or two years have passed, you'll curse the name of that man, when you look at the mess he has made of the army. Peace is all very well — universal peace. The only way we can secure it is by being a good deal stronger than we are at present."

" That is your point of view," Hebblethwaite reminded him. " I tell you frankly that I incline towards Busby's."

" Then you'll eat your words," Wyatt asserted, " before many months are out. I, too, have been in Germany lately, although I was careful to go as a

tourist, and I have picked up a little information.
I tell you it isn't for nothing that Germany has a
complete list of the whole of her rolling stock, the
actual numbers in each compartment registered and
reserved for the use of certain units of her troops.
I tell you that from one end of the country to the
other her state of military preparedness is amazing.
She has but to press a button, and a million men
have their rifles in their hands, their knapsacks on
their backs, and each regiment knows exactly at
which station and by what train to embark. She is
making Zeppelins night and day, training her men
till they drop with exhaustion. Krupp's works are
guarded by double lines of sentries. There are secrets there which no one can penetrate. And all
the time she is building ships feverishly. Look here
— you know my cousin, Lady Emily Fakenham?"

"Of course!"

"Only yesterday," Wyatt continued impressively,
"she showed me a letter — I read it, mind — from
a cousin of Prince Hohenlowe. She met him at
Monte Carlo this year, and they had a sort of flir-
tation. In the postscript he says: 'If you take
my advice, don't go to Dinard this August. Don't
be further away from home than you can help at all
this summer.' What do you think that meant?"

"It sounds queer," Hebblethwaite admitted.

"Germany is bound to have a knock at us," Spencer Wyatt went on. "We've talked of it so long
that the words pass over our heads, as it were, but
she means it. And I tell you another thing. She
means to do it while there's a Radical Government

in power here, and before Russia finishes her reorganisation scheme. I am not a soldier, Hebblethwaite, but the fellows we've got up at the top — not the soldiers themselves but the chaps like old Busby and Simons — are simply out and out rotters. That's plain speaking, isn't it, but you and I are the two men concerned in the government of this country who do talk common sense to one another. We've fine soldiers and fine organisers, but they've been given the go-by simply because they know their job and would insist upon doing it thoroughly, if at all. Russia will have another four million men ready to be called up by the end of 1915, and not only that, but what is more important, is that she'll have the arms and the uniforms for them. Germany isn't going to wait for that. I've thought it all out. We are going to get it in the neck before seven or eight months have passed, and if you want to know the truth, Hebblethwaite, that's why I have taken a risk and ordered these ships. The navy is my care, and it's my job to see that we keep it up to the proper standard. Whose votes rob me of my extra battleships? Why, just a handful of Labour men and Irishmen and cocoa Liberals, who haven't an Imperial idea in their brains, who think war belongs to the horrors of the past, and think they're doing their duty by what they call ' keeping down expenses.' Hang it, Hebblethwaite, it's worse than a man who won't pay fire insurance for his house in a dangerous neighbourhood, so as to save a bit of money! What I've done I stick to. Split on me, if you want to."

" I don't think I shall do that," Hebblethwaite said, " but honestly, Wyatt, I can't follow you in your war talk. We got over the Agadir trouble. We've got over a much worse one — the Balkan crisis. There isn't a single contentious question before us just now. The sky is almost clear."

" Believe me," Wyatt insisted earnestly, " that's just the time to look for the thunderbolt. Can't you see that when Germany goes to war, it will be a war of conquest, the war which she has planned for all these years? She'll choose her own time, and she'll make a *casus belli*, right enough, when the time comes. Of course, she'd have taken advantage of the position last year, but she simply wasn't ready. If you ask me, I believe she thinks herself now able to lick the whole of Europe. I am not at all sure, thanks to Busby and our last fifteen years' military administration, that she wouldn't have a good chance of doing it. Any way, I am not going to have my fleet cut down."

" The country is prosperous," Hebblethwaite acknowledged. " We can afford the ships."

" Then look here, old chap," Wyatt begged, " I am not pleading for my own sake, but the country's. Keep your mouth shut. See what the next month or two brings. If there's trouble — well, I don't suppose I shall be jumped on then. If there isn't, and you want a victim, here I am. I disobeyed orders flagrantly. My resignation is in my desk at any moment."

Hebblethwaite glanced at the clock.

" I am very hungry," he said, " and I have a long

way to go for dinner.   We'll let it go at that, Wyatt.
I'll try and keep things quiet for you.   If it comes
out, well, you know the risk you run."

"I know the bigger risk we are all running,"
Wyatt declared, as he took a cigarette from an open
box on the table by his side and turned towards the
door.   "I'll manage the turtle soup now, with luck.
You're a good fellow, Hebblethwaite.   I know it
goes against the grain with you, but, by Jove, you
may be thankful for this some time!"

The Right Honourable John William Hebblethwaite took the hat from his footman, stepped into
his car, and was driven rapidly away.   He leaned
back among the cushions, more thoughtful than
usual.   There was a yellow moon in the sky, pale
as yet.   The streets were a tangled vortex of motor-
cars and taxies, all filled with men and women in evening dress.   It was the height of a wonderful season.
Everywhere was dominant the note of prosperity,
gaiety, even splendour.   The houses in Park Lane,
flower-decked, displayed through their wide-flung
windows a constant panorama of brilliantly-lit rooms.
Every one was entertaining.   In the Park on the
other side were the usual crowd of earnest, hard-
faced men and women, gathered in little groups
around the orator of the moment.   Hebblethwaite
felt a queer premonition that evening.   A man of
sanguine temperament, thoroughly contented with
himself and his position, he seemed almost for the
first time in his life, to have doubts, to look into
the future, to feel the rumblings of an earthquake,
the great dramatic cry of a nation in the throes of

suffering. Had they been wise, all these years, to have legislated as though the old dangers by land and sea had passed? — to have striven to make the people fat and prosperous, to have turned a deaf ear to every note of warning? Supposing the other thing were true! Supposing Norgate and Spencer Wyatt had found the truth! What would history have to say then of this Government of which he was so proud? Would it be possible that they had brought the country to a great prosperity by destroying the very bulwarks of its security?

The car drew up with a jerk, and Hebblethwaite came back to earth. Nevertheless, he promised himself, as he hastened across the pavement, that on the morrow he would pay a long-delayed visit to the War Office.

CHAPTER XXIII

Anna was seated, a few days later, with her dearest friend, the Princess of Thurm, in a corner of the royal enclosure at Ascot. For the first time since their arrival they found themselves alone. From underneath her parasol the Princess looked at her friend curiously.

"Anna," she said, "something has happened to you."

"Perhaps, but explain yourself," Anna replied composedly.

"It is so simple. There you sit in a Doucet gown, perfection as ever, from the aigrette in your hat to those delicately pointed shoes. You have been positively hunted by all the nicest men — once or twice, indeed, I felt myself neglected — and not a smile have I seen upon your lips. You go about, looking just a little beyond everything. What did you see, child, over the tops of the trees in the paddock, when Lord Wilton was trying so hard to entertain you?"

"An affair of moods, I imagine," Anna declared. "Somehow I don't feel quite in the humour for Ascot to-day. To be quite frank," she went on, turning her head slowly, "I rather wonder that you do, Mildred."

The Princess raised her eyebrows.

"Why not? Everything, so far as I am concerned, is *couleur de rose*. Madame Blanche declared yesterday that my complexion would last for twenty years. I found a dozen of the most adorable hats in Paris. The artist who designs my frocks was positively inspired the last time I sat to him. I am going to see Maurice in a few weeks, and meanwhile I have several new flirtations which interest me amazingly. As for you, my child, one would imagine that you had lost your taste for all frivolity. You are as cold as granite. Be careful, dear. The men of to-day, in this country, at any rate, are spoilt. Sometimes they are even uncourtier-like enough to accept a woman's refusal."

"Well," Anna observed, smiling faintly, "even a lifetime at Court has not taught me to dissimulate. I am heavy-hearted, Mildred. You wondered what I was looking at when I gazed over those green trees under which all those happy people were walking. I was looking out across the North Sea. I was looking through Belgium to Paris. I saw a vast curtain roll up, and everything beyond it was a blood-stained panorama."

A shade rested for a moment on her companion's fair face. She shrugged her shoulders.

"We've known for a long time, dear, that it must come."

"But all the same, in these last moments it is terrible," Anna insisted. "Seriously, Mildred, I wonder that I should feel it more than you. You are absolutely English. Your father is English, your mother is English. It is only your husband that is Austrian. You have lived in Austria only for seven years. Has that been sufficient to destroy all your patriotism, all your love for your own country?"

The Princess made a little grimace.

"My dear Anna," she said, "I am not so serious a person as you are. I am profoundly, incomprehensibly selfish. The only human being in the whole world for whom I have had a spark of real affection is Maurice, and I adore him. What he has told me to do, I have done. What makes him happy makes me happy. For his sake, even, I have forgotten and shall always forget that I was born an Englishwoman. Circumstances, too," she went on thoughtfully, "have made it so easy. England is such a changed country. When I was a child, I could read of the times when our kings really ruled, of our battles for dominion, of our fight for colonies, of our building up a great empire, and I could feel just a little thrill. I can't now. We have gone ahead of Napoleon. From a nation of shop-keepers we have become a nation of general dealers — a fat, over-confident, bourgeois people. Socialism has its hand upon the throat of the classes. Park Lane, where our aristocracy lived, is filled with the mansions of South African Jews, whom one must meet here or keep out of society altogether. Our country houses have gone the same way. Our Court set is dowdy, dull to a degree, and common in a different fashion. You are right. I have lost my love for England, partly because of my marriage, partly because of those things which have come to England herself."

For the first time there was a little flush of colour in Anna's exquisitely pale cheeks. There was even animation in her tone as she turned towards her friend.

" Mildred," she exclaimed, " it is splendid to hear you say what is really in your mind! I am so glad you have spoken to me like this. I feel these things, too. Now I am not nearly so English as you. My mother was English and my father Austrian. Therefore, only half of me should be English. Yet, although I am so much further removed from England than you are, I have suddenly felt a return of all my old affection for her."

" You are going to tell me why? " her companion begged.

" Of course! It is because I believe — it is too ridiculous — but I believe that I am in your position with the circumstances reversed. I am beginning to care in the most foolish way for an unmistakable Englishman."

" If we had missed this little chance of conversation," the Princess declared, " I should have been miserable for the rest of my life! There is the Duke hanging about behind. For heaven's sake, don't turn. Thank goodness he has gone away! Now go on, dear. Tell me about him at once. I can't imagine who it may be. I have watched you with so many men, and I know quite well, so long as that little curl is at the corner of your lips, that they none of them count. Do I know him? "

" I do not think so," Anna replied. " He is not a very important person."

" It isn't the man you were dining with in the Café de Berlin when Prince Karl came in? "

" Yes, it is he! "

The Princess made a little grimace.

" But how unsuitable, my dear," she exclaimed, " if you are really in earnest! What is the use of your thinking of an Englishman? He is quite nice, I know. His mother and my mother were friends, and we met once or twice. He was very kind to me in Paris, too. But for a serious affair —"

" Well, it may not come to that," Anna interrupted, " but there it is. I suppose that it is partly for his sake that I feel this depression."

" I should have thought that he himself would have been a little out of sympathy with his country just now," the Princess remarked. " They tell me that the Foreign Office ate humble pie with the Kaiser for that affair shockingly. They not only removed him from the Embassy, but they are going to give him nothing in Europe. I heard for a fact that the Kaiser requested that he should not be attached to any Court with which Germany had diplomatic relations."

Anna nodded. " I believe that it is true," she admitted, " but I am not sure that he realises it himself. Even if he does, well, you know the type. He is English to the backbone."

" But there are Englishmen," the Princess insisted earnestly, " who are amenable to common sense. There are Englishmen who are sorrowing over the decline of their own country and who would not be so greatly distressed if she were punished a little."

" I am afraid Mr. Norgate is not like that," Anna observed drily. "However, one cannot be sure. Bother! I thought people were very kind to leave us so long in peace. Dear Prince, how clever of you to find out our retreat!"

The Ambassador stood bareheaded before them.

"Dear ladies," he declared, " you are the lodestones which would draw one even through these gossamer walls of lace and chiffons, of draperies as light as the sunshine and perfumes as sweet as Heine's poetry."

"Very pretty," Anna laughed, "but what you really mean is that you were looking for two of your very useful slaves and have found them."

The Ambassador glanced around. Their isolation was complete.

"Ah! well," he murmured, " it is a wonderful thing to be so charmingly aided towards such a wonderful end."

"And to have such complete trust in one's friends," Anna remarked, looking him steadfastly in the face.

The Prince did not flinch. His smile was perfectly courteous and acknowledging.

"That is my happiness," he admitted. "I will tell you the reason which directed my footsteps this way," he added, drawing a small betting book from his pocket. "You must back Prince Charlie for the next race. I will, if you choose, take your commissions. I have a man waiting at the rails."

"Twenty pounds for me, please," the Princess de-

clared.   " I have the horse marked on my card, but
I had forgotten for the moment."

"And the same for me," Anna begged.   "But did
you really come only to bring us this valuable tip,
Prince? "

The Ambassador stooped down.

" There is a dispatch on its way to me," he said
softly, " which I believe concerns you.   It might be
necessary for you to take a short journey within the
next few days."

" Not back to Berlin? " Anna exclaimed.

Their solitude had been invaded by now, and the
Princess was talking to two or three men who were
grouped about her chair.   The Ambassador stooped
a little lower.

" To Rome," he whispered.

CHAPTER XXIV

Back from the dusty roads, the heat and noise of the long day, Anna was resting on the couch in her sitting-room. A bowl of roses and a note which she had read three or four times stood on a little table by her side. One of the blossoms she had fastened into the bosom of her loose gown. The blinds were drawn, the sounds of the traffic outside were muffled and distant. Her bath had been just the right temperature, her maid's attention was skilful and delicate as ever. She was conscious of the drowsy sweet perfume of the flowers, the pleasant sense of powdered cleanliness. Everything should have conduced to rest, but she lay there with her eyes wide-open. There was so much to think about, so much that was new finding its way into her stormy young life.

" Madame ! "

Anna turned her head. Her maid had entered noiselessly from the inner room and was standing by her side.

" Madame does not sleep? There is a person outside who waits for an interview. I have denied him, as all others. He gave me this."

Anna almost snatched the piece of paper from her maid's fingers. She glanced at the name, and the disappointment which shone in her eyes was very apparent.   It was succeeded by an impulse of surprise.

" You can show him in," she directed.

Selingman appeared a few moments later — Selingman, cool, rosy, and confident, on the way to his be-
loved bridge club.   He took the hand which Anna,
without moving, held out to him, and raised it gal-
lantly to his lips.

" I thought it was understood, my crockery
friend," she murmured, " that in London we did not
interchange visits."

" Most true, gracious lady," he admitted, " but
there are circumstances which can alter the most immovable decisions.   At this moment we are con-
fronted with one.   I come to discuss with you the
young Englishman, Francis Norgate."

She turned her head a little.   Her eyes were full of
enquiry.

" To discuss him with me? "

Selingman's eyes as though by accident fell upon
the roses and the note.

" Ah, well," she murmured, " go on."

" It is wonderful," Selingman proceeded, " to be
able to tell the truth.   I speak to you as one com-
rade to another.   This young man was your companion at the Café de Berlin.   For the indiscretion
of behaving like a bull-headed but courageous young
Englishman, he is practically dismissed from the
Service.   He comes back smarting with the injustice
of it.   Chance brings him in my way.   I proceed to
do my best to make use of this opportunity."

" So like you, dear Herr Selingman! " Anna murmured.

Selingman beamed.

"Ever gracious, dear lady. Well, to continue, then. Here I find a young Englishman of exactly the order and position likely to be useful to us. I approach him frankly. He has been humiliated by the country he was willing to serve. I talk to him of that country. 'You are English, of course,' I remind him, 'but what manner of an England is it to-day which claims you?' It is a very telling argument, this. Upon the classes of this country, democracy has laid a throttling hand. There is a spirit of discontent, they say, among the working-classes, the discontent which breeds socialism. There is a worse spirit of discontent among the upper classes here, and it is the discontent which breeds so-called traitors."

"I can imagine all the rest," Anna interposed coolly. "How far have you succeeded?"

"The young man," Selingman told her, "has accepted my proposals. He has drawn three months' salary in advance. He furnished me yesterday with details of a private conversation with a well-known Cabinet Minister."

Anna turned her head. "So soon!" she murmured.

"So soon," Selingman repeated. "And now, gracious lady, here comes my visit to you. We have a recruit, invaluable if he is indeed a recruit at heart, dangerous if he has the brains and wit to choose to make himself so. I, on my way through life, judge men and women, and I judge them — well, with few exceptions, unerringly, but at the back of my brain there lingers something of mistrust of this young man. I have seen others in his position accept similar proposals. I have seen the struggles of shame, the doubts, the assertion of some part of a man's lower nature reconciling him in the end to accepting the pay of a foreign country. I have seen none of these things in this young man — simply a cold and deliberate acceptance of my proposals. He conforms to no type. He sets up before me a problem which I myself have failed wholly to solve. I come to you, dear lady, for your aid."

"I am to spy upon the spy," she remarked.

"It is an easy task," Selingman declared. "This young man is your slave. Whatever your daily business may be here, some part of your time, I imagine, will be spent in his company. Let me know what manner of man he is. Is this innate corruptness which brings him so easily to the bait, or is it the stinging smart of injustice from which he may well be suffering? Or, failing these, has he dared to set his wits against mine, to play the double traitor? If even a suspicion of this should come to you, there must be an end of Mr. Francis Norgate."

Anna toyed for a moment with the rose at her bosom. Her eyes were looking out of the room. Once again she was conscious of a curious slackening of purpose, a confusion of issues which had once seemed to her so clear.

"Very well," she promised. "I will send you a report in the course of a few days."

"I should not," Selingman continued, rising, "venture to trouble you, Baroness, as I know the sphere of your activities is far removed from mine, but chance has put you in the position of being able to ascertain definitely the things which I desire to know. For our common sake you will, I am sure, seek to discover the truth."

"So far as I can, certainly," Anna replied, "but I must admit that I, like you, find Mr. Norgate a little incomprehensible."

"There are men," Selingman declared, "there have been many of the strongest men in history, impenetrable to the world, who have yielded their secrets readily to a woman's influence. The diplomatists in life who have failed have been those who have underrated the powers possessed by your wonderful sex."

"Among whom," Anna remarked, "no one will ever number Herr Selingman."

"Dear Baroness," Selingman concluded, as the maid whom Anna had summoned stood ready to show him out, "it is because in my life I have been brought into contact with so many charming examples of your power."

Once more silence and solitude. Anna moved restlessly about on her couch. Her eyes were a little hot. That future into which she looked seemed to become more than ever a tangled web. At half-past seven her maid reappeared.

"Madame will dress for dinner?"

Anna swung herself to her feet. She glanced at the clock.

"I suppose so," she assented.

" I have three gowns laid out," the maid continued respectfully. " Madame would look wonderful in the light green."

" Anything," Anna yawned.

The telephone bell tinkled. Anna took down the receiver herself.

" Yes? " she asked.

Her manner suddenly changed. It was a familiar voice speaking. Her maid, who stood in the background, watched and wondered.

" It is you, Baroness! I rang up to see whether there was any chance of your being able to dine with me? I have just got back to town."

" How dared you go away without telling me!" she exclaimed. " And how can I dine with you? Do you not realise that it is Ascot Thursday, and I have had many invitations to dine to-night? I am going to a very big dinner-party at Thurm House."

" Bad luck!" Norgate replied disconsolately. " And to-morrow? "

" I have not finished about to-night yet," Anna continued. " I suppose you do not, by any chance, want me to dine with you very much? "

" Of course I do," was the prompt answer. " You see plenty of the Princess of Thurm and nothing of me, and there is always the chance that you may have to go abroad. I think that it is your duty —"

" As a matter of duty," Anna interrupted, " I ought to dine at Thurm House. As a matter of pleasure, I shall dine with you. You will very likely not enjoy yourself. I am going to be very cross indeed. You have neglected me shamefully. It is only these wonderful roses which have saved you."

" So long as I am saved," he murmured, " tell me, please, where you would like to dine? "

" Any place on earth," she replied. " You may call for me here at half-past eight. I shall wear a hat and I would like to go somewhere where our people do not go."

Anna set down the telephone. The listlessness had gone from her manner. She glanced at the clock and ran lightly into the other room.

" Put all that splendour away," she ordered her maid cheerfully. " To-night we shall dazzle no one. Something perfectly quiet and a hat, please. I dine in a restaurant. And ring the bell, Marie, for two apéritifs — not that I need one. I am hungry, Marie. I am looking forward to my dinner already. I think something dead black. I am looking well to-night. I can afford to wear black."

Marie beamed.

" Madame has recovered her spirits," she remarked demurely.

Anna was suddenly silent. Her light-heartedness was a revelation. She turned to her maid.

" Marie," she directed, " you will telephone to Thurm House. You will ask for Lucille, the Princess's maid. You will give my love to the Princess. You will say that a sudden headache has prostrated me. It will be enough. You need say no more. To-morrow I lunch with the Princess, and she will understand."

CHAPTER XXV

" Confess," Anna exclaimed, as she leaned back in her chair, " that my idea was excellent! Your little restaurant was in its way perfection, but the heat — does one feel it anywhere, I wonder, as one does in London? "

" Here, at any rate, we have air," Norgate remarked appreciatively.

" We are far removed," she went on, " from the clamour of diners, that babel of voices, the smell of cooking, the meretricious music. We look over the house-tops. Soon, just behind that tall building there, you will see the yellow moon."

They were taking their coffee in Anna's sitting-room, seated in easy-chairs drawn up to the wide-flung windows. The topmost boughs of some tall elm trees rustled almost in their faces. Away before them spread the phantasmagoria of a wilderness of London roofs, softened and melting into the dim blue obscurity of the falling twilight. Lights were flashing out everywhere, and above them shone the stars. Norgate drew a long breath of content.

" It is wonderful, this," he murmured.

" We are at least alone," Anna said, " and I can talk to you. I want to talk to you. Should you be very much flattered, I wonder, if I were to say that

I have been thinking of little else for the last three or four days than how to approach you, how to say something to you without any fear of being misunderstood, how to convince you of my own sincerity? "

" If I am not flattered," he answered, looking at her keenly, " I am at least content.   Please go on."

" You are one of those, I believe," she continued earnestly, " who realise that somewhere not far removed from the splendour of these summer days, a storm is gathering.   I am one of those who know. England has but a few more weeks of this self-confident, self-esteeming security.   Very soon the shock will come.   Oh! you sit there, my friend, and you are very monosyllabic, but that is because you do not wholly trust me."

He swung suddenly round upon her and there was an unaccustomed fire in his eyes.

" May it not be for some other reason? " he asked quickly.

There was a moment's silence.   Her own face seemed paler than ever in the strange half light, but her eyes were wonderful.   He told himself with passionate insistence that they were the eyes of a truthful woman.

" Tell me," she begged, " what reason? "

He leaned towards her.

" It is so hopeless," he said.   " I am just a broken diplomat whose career is ended almost before it is begun, and you — well, you have everything at your feet.   It is foolish of me, isn't it, but I love you."

He took her hand, and she did not withdraw it.

" If it is foolish," she murmured, " then I am

foolish, too. Perhaps you can guess now why I came to London."

He drew her into his arms. She made no resistance. Her lips, even, were seeking his. It seemed to him in those breathless moments that a greater thing than even the destiny of nations was born into the world. There was a new vigour in his pulses as she gently pushed him back, a new splendour in life.

"Dear," she exclaimed, "of course we are both very foolish, and yet, I do not know. I have been wondering why this has not come to me long ago, and now that it has come I am happy."

"You care — you really care?" he insisted passionately.

"Of course I do," she told him, quietly enough and yet very convincingly. "If I did not care I should not be here. If I did not care, I should not be going to say the things to you which I am going to say now. Sit back in your chair, please, hold my hand still, smoke if you will, but listen."

He obeyed. A deeper seriousness crept into her tone, but her face was still soft and wonderful. The new things were lingering there.

"I want to tell you first," she said, "what I think you already know. The moment for which Germany has toiled so long, from which she has never faltered, is very close at hand. With all her marvellous resources and that amazing war equipment of which you in this country know little, she will soon throw down the gage to England. You are an Englishman, Francis. You are not going to forget it, are you?"

"Forget it?" he repeated.

"I know," she continued slowly, "that Selingman has made advances to you. I know that he has a devilish gift for enrolling on his list men of honour and conscience. He has the knack of subtle argument, of twisting facts and preying upon human weaknesses. You have been shockingly treated by your Foreign Office. You yourself are entirely out of sympathy with your Government. You know very well that England, as she is, is a country which has lost her ideals, a country in which many of her sons might indeed, without much reproach, lose their pride. Selingman knows this. He knows how to work upon these facts. He might very easily convince you that the truest service you could render your country was to assist her in passing through a temporary tribulation."

He looked at her almost in surprise.

"You seem to know the man's methods," he observed.

"I do," she answered, "and I detest them. Now, Francis, please tell me the truth. Is your name, too, upon that long roll of those who are pledged to assist his country?"

"It is," he admitted.

She drew a little away.

"You admit it? You have already consented?"

"I have drawn a quarter's salary," Norgate confessed. "I have entered Selingman's corps of the German Secret Service."

"You mean that you are a traitor!" she exclaimed.

" A traitor to the false England of to-day," Norgate replied, " a friend, I hope, of the real England."

She sat quite still for some moments.

" Somehow or other," she said, " I scarcely fancied that you would give in so easily."

" You seem disappointed," he remarked, " yet, after all, am I not on your side? "

" I suppose so," she answered, without enthusiasm.

There was another and a more prolonged silence. Norgate rose at last to his feet. He walked restlessly to the end of the room and back again. A dark mass of clouds had rolled up; the air seemed almost sulphurous with the presage of a coming storm. They looked out into the gathering darkness.

" I don't understand," he said. " You are Austrian; that is the same as German. I tell you that I have come over on your side. You seem disappointed."

" Perhaps I am," she admitted, standing up, too, and linking her arm through his. " You see, my mother was English, and they say that I am entirely like her. I was brought up here in the English country. Sometimes my life at Vienna and Berlin seems almost like a dream to me, something unreal, as though I were playing at being some other woman. When I am back here, I feel as though I had come home. Do you know really that nothing would make me happier than to hear or think nothing about duty, to just know that I had come back to England to stay, and that you were English, and that we were going to live just the sort of life I pictured to myself that two people could live so happily over here, without too much ambition, without intrigue, simply and honestly. I am a little weary of cities and courts, Francis. To-night more than ever England seems to appeal to me, to remind me that I am one of her daughters."

" Are you trying me, Anna? " he asked hoarsely.

" Trying you? Of course not! " she answered. " I am speaking to you just simply and naturally, because you are the one person in the world to whom I may speak like that."

" Then let's drop it, both of us! " he exclaimed, holding her arm tightly to his. " Courts and cities can do without you, and Selingman can do without me. We'll take a cottage somewhere and live through these evil days."

She shook her head.

" You and I are not like that, Francis," she declared. " When the storm breaks, we mustn't be found hiding in our holes. You know that quite well. It is for us to decide what part we may play. You have chosen. So, in a measure, have I. To-morrow I am going on a secret mission to Italy."

" Anna! " he cried in dismay.

" Alas, yes! " she repeated. " We may not even meet again, Francis, till the map of Europe has been rewritten with the blood of many of our friends and millions of our country-people. But I shall think of you, and the kiss you will give me now shall be the last upon my lips."

" You can go away? " he demanded. " You can leave me like this? "

"I must," she answered simply. "I have work before me. Good-by, Francis! Somehow I knew what was coming. I believe that I am glad, dear, but I must think about it, and so must you."

Norgate left the hotel and walked out amid the first mutterings of the storm. He found a taxi and drove to his rooms. For an hour he sat before his window, watching the lightning play, fighting the thoughts which beat upon his brain, fighting all the time a losing battle. At midnight the storm had ceased. He walked back through the rain-streaming streets. The air was filled with sweet and pungent perfumes. The heaviness had passed from the atmosphere. His own heart was lighter; he walked swiftly. Outside her hotel he paused and looked up at the window. There was a light still burning in her room. He even fancied that he could see the outline of her figure leaning back in the easy-chair which he had wheeled up close to the casement. He entered the hotel, stepped into the lift, ascended to her floor, and made his way with tingling pulses and beating heart along the corridor. He knocked softly at her door. There was a little hesitation, then he heard her voice on the other side.

"Who is that?"

"It is I,—Francis," he answered softly. "Let me in."

There was a little exclamation. She opened the door, holding up her finger.

"Quietly," she whispered. "What is it, Francis? Why have you come back? What has happened to you?"

He drew her into the room. She herself looked weary, and there were lines under her eyes. It seemed, even, as though she might have been weeping. But it was a new Norgate who spoke. His words rang out with a fierce vigour, his eyes seemed on fire.

"Anna," he cried, "I can't fence with you. I can't lie to you. I can't deceive you. I've tried these things, and I went away choking. I had to come back. You shall know the truth, even though you betray me. I am no man of Selingman's. I have taken his paltry money — it went last night to a hospital. I am for England — God knows it! — the England of any government, England, however misguided or mistaken. I want to do the work for her that's easiest and that comes to me. I am on Selingman's roll. What do you think he'll get from me? Nothing that isn't false, no information that won't mislead him, no facts save those I shall distort until they may seem so near the truth that he will build and count upon them. Every minute of my time will be spent to foil his schemes. They don't believe me in Whitehall, or Selingman would be at Bow Street to-morrow morning. That's why I am going my own way. Tell him, if you will. There is only one thing strong enough to bring me here, to risk everything, and that's my love for you."

She was in his arms, sobbing and crying, and yet laughing. She clutched at him, drew down his face and covered his lips with kisses.

"Oh! I am so thankful," she cried, "so thankful! Francis, I ached — my heart ached to have you sit there and talk as you did. Now I know that you are the man I thought you were. Francis, we will work together."

"You mean it?"

"I do. England was my mother's country, England shall be my husband's country. I will tell you many things that should help. From now my work shall be for you. If they find me out, well, I will pay the price. You shall run your risk, Francis, for your country, and I must take mine; but at least we'll keep our honour and our conscience and our love. Oh, this is a better parting, dear! This is a better good night!"

CHAPTER XXVI

Mrs. Benedek was the first to notice the transformation which had certainly taken place in Norgate's appearance. She came and sat by his side upon the cushioned fender.

" What a metamorphosis! " she exclaimed. " Why, you look as though Providence had been showering countless benefits upon you."

There were several people lounging around, and Mrs. Benedek's remark certainly had point.

" You look like Monty, when he's had a winning week," one of them observed.

" It is something more than gross lucre," a young man declared, who had just strolled up. " I believe that it is a good fat appointment. Rome, perhaps, where every one of you fellows wants to get to, nowadays."

" Or perhaps," the Prince intervened, with a little bow, " Mrs. Benedek has promised to dine with you? She is generally responsible for the gloom or happiness of us poor males in this room."

Norgate smiled.

" None of these wonderful things have happened — and yet, something perhaps more wonderful," he announced. " I am engaged to be married."

There was a mingled chorus of exclamations and

congratulations. Selingman, who had been standing on the outskirts of the group, drew a little nearer. His face wore a somewhat puzzled expression.

"And the lady?" he enquired. "May we not know the lady's name? That is surely important?"

"It is the Baroness von Haase," Norgate replied. "You probably know her by name and repute, at least, Mr. Selingman. She is an Austrian, but she is often at Berlin."

Selingman stretched out his great hand. For some reason or other, the announcement seemed to have given him real pleasure.

"Know her? My dear young friend, while I may not claim the privilege of intimate friendship with her, the Baroness is a young lady of the greatest distinction and repute in Berlin. I congratulate you. I congratulate you most heartily. The anger of our young princeling is no longer to be wondered at. I cannot tell you how thoroughly interesting this news is to me."

"You are very good indeed, I am sure, all of you," Norgate declared, answering the general murmur of kindly words. "The Baroness doesn't play bridge, but I'd like to bring her in one afternoon, if I may."

"I have had the honour of meeting the Baroness von Haase several times," Prince Lenemaur said. "It will give me the utmost pleasure to renew my acquaintance with her. These alliances are most pleasing. Since I have taken up my residence in this country, I regard them with the utmost favour They do much to cement the good feeling between

Germany, Austria, and England, which is so desirable."

" English people," Mrs. Benedek remarked, " will at least have the opportunity of judging Austrian women from the proper standpoint. Anna is one of the most accomplished and beautiful women in either Vienna or Berlin. I hope so much that she will not have forgotten me altogether."

They all drifted presently back to the bridge tables. Norgate, however, excused himself. He had some letters to write, he declared, and presently he withdrew to the little drawing-room. In about a quarter of an hour, as he had expected, the door opened, and Selingman entered. He crossed the room at once to where Norgate was writing and laid his hand upon his shoulder.

" Young man," he said, " I wish to talk with you. Bring your chair around. Sit there so that the light falls upon your face. So! Now let me see. Where does that door lead to? "

" Into the secretary's room, but it is locked," Norgate told him.

" So! And the outer one I myself have carefully closed. We talk here, then, in private. This is great news which you have brought this afternoon."

" It is naturally of some interest to me," Norgate assented, " but I scarcely see —"

" It is of immense interest, also, to me," Selingman interrupted. " It may be that you do not know this at present. It may be that I anticipate, but if so, no matter. Between you and your fiancée there will naturally be no secrets. You are perhaps already aware that she holds a high position amongst those who are working for the power and development and expansion of our great empire? "

" I have gathered something of the sort," Norgate admitted. " I know, of course, that she is a personal favourite of the Emperor's, and *persona grata* at the Court of Berlin."

" You have no scruple, then, about marrying a woman who belongs to a certain clique, a certain school of diplomacy which you might, from a superficial point of view, consider inimical to your country's interests? "

" I have no scruple at all in marrying the Baroness von Haase," Norgate replied firmly. " As for the rest, you and I have discussed fully the matter of the political relations between our countries. I have shown you practically have I not, what my own views are? "

" That is true, my young friend," Selingman confessed. " We have spoken together, man to man, heart to heart. I have tried to show you that even though we should stand with sword outstretched across the seas, yet in the hearts of our people there dwells a real affection, real good-will towards your country. I think that I have convinced you. I have come, indeed, to have a certain amount of confidence in you. That I have already proved. But your news to-day alters much. There are grades of that society which you have joined, rings within rings, as you may well imagine. I see the prospect before me now of making much greater and more valuable use of you. It was your brain, and a certain impatience with the political conduct of your country, which brought you over to our side. Why should not that become an alliance — an absolute alliance? Your interests are drawn into ours. You have now a real and great reason for throwing in your lot with us. Let me look at you. Let me think whether I may not venture upon a great gamble."

Norgate did not flinch. He appeared simply a little puzzled. Selingman's blue, steel-like eyes seemed striving to reach the back of his brain.

" All the things that we accomplish in my country," the latter continued, " we do by method and order. We do them scientifically. We reach out into the future. So far as we can, we foresee everything. We leave little to chance. Yet there are times when one cannot deal in certainties. Young man, the news which you have told us this afternoon has brought us to this pitch. I am inclined to gamble — to gamble upon you."

" Is there any question of consulting me in this? " Norgate asked coolly.

Selingman brushed the interruption on one side.

" I now make clear to you what I mean," he continued. " You have joined my little army of helpers, those whom I have been able to convince of the justice and reasonableness of Germany's ultimate aim. Now I want more from you. I want to make of you something different. More than anything in the world, for the furtherance of my schemes here, I need a young Englishman of your position and with your connections, to whom I can give my whole confi-

dence, who will act for me with implicit obedience,
without hesitation. Will you accept that post,
Francis Norgate?"

"If you think I am capable of it," Norgate replied promptly.

"You are capable of. it," Selingman asserted.
"There is only one grim possibility to be risked.
Are you entirely trustworthy? Would you flinch at
the danger moment? Before this afternoon I hesitated. It is your alliance with the Baroness which
gives me that last drop of confidence which was
necessary."

"I am ready to do your work," Norgate said.
"I can say no more. My own country has no use
for me. My own country seems to have no use for
any one at all just now who thinks a little beyond
the day's eating and drinking and growing fat."

Selingman nodded his head. The note of bitterness in the other's tone was to his liking.

"Of rewards, of benefits, I shall not now speak,"
he proceeded. "You have something in you of the
spirit of men who aim at the greater things. There
is, indeed, in your attitude towards life something
of the idealism, the ever-stretching heavenward culture of my own people. I recognise that spirit in
you, and I will not give a lower tone to our talk this
afternoon by speaking of money. Yet what you
wish for you may have. When the time comes, what
further reward you may desire, whether it be rank
or high position, you may have, but for the present
let it be sufficient that you are my man."

He held out his hand, and all the time his eyes

never left Norgate's. Gone the florid and beaming geniality of the man, his easy good-humour, his air of good-living and rollicking gaiety. There were lines in his forehead. The firm contraction of his lips brought lines even across his plump cheeks. It was the face, this, of a strong man and a thinker. He held Norgate's fingers, and Norgate never flinched.

" So! " he said at last, as he turned away. " Now you are indeed in the inner circle, Mr. Francis Norgate. Good! Listen to me, then. We will speak of war, the war that is to come, the war that is closer at hand than even you might imagine."

" War with England? " Norgate exclaimed.

Selingman struck his hands together.

" No! " he declared. " You may take it as a compliment, if you like — a national compliment. We do not at the present moment desire war with England. Our plan of campaign, for its speedy and successful accomplishment, demands your neutrality. The North Sea must be free to us. Our fleet must be in a position to meet and destroy, as it is well able to do, the Russian and the French fleets. Now you know what has kept Germany from war for so long."

" You are ready for it, then? " Norgate remarked.

" We are over-ready for it," Selingman continued. " We are spoiling for it. We have piled up enormous stores of ordnance, ammunition, and all the appurtenances of warfare. Our schemes have been cut and dried to the last detail. Yet time after time we have been forced to stay our hand. Need I tell you why? It is because, in all those small diplomatic

complications which have arisen and from which war
might have followed, England has been involved. We
want to choose a time and a cause which will give
England every opportunity of standing peacefully
on one side. That time is close at hand. From all
that I can hear, your country is, at the present moment, in danger of civil war. Your Ministers who
are most in favour are Radical pacifists. Your army
has never been so small or your shipbuilding programme more curtailed. Besides, there is no warlike
spirit in your nation; you sleep peacefully. I think
that our time has come. You will not need to strain
your ears, my friend. Before many weeks have
passed, the tocsin will be sounding. Does that move
you? Let me look at you."

Norgate's face showed little emotion. Selingman
nodded ponderously.

"Surely," Norgate asked, "Germany will wait for
some reasonable pretext?"

"She will find one through Austria," Selingman
replied. "That is simple. Mind, though this may
seem to you a war wholly of aggression, and though
I do not hesitate to say that we have been prepared
for years for a war of aggression, there are other
factors which will come to light. Only a few months
ago, an entire Russian scheme for the invasion of
Germany next spring was discovered by one of our
Secret Service agents."

Norgate nodded.

"One question more," he said. "Supposing Germany takes the plunge, and then England, contrary
to anticipation, desides to support France?"

Selingman's face darkened. A sudden purposeless anger shook his voice.

"We choose a time," he declared, "when England's hands are tied. She is in no position to go to war with any one. I have many reports reaching me every day. I have come to the firm conclusion that we have reached the hour. England will not fight."

"And what will happen to her eventually?" Norgate asked.

Selingman smiled slowly.

"When France is crushed," he explained, "and her northern ports garrisoned by us, England must be taught just a little lesson, the lesson of which you and I have spoken, the lesson which will be for her good. That is what we have planned. That is how things will happen. Hush! There is some one coming. It is finished, this. Come to me to-morrow morning. There is work for you."

CHAPTER XXVII

Later on that evening, Norgate walked up and down the platform at Charing-Cross with Anna. Her arm rested upon his; her expression was animated and she talked almost eagerly. Norgate carried himself like a man who has found a new thing in life. He was feeling none of the depression of the last few days.

"Dear," Anna begged, "you won't forget, will you, all the time that I am away, that you must never for a single moment relax your caution? Selingman speaks of trust. Well, he gambles, it is true, yet he protects himself whenever he can. You will not move from early morning until you go to bed at night, without being watched. To prove what I say — you see the man who is reading an evening paper under the gas-lamp there? Yes? He is one of Selingman's men. He is watching us now. More than once he has been at our side. Scraps of conversation, or anything he can gather, will go back to Selingman, and Selingman day by day pieces everything together. Don't let there be a single thing which he can lay hold of."

"I'll lead him a dance," Norgate promised, nodding a little grimly. "As for that, Anna dear, you needn't be afraid. If ever I had any wits, they'll be awake during the next few weeks."

" When I come back from Rome," Anna went on,
" I shall have more to tell you. I believe that I
shall be able to tell you even the date of the great
happening. I wonder what other commissions he
will give you. The one to-night is simple. Be careful, dear. Think — think hard before you make up
your mind. Remember that there is some duplicity
which might become suddenly obvious. An official
statement might upset everything. These English
papers are so garrulous. You might find yourself
hard-pressed for an explanation."

" I'll be careful, dear," Norgate assured her, as
they stood at last before the door of her compartment. " And of ourselves? "

She lifted her veil.

" We have so little time," she murmured.

" But have you thought over what I suggested? "
he begged.

She laughed at him softly.

" It sounds quite attractive," she whispered.
" Shall we talk of it when I come back from Italy?
Good-by, dear! Of course, I do not really want to
kiss you, but our friend under the gas-lamp is looking — and you know our engagement! It is so satisfactory to dear Mr. Selingman. It is the one genuine thing about us, isn't it? So good-by! "

The long train drew out from the platform a few
minutes later. Norgate lingered until it was out of
sight. Then he took a taxi and drove to the House
of Commons. He sent in a card addressed to David
Bullen, Esq., and waited for some time. At last a
young man came down the corridor towards him.

"I am Mr. Bullen's private secretary," he announced. "Mr. Bullen cannot leave the House for some time. Would you care to go into the Strangers' Gallery, or will you wait in his room?"

"I should like to listen to the debate, if it is possible," Norgate decided.

A place was found for him with some difficulty. The House was crowded. The debate concerned one of the proposed amendments to the Home Rule Bill, not in itself important, yet interesting to Norgate on account of the bitter feeling which seemed to underlie the speeches of the extreme partisans on either side. The debate led nowhere. There was no division, no master mind intervening, yet it left a certain impression on Norgate's mind. At a little before ten, the young man who had found him his place touched his shoulder.

"Mr. Bullen will see you now, sir," he said.

Norgate followed his conductor through a maze of passages into a barely-furnished but lofty apartment. The personage whom he had come to see was standing at the further end, talking somewhat heatedly to one or two of his supporters. At Norgate's entrance, however, he dismissed them and motioned his visitor to a chair. He was a tall, powerful-looking man, with the eyes and forehead of a thinker. There was a certain laconic quality in his speech which belied his nationality.

"You come to me, I understand, Mr. Norgate," he began, "on behalf of some friends in America, not directly, but representing a gentleman who in his letter did not disclose himself. It sounds rather complicated, but please talk to me. I am at your service."

"I am sorry for the apparent mystery," Norgate said, as he took the seat to which he was invited. "I will make up for it by being very brief. I have come on behalf of a certain individual — whom we will call, if you please, Mr. X——. Mr. X—— has powerful connections in America, associated chiefly with German-Americans. As you know from your own correspondence with an organisation over there, the situation in Ireland is intensely interesting to them at the present moment."

"I have gathered that, sir," Mr. Bullen confessed. "The help which the Irish and Americans have sent to Dublin has scarcely been of the magnitude which one might have expected, but one is at least assured of their sympathy."

"It is partly my mission to assure you of something else," Norgate declared. "A secret meeting has been held in New York, and a sum of money has been promised, the amount of which would, I think, surprise you. The conditions attached to this gift, however, are peculiar. They are inspired by a profound disbelief in the *bona fides* of England and the honourableness of her intentions so far as regards the administration of the bill when passed."

Mr. Bullen, who at first had seemed a little puzzled, was now deeply interested. He drew his chair nearer to his visitor's.

"What grounds have you, or those whom you represent, for saying that?" he demanded.

"None that I can divulge," Norgate replied. "Yet they form the motive of the offer which I am about to make to you. I am instructed to say that the sum of a million pounds will be paid into your funds on certain guarantees to be given by you. It is my business here to place these guarantees before you and to report as to your attitude concerning them."

"One million pounds!" Mr. Bullen murmured, breathlessly.

"There are the conditions," Norgate reminded him.

"Well?"

"In the first place," Norgate continued, "the subscribers to this fund, which is by no means exhausted by the sum I mention, demand that you accept no compromise, that at all costs you insist upon the whole bill, and that if it is attempted at the last moment to deprive the Irish people by trickery of the full extent of their liberty, you do not hesitate to encourage your Nationalist party to fight for their freedom."

Mr. Bullen's lips were a little parted, but his face was immovable.

"Go on."

"In the event of your doing so," Norgate continued, "more money, and arms themselves if you require them, will be available, but the motto of those who have the cause of Ireland entirely at heart is, 'No compromise!' They recognise the fact that you are in a difficult position. They fear that you have allowed yourself to be influenced, to be weak-

ened by pressure so easily brought upon you from
high quarters."

"I understand," Mr. Bullen remarked.   "Go on."

"There is a further condition," Norgate proceeded, "though that is less important. The position in Europe at the present moment seems to indi-
cate a lasting peace, yet if anything should happen
that that peace should be broken, you are asked to
pledge your word that none of your Nationalist
volunteers should take up arms on behalf of England until that bill has become law and is in oper-
ation. Further, if that unlikely event, a war, should
take place, that you have the courage to keep your
men solid and armed, and that if the Ulster volunteers, unlike your men, decide to fight for England,
as they very well might do, that you then proceed
to take by force what it is not the intention of England to grant you by any other means."

Mr. Bullen leaned back in his chair.   He picked up
a penholder and played with it for several moments.
"Young man," he asked at last, "who is Mr.
X——?"

"That, in the present stage of our negotiations,"
Norgate answered coolly, "I am not permitted to
tell you."

"May I guess as to his nationality?" Mr. Bullen
enquired.

"I cannot prevent your doing that."

"The speculation is an interesting one," Mr.
Bullen went on, still fingering the penholder. "Is
Mr. X—— a German?"

Norgate was silent.

"I cannot answer questions," he said, "until you have expressed your views."

"You can have them, then," Mr. Bullen declared. "You can go back to Mr. X—— and tell him this. Ireland needs help sorely to-day from all her sons, whether at home or in foreign countries. More than anything she needs money. The million pounds of which you speak would be a splendid contribution to what I may term our war chest. But as to my views, here they are. It is my intention, and the intention of my Party, to fight to the last gasp for the literal carrying out of the bill which is to grant us our liberty. We will not have it whittled away or weakened one iota. Our lives, and the lives of greater men, have been spent to win this measure, and now we stand at the gates of success. We should be traitors if we consented to part with a single one of the benefits it brings us. Therefore, you can tell Mr. X—— that should this Government attempt any such trickery as he not unreasonably suspects, then his conditions will be met. My men shall fight, and their cause will be just."

"So far," Norgate admitted, "this is very satisfactory."

"To pass on," Mr. Bullen continued, "let me at once confess that I find something sinister, Mr. Norgate, in this mysterious visit of yours, in the hidden identity of Mr. X——. I suspect some underlying motive which prompts the offering of this million pounds. I may be wrong, but it seems to me that I can see beneath it all the hand of a foreign enemy of England."

"Supposing you were right, Mr. Bullen," Norgate said, "what is England but a foreign enemy of Ireland?"

A light flashed for a moment in Mr. Bullen's eyes. His lip curled inwards.

"Young man," he demanded, "are you an Englishman?"

"I am," Norgate admitted.

"You speak poorly, then. To proceed to the matter in point, my word is pledged to fight. I will plunge the country I love into civil war to gain her rights, as greater patriots than I have done before. But the thing which I will not do is to be made the cat's-paw, or to suffer Ireland to be made the cat's-paw, of Germany. If war should come before the settlement of my business, this is the position I should take. I would cross to Dublin, and I would tell every Nationalist Volunteer to shoulder his rifle and to fight for the British Empire, and I would go on to Belfast — I, David Bullen — to Belfast, where I think that I am the most hated man alive, and I would stand side by side with the leader of those men of Ulster, and I would beg them to fight side by side with my Nationalists. And when the war was over, if my rights were not granted, if Ireland were not set free, then I would bid my men take breathing time and use all their skill, all the experience they had gained, and turn and fight for their own freedom against the men with whom they had struggled in the same ranks. Is that million pounds to be mine, Mr. Norgate?"

Norgate shook his head.

" Nor any part of it, sir," he answered.

" I presume," Mr. Bullen remarked, as he rose, " that I shall never have the pleasure of meeting Mr. X—— ? "

" I most sincerely hope," Norgate declared fervently, " that you never will. Good-day, Mr. Bullen ! "

He held out his hand. Mr. Bullen hesitated.

" Sir," he said, " I am glad to shake hands with an Irishman. I am willing to shake hands with an honest Englishman. Just where you come in, I don't know, so good evening. You will find my secretary outside. He will show you how to get away."

For a moment Norgate faltered. A hot rejoinder trembled upon his lips. Then he remembered himself and turned on his heel. It was his first lesson in discipline. He left the room without protest.

CHAPTER XXVIII

Mr. Hebblethwaite turned into Pall Mall, his hands behind his back, his expression a little less indicative of bland good humour than usual. He had forgotten to light his customary cigarette after the exigencies of a Cabinet Council. He had even forgotten to linger for a few minutes upon the doorstep in case any photographer should be hanging around to take a snapshot of a famous visitor leaving an historic scene, and quite unconsciously he ignored the salutation of several friends. It was only by the merest chance that he happened to glance up at the corner of the street and recognised Norgate across the way. He paused at once and beckoned to him.

"Well, young fellow," he exclaimed, as they shook hands, "how's the German spy business going?"

"Pretty well, thanks," Norgate answered coolly. "I am in it twice over now. I'm marrying an Austrian lady shortly, very high up indeed in the Diplomatic Secret Service of her country. Between us you may take it that we could read, if we chose, the secrets of the Cabinet Council from which you have just come."

"Any fresh warnings, eh?"

Norgate turned and walked by his friend's side.

"It is no use warning you," he declared. "You've a hide as thick as a rhinoceros. Your complacency is bomb-proof. You won't believe anything until it's too late."

"Confoundedly disagreeable companion you make, Norgate," the Cabinet Minister remarked irritably. "You know quite as well as I do that the German scare is all bunkum, and you only hammer it in either to amuse yourself or because you are of a sensational turn of mind. All the same —"

"All the same, what?" Norgate interrupted.

Hebblethwaite took his young friend's arm and led him into his club.

"We will take an apéritif in the smoking-room," he said. "After that I will look in my book and see where I am lunching. It is perhaps not the wisest thing for a Cabinet Minister to talk in the street. Since the Suffragette scares, I have quite an eye for a detective, and there has been a fellow within a few yards of your elbow ever since you spoke to me."

"That's all right," Norgate reassured him. "Let's see, it's Tuesday, isn't it? I call him Boko. He never leaves me. My week-end shadowers are a trifle less assiduous, but Boko is suspicious. He has deucedly long ears, too."

"What the devil are you talking about?" Hebblethwaite demanded, as they sat down.

"The fact of it is," Norgate explained, "they don't altogether trust me in my new profession. They give me some important jobs to look after, but they watch me night and day. What they'd do if I turned 'em up, I can't imagine. By-the-by, if you do hear of my being found mysteriously shot or poisoned or something of that sort, don't you take on any theory as to suicide. It will be murder, right enough. However," he added, raising his glass to his lips and nodding, " they haven't found me out yet."

" I hear," Hebblethwaite muttered, " that the bookstalls are loaded with this sort of rubbish. You do it very well, though."

" Oh! I am the real thing all right," Norgate declared. " By-the-by, what's the matter with you? "

" Nothing," Hebblethwaite replied. " When you come to think of it, sitting here and feeling the reviving influence of this remarkably well-concocted beverage, I can confidently answer ' Nothing.' And yet, a few minutes ago, I must admit that I was conscious of a sensation of gloom. You know, Norgate, you're not the only idiot in the world who goes about seeing shadows. For the first time in my life I begin to wonder whether we haven't got a couple of them among us. Of course, I don't take any notice of Spencer Wyatt. It's his job. He plays the part of popular hero — National Anthem, God Save the Empire, and all that sort of thing. He must keep in with his admirals and the people, so of course he's always barking for ships. But White, now. I have always looked upon White as being absolutely the most level-headed, sensible, and peace-adoring Minister this country ever had."

" What's wrong with him? " Norgate asked.

" I cannot," Hebblethwaite regretted, " talk confidentially to a German spy."

"Getting cautious as the years roll on, aren't you?" Norgate sighed. "I hoped I was going to get something interesting out of you to cable to Berlin."

"You try cabling to Berlin, young fellow," Hebblethwaite replied grimly, "and I'll have you up at Bow Street pretty soon! There's no doubt about it, though, old White has got the shivers for some reason or other. To any sane person things were never calmer and more peaceful than at the present moment, and White isn't a believer in the German peril, either. He is half inclined to agree with old Busby. He got us out of that Balkan trouble in great style, and all I can say is that if any nation in Europe wanted war then, she could have had it for the asking."

"Well, exactly what is the matter with White at the present moment?" Norgate demanded.

"Got the shakes," Hebblethwaite confided. "Of course, we don't employ well-born young Germans who are undergoing a period of rustication, as English spies, but we do get to know a bit what goes on there, and the reports that are coming in are just a little curious. Rolling stock is being called into the termini of all the railways. Staff officers in mufti have been round all the frontiers. There's an enormous amount of drilling going on, and the ordnance factories are working at full pressure, day and night."

"The manœuvres are due very soon," Norgate reminded his friend.

"So I told White," Hebblethwaite continued, "but

manœuvres, as he remarked, don't lead to quite so much feverish activity as there is about Germany just now. Personally, I haven't a single second's anxiety. I only regret the effect that this sort of feeling has upon the others. Thank heavens we are a Government of sane, peace-believing people!"

" A Government of fat-headed asses who go about with your ears stuffed full of wool," Norgate declared, with a sudden bitterness. " What you've been telling me is the truth. Germany's getting ready for war, and you'll have it in the neck pretty soon."

Hebblethwaite set down his empty glass. He had recovered his composure.

" Well, I am glad I met you, any way, young fellow," he remarked. " You're always such an optimist. You cheer one up. Sorry I can't ask you to lunch," he went on, consulting his book, " but I find I am motoring down for a round of golf this afternoon."

" Yes, you would play golf!" Norgate grunted, as they strolled towards the door. " You're the modern Nero, playing golf while the earthquake yawns under London."

" Play you some day, if you like," Hebblethwaite suggested, as he called for a taxi. " They took my handicap down two last week at Walton Heath — not before it was time, either. By-the-by, when can I meet the young lady? My people may be out of town next week, but I'll give you both a lunch or a dinner, if you'll say the word. Thursday night, eh?"

"At present," Norgate replied, "the Baroness is in Italy, arranging for the mobilisation of the Italian armies, but if she's back for Thursday, we shall be delighted. She'll be quite interested to meet you. A keen, bright, alert politician of your type will simply fascinate her."

"We'll make it Thursday night, then, at the Carlton," Hebblethwaite called out from his taxi. "Take care of Boko. So long!"

At the top of St. James's Street, Norgate received the bow of a very elegantly-dressed young woman who was accompanied by a well-known soldier. A few steps further on he came face to face with Selingman.

"A small city, London," the latter declared. "I am on my way to the Berkeley to lunch. Will you come with me? I am alone to-day, and I hate to eat alone. Miss Morgen has deserted me shamefully."

"I met her a moment or two ago," Norgate remarked. "She was with Colonel Bowden."

Selingman nodded. "Rosa has been taking a great interest in flying lately. Colonel Bowden is head of the Flying Section. Well, well, one must expect to be deserted sometimes, we older men."

"Especially in so great a cause," Norgate observed drily.

Selingman smiled enigmatically.

"And you, my young friend," he enquired, "what have you been doing this morning?"

"I have just left Hebblethwaite," Norgate answered.

" There was a Cabinet Council this morning, wasn't there? "

Norgate nodded.

" An unimportant one, I should imagine. Hebblethwaite seemed thoroughly satisfied with himself and with life generally. He has gone down to Walton Heath to play golf."

Selingman led the way into the restaurant.

" Very good exercise for an English Cabinet Minister," he remarked, " capital for the muscles! "

CHAPTER XXIX

"I had no objection," Norgate remarked, a few hours later, "to lunching with you at the Berkeley — very good lunch it was, too — but to dine with you in Soho certainly seems to require some explanation. Why do we do it? Is it my punishment for a day's inactivity, because if so, I beg to protest. I did my best with Hebblethwaite this morning, and it was only because there was nothing for him to tell me that I heard nothing."

Selingman spread himself out at the little table and talked in voluble German to the portly head-waiter in greasy clothes. Then he turned to his guest.

"My young friend," he enjoined, "you should cultivate a spirit of optimism. I grant you that the place is small and close, that the odour of other people's dinners is repellent, that this cloth, perhaps, is not so clean as it once was, or the linen so fine as we are accustomed to. But what would you have? All sides of life come into the great scheme. It is here that we shall meet a person whom I need to meet, a person whom I do not choose to have visit me at my home, whom I do not choose to be seen with in any public place of great repute."

"I should say we were safe here from knocking

against any of our friends!" Norgate observed.
"Anyhow, the beer's all right."

They were served with light-coloured beer in tall,
chased tumblers. Selingman eyed his with approval.

"A nation," he declared, "which brews beer like
this, deserves well of the world. You did wisely,
Norgate, to become ever so slightly associated with
us. Now examine carefully these *hors d'œuvres*. I
have talked with Karl, the head-waiter. Instead of
eighteen pence, we shall pay three shillings each for
our dinner. The whole resources of the establishment are at our disposal. Fresh tins of *delicatessen*,
you perceive. Do not be afraid that you will go
away hungry."

"I am more afraid," Norgate grumbled, "that I
shall go away sick. However!"

"You may be interested to hear," announced
Selingman, glancing up, "that our visit is not in
vain. You perceive the two men entering? The
nearest one is a Bulgarian. He is a creature of
mine. The other is brought here by him to meet us.
It is good."

The newcomers made their way along the room.
One, the Bulgarian, was short and dark. He wore a
well-brushed blue serge suit with a red tie, and a
small bowler hat. He was smoking a long, brown
cigarette and he carried a bundle of newspapers.
Behind him came a youth with a pale, sensitive face
and dark eyes, ill-dressed, with the grip of poverty
upon him, from his patched shoes to his frayed collar
and well-worn cap. Nevertheless, he carried himself
as though indifferent to these things. His compan-

ion stopped short as he neared the table at which the two men were sitting, and took off his hat, greeting Selingman with respect.

"My friend Stralhaus!" Selingman exclaimed. "It goes well, I trust? You are a stranger. Let me introduce to you my secretary, Mr. Francis Norgate."

Stralhaus bowed and turned to his young companion.

"This," he said, "is the young man with whom you desired to speak. We will sit down if we may. Sigismund, this is the great Herr Selingman, philanthropist and millionaire, with his secretary, Mr. Norgate. We take dinner with him to-night."

The youth shook hands without enthusiasm. His manner towards Selingman was cold. At Norgate he glanced once or twice with something approaching curiosity. Stralhaus proceeded to make conversation.

"Our young friend," he explained, addressing Norgate, "is an exile in London. He belongs to an unfortunate country. He is a native of Bosnia."

The boy's lip curled.

"It is possible," he remarked, "that Mr. Norgate has never even heard of my country. He is very little likely to know its history."

"On the contrary," Norgate replied, "I know it very well. You have had the misfortune, during the last few years, to come under Austrian rule."

"Since you put it like that," the boy declared, "we are friends. I am one of those who cry out to Heaven in horror at the injustice which has been done. We love liberty, we Bosnians. We love our own people and our own institutions, and we hate Austria. May you never know, sir, what it is to be ruled by an alien race!"

"You have at least the sympathy of many nations who are powerless to interfere," Selingman said quietly. "I read your pamphlet, Mr. Henriote, with very great interest. Before we leave to-night, I shall make a proposal to you."

The boy seemed puzzled for a moment, but Stralhaus intervened with some commonplace remark.

"After dinner," he suggested, "we will talk."

Certainly during the progress of the meal Henriote said little. He ate, although obviously half famished, with restraint, but although Norgate did his best to engage him in conversation, he seemed taciturn, almost sullen. Towards the end of dinner, when every one was smoking and coffee had been served, Selingman glanced at his watch.

"Now," he said, "I will tell you, my young Bosnian patriot, why I sent for you. Would you like to go back to your country, in the first place?"

"It is impossible!" Henriote declared bitterly. "I am exile. I am forbidden to return under pain of death."

Selingman opened his pocket-book, and, searching among his papers, produced a thin blue one which he opened and passed across the table.

"Read that," he ordered shortly.

The young man obeyed. A sudden exclamation broke from his lips. A pink flush, which neither the wine nor the food had produced, burned in his cheeks. He sat hunched up, leaning forward, his eyes devouring the paper. When he had finished, he still gripped it.

" It is my pardon! " he cried. " I may go back home — back to Bosnia! "

" It is your free pardon," Selingman replied, " but it is granted to you upon conditions. Those conditions, I may say, are entirely for your country's sake and are framed by those who feel exactly as you feel — that Austrian rule for Bosnia is an injustice."

" Go on," the young man muttered. " What am I to do? "

" You are a member," Selingman went on, " of the extreme revolutionary party, a party pledged to stop at nothing, to drive your country's enemies across her borders. Very well, listen to me. The pardon which you have there is granted to you without any promise having been asked for or given in return. It is I alone who dictate terms to you. Your country's position, her wrongs, and the abuses of the present form of government, can only be brought before the notice of Europe in one way. You are pledged to do that. All that I require of you is that you keep your pledge."

The young man half rose to his feet with excitement.

" Keep it! Who is more anxious to keep it than I? If Europe wants to know how we feel, she shall know! We will proclaim the wrongs of our country so that England and Russia, France and Italy, shall hear and judge for themselves. If you need deeds to rivet the attention of the world upon our sufferings, then there shall be deeds. There shall —"

He stopped short. A look of despair crossed his face.

"But we have no money!" he exclaimed. "We patriots are starving. Our lands have been confiscated. We have nothing. I live over here Heaven knows how — I, Sigismund Henriote, have toiled for my living with Polish Jews and the outcasts of Europe."

Selingman dived once more into his pocket-book. He passed a packet across the table.

"Young man," he said, "that sum has been collected for your funds by the friends of your country abroad. Take it and use it as you think best. All that I ask from you is that what you do, you do quickly. Let me suggest an occasion for you. The Archduke of Austria will be in your capital almost as soon as you can reach home."

The boy's face was transfigured. His great eyes were lit with a wonderful fire. His frame seemed to have filled out. Norgate looked at him in wonderment. He was like a prophet; then suddenly he grew calm. He placed his pardon, to which was attached his passport, and the notes, in his breast-coat pocket. He rose to his feet and took the cap from the floor by his side.

"There is a train to-night," he announced. "I wish you farewell, gentlemen. I know nothing of you, sir," he added, turning to Selingman, "and I ask no questions. I only know that you have pointed towards the light, and for that I thank you.   Good night, gentlemen!"

He left them and walked out of the restaurant like a man in a dream.   Selingman helped himself to a liqueur and passed the bottle to Norgate.

"It is in strange places that one may start sometimes the driving wheels of Fate," he remarked.

CHAPTER XXX

Anna almost threw herself from the railway carriage into Norgate's arms. She kissed him on both cheeks, held him for a moment away from her, then passed her arm affectionately through his.

"You dear!" she exclaimed. "Oh, how weary I am of it! Nearly a week in the train! And how well you are looking! And I am not going to stay a single second bothering about luggage. Marie, give the porter my dressing-case. Here are the keys. You can see to everything."

Norgate, carried almost off his feet by the delight of her welcome, led her away towards a taxicab.

"I am starving," she told him. "I would have nothing at Dover except a cup of tea. I knew that you would meet me, and I thought that we would have our first meal in England together. You shall take me somewhere where we can have supper and tell me all the news. I don't look too hideous, do I, in my travelling clothes?"

"You look adorable," he assured her, "and I believe you know it."

"I have done my best," she confessed demurely. "Marie took so much trouble with my hair. We had the most delightful coupé all to ourselves. Fancy, we are back again in London! I have been to Italy, I have spoken to kings and prime ministers, and I am back again with you. And queerly enough, not until to-morrow shall I see the one person who really rules Italy."

" Who is that? " he asked.

" I am not sure that I shall tell you everything," she decided. " You have not opened your mouth to me yet. I shall wait until supper-time. Have you changed your mind since I went away? "

" I shall never change it," he assured her eagerly. " We are in a taxicab and I know it's most unusual and improper, but —"

" If you hadn't kissed me," she declared a moment later as she leaned forward to look in the glass, " I should not have eaten a mouthful of supper."

They drove to the Milan Grill. It was a little early for the theatre people, and they were almost alone in the place. Anna drew a great sigh of content as she settled down in her chair.

" I think I must have been lonely for a long time," she whispered, " for it is so delightful to get back and be with you. Tell me what you have been doing? "

" I have been promoted," Norgate announced. " My prospective alliance with you has completed Selingman's confidence in me. I have been entrusted with several commissions."

He told her of his adventures. She listened breathlessly to the account of his dinner in Soho.

" It is queer how all this is working out," she observed. " I knew before that the trouble was to come through Austria. The Emperor was very anxious indeed that it should not. He wanted to

have his country brought reluctantly into the struggle. Even at this moment I believe that if he thought
there was the slightest chance of England becoming
embroiled, he would travel to Berlin himself to plead
with the Kaiser. I really don't know why, but the
one thing in Austria which would be thoroughly unpopular would be a war with England."

" Tell me about your mission? " he asked.

" To a certain point," she confessed, with a little
grimace, " it was unsuccessful. I have brought a
reply to the personal letter I took over to the King.
I have talked with Guillamo, the Secretary of State
for Foreign Affairs, with whom, of course, everything is supposed to rest. What I have brought
with me, however, and what I heard from Guillamo,
are nothing but a repetition of the assurances given
to our Ambassador. The few private words which
I was to get I have failed in obtaining, simply because the one person who could have spoken them is
here in London."

" Who is that? " he enquired curiously.

" The Comtesse di Strozzi," she told him. " It is
she who has directed the foreign policy of Italy
through Guillamo for the last ten years. He does
nothing without her. He is like a lost child, indeed,
when she is away. And where do you think she is?
Why, here in London. She is staying at the Italian
Embassy. Signor Cardina is her cousin. The great
ball to-morrow night, of which you have read, is in
her honour. You shall be my escort. At one time
I knew her quite well."

" The Comtesse di Strozzi! " he exclaimed.

"Why, she spent the whole of last season in Paris. I saw quite a great deal of her."

"How odd!" Anna murmured. "But how delightful! We shall be able to talk to her together, you and I."

"It is rather a coincidence," he admitted. "She had a sort of craze to visit some of the places in Paris where it is necessary for a woman to go incognito, and I was always her escort. I heard from her only a few weeks ago, and she told me that she was coming to London."

Anna shook her head at him gaily.

"Well," she said, "I won't indulge in any ante-jealousies. I only hope that through her we shall get to know the truth. Are things here still quiet?"

"Absolutely."

"Also in Paris. Francis, I feel so helpless. On my way I thought of staying over, of going to see the Minister of War and placing certain facts before him. And then I realised how little use it would all be. They won't believe us, Francis. They would simply call us alarmists. They won't believe that the storm is gathering."

"Don't I know it!" Norgate assented earnestly. "Why, Hebblethwaite here has always been a great friend of mine. I have done all I can to influence him. He simply laughs in my face. To-day, for the first time, he admitted that there was a slight uneasiness at the Cabinet Meeting, and that White had referred to a certain mysterious activity throughout Germany. Nevertheless, he has gone down to Walton Heath to play golf."

She made a little grimace.

"Your great Drake," she reminded him, "played bowls when the Armada sailed. Your Cabinet Ministers will be playing golf or tennis. Oh, what a careless country you are! — a careless, haphazard, blind, pig-headed nation to watch over the destinies of such an Empire! I'm so tired of politics, dear. I am so tired of all the big things that concern other people. They press upon one. Now it is finished. You and I are alone. You are my lover, aren't you? Remind me of it. If you will, I will discuss the subject you mentioned the other day. Of course I shall say 'No!' I am not nearly ready to be married yet. But I should like to hear your arguments."

Their heads grew closer and closer together. They were almost touching when Selingman and Rosa Morgen came in. Selingman paused before their table.

"Well, well, young people!" he exclaimed. "Forgive me, Baroness, if I am somewhat failing in respect, but the doings of this young man have become some concern of mine."

Her greeting was tinged with a certain condescension. She had suddenly stiffened. There was something of the *grande dame* in the way she held up the tips of her fingers.

"You do not disapprove, I trust?"

"Baroness," Selingman declared earnestly, "it is an alliance for which no words can express my approval. It comes at the one moment. It has riveted to us and our interests one whose services will never be forgotten. May I venture to hope that your journey to Italy has been productive? "

" Not entirely as we had hoped," Anna replied, " yet the position there is not unfavourable."

Selingman glanced towards the table at which Miss Morgen had already seated herself.

" I must not neglect my duties," he remarked, turning away.

" Especially," Anna murmured, glancing across the room, " when they might so easily be construed into pleasures."

Selingman beamed amiably.

" The young lady," he said, " is more than orna-mental — she is extremely useful. From the fact that I may not be privileged to present her to you, I must be careful that she cannot consider herself neglected. And so good night, Baroness! Good night, Norgate! "

He passed on. The Baroness watched him as he took his place opposite his companion.

" Is it my fancy," Norgate asked, " or does Se-lingman not meet entirely with your approval? "

She shrugged her shoulders.

" It is not that," she replied. " He is a great man, in his way, the Napoleon of the bourgeoisie, but then he is one of them himself. He collects the whole scheme of information as to the social life and opin-ions — the domestic particulars, I call them — of your country. Details of your industries are at his finger-tips. He and I do not come into contact. I am the trusted agent of both sovereigns, but it is only in high diplomatic affairs that I ever intervene.

Selingman, it is true, may be considered the greatest spy who ever breathed, but a spy he is. If we could only persuade your too amiable officials to believe one-tenth of what we could tell them, I think our friend there would breakfast in an English fortress, if you have such a thing."

"We should only place him under police supervision," declared Norgate, "and let him go. It's just our way, that's all."

She waved the subject of Selingman on one side, but almost at that moment he stood once more before them. He held an evening paper in his hand.

"I bring you the news," he announced. "A terrible tragedy has happened. The Archduke of Austria and his Consort have been assassinated on their tour through Bosnia."

For a moment neither Anna nor Norgate moved. Norgate felt a strange sense of sickening excitement. It was as though the curtain had been rung up!

"Is the assassin's name there?" he asked.

"The crime," Selingman replied, "appears to have been committed by a young Servian student. His name is Sigismund Henriote."

CHAPTER XXXI

They paused at last, breathless, and walked out of the most wonderful ballroom in London into the gardens, aglow with fairy lanterns whose brilliance was already fading before the rising moon. They found a seat under a tall elm tree, and Anna leaned back. It was a queer mixture of sounds which came to their ears; in the near distance, the music of a wonderful orchestra rising and falling; further away, the roar of the great city still awake and alive outside the boundary of those grey stone walls.

"Of course," she murmured, "this is the one thing which completes my subjugation. Fancy an Englishman being able to waltz! Almost in that beautiful room I fancied myself back in Vienna, except that it was more wonderful because it was you."

"You are turning my head," he whispered. "This is like a night out of Paradise. And to think that we are really in the middle of London!"

"Ah! do not mention London," she begged, "or else I shall begin to think of Sodom and Gomorrah. After all, why need one live for anything else except the present?"

"There is the Comtesse," he reminded her disconsolately.

She sighed.

"How horrid of you!"

"Let us forget her, then," he begged. "We will

go into the marquee there and have supper, and afterwards dance again. We'll steal to-night out of the calendar. We'll call it ours and play with it as we please."

She shook her head.

"No," she decided, "you have reminded me of our duty, and you are quite right. You were brought here to talk to the Comtesse. I do not know why, but she is in a curiously impenetrable frame of mind. I tried hard to get her to talk to me, but it was useless; you must see what you can do. Fortunately, she seems to be absolutely delighted to have met you again. You have a dance with her, have you not?"

He drew out his programme reluctantly.

"The next one, too," he sighed.

Anna rose quickly to her feet.

"How absurd of me to forget! Take me inside, please, and go and look for her at once."

"It's all very well," Norgate grumbled, "but the last time I saw her she was about three deep among the notabilities. I really don't feel that I ought to jostle dukes and ambassadors to claim a dance."

"You must not be so foolish," Anna insisted. "The Comtesse cares nothing for dukes and ambassadors, but she is most ridiculously fond of good-looking young men. Mind, you will do better with her if you speak entirely outside all of us. She is a very peculiar woman. If one could only read the secrets she has stored up in her brain! Sometimes she is so lavish with them, and at other times, and with other people, it seems as though it would take an earthquake to force a sentence from her lips.

There she is, see, in that corner. Never mind the people around her. Go and do your duty."

Norgate found it easier than he had expected. She no sooner saw him coming than she rose to her feet and welcomed him. She laid her fingers upon his arm, and they moved away towards the ballroom.

" I am afraid," he apologised, " that I am rather an intruder. You all seemed so interested in listening to the Duke."

" On the contrary, I welcome you as a deliverer," she declared. " I have heard those stories so often, and worse than having heard them is the necessity always to smile. The Duke is a dear good person, and he has been exceedingly kind to me during the whole of my stay, but oh, how one sometimes does weary oneself of this London of yours! Yet I love it. Do you know that you were almost the first person I asked for when I arrived here? They told me that you were in Berlin."

" I was," he admitted. " I am in the act of being transferred."

" Fortunate person!" she murmured. " You speak the language of all capitals, but I cannot fancy you in Berlin."

They had reached the edge of the ballroom. He hesitated.

" Do you care to dance or shall we go outside and talk? "

She smiled at him. " Both, may we not? You dear, discreet person, when I think of the strange places where I have danced with you — Perhaps it is better not to remember! "

They moved away to the music and later on found their way into the garden. The Comtesse was a little thoughtful.

" You are a great friend of Anna's, are you not? " she enquired.

" We are engaged to be married," he answered simply.

She made a little grimace.

" Ah ! " she sighed, " you nice men, it comes to you all. You amuse yourselves with us for a time, and then the real feeling comes, and where are we? But it is queer, too," she went on thoughtfully, " that Anna should marry an Englishman, especially just now."

" Why ' especially just now'? "

The Comtesse evaded the question.

" Anna seemed always," she said, " to prefer the men of her own country. Oh, what music ! Shall we have one turn more, Mr. Francis Norgate? It is the waltz they played — but who could expect a man to remember ! "

They plunged again into the crowd of dancers. The Comtesse was breathless yet exhilarated when at last they emerged.

" But you dance, as ever, wonderfully ! " she cried. " You make me think of those days in Paris. You make me even sad."

" They remain," he assured her, " one of the most pleasant memories of my life."

She patted his hand affectionately. Then her tone changed.

" Almost," she declared, " you have driven all

other things out of my mind. What is it that Anna is so anxious to know from me? You are in her confidence, she tells me."

" Entirely."

" That again is strange," the Comtesse continued, " when one considers your nationality, yet Anna herself has assured me of it. Do you know that she is a person whom I very much envy? Her life is so full of variety. She is the special protégée of the Emperor. No woman at Vienna is more trusted."

" I am not sure," Norgate observed, " that she was altogether satisfied with the results of her visit to Rome."

The Comtesse's fan fluttered slowly back and forth. She looked for a moment or two idly upon the brilliant scene. The smooth garden paths, the sheltered seats, the lawns themselves, were crowded with little throngs of women in exquisite toilettes, men in uniform and Court dress. There were well-known faces everywhere. It was the crowning triumph of a wonderful London season.

" Anna's was a very difficult mission," the Comtesse pointed out confidentially. " There is really no secret about these matters. The whole world knows of Italy's position. A few months ago, at the time of what you call the Balkan Crisis, Germany pressed us very hard for a definite assurance of our support, under any conditions, of the Triple Alliance. I remember that Andrea was three hours with the King that day, and our reply was unacceptable in Berlin. It may have helped to keep the peace. One cannot tell. The Kaiser's present letter is simply a repetition of his feverish attempt to probe our intentions."

" But at present," Norgate ventured, " there is no Balkan Crisis."

The Comtesse looked at him lazily out of the corners of her sleepy eyes.

" Is there not? " she asked simply. " I have been away from Italy for a week or so, and Andrea trusts nothing to letters. Yesterday I had a dispatch begging me to return. I go to-morrow morning. I do not know whether it is because of the pressure of affairs, or because he wearies himself a little without me."

" One might easily imagine the latter," Norgate remarked. " But is it indeed any secret to you that there is a great feeling of uneasiness throughout the Continent, an extraordinary state of animation, a bustle, although a secret bustle, of preparation in Germany? "

" I have heard rumours of this," the Comtesse confessed.

" When one bears these things in mind and looks a little into the future," Norgate continued, " one might easily believe that the reply to that still unanswered letter of the Kaiser's might well become historical."

" You would like me, would you not," she asked, " to tell you what that reply will most certainly be? "

" Very much! "

" You are an Englishman," she remarked thoughtfully, " and intriguing with Anna. I fear that I do not understand the position."

" Must you understand it? "

" Perhaps not," she admitted. " It really matters very little. I will speak to you just in the only way I can speak, as a private individual. I tell you that I do not believe that Andrea will ever, under any circumstances, join in any war against England, nor any war which has for its object the crushing of France. In his mind the Triple Alliance was the most selfish alliance which any country has ever entered into, but so long as the other two Powers understood the situation, it was scarcely Italy's part to point out the fact that she gained everything by it and risked nothing. Italy has sheltered herself for years under its provisions, but neither at the time of signing it, nor at any other time, has she had the slightest intention of joining in an aggressive war at the request of her allies. You see, her Government felt themselves safe — and I think that that was where Andrea was so clever — in promising to fulfil their obligations in case of an attack by any other Power upon Germany or Austria, because it was perfectly certain to Andrea, and to every person of common sense, that no such aggressive attack would ever be made. You read Austria's demands from Servia in the paper this morning? "

" I did," Norgate admitted. " No one in the world could find them reasonable."

" They are not meant to be reasonable," the Comtesse pointed out. " They are the foundation from which the world quarrel shall spring. Russia must intervene to protect Servia from their hideous injustice. Germany and Austria will throw down the gage. Germany may be right or she may be wrong, but she believes she can count on Great Britain's neutrality. She needs our help and believes she will get it. That is because German diplomacy always believes that it is going to get what it wants. Now, in a few words, I will tell you what the German Emperor would give me a province to know. I will tell you that no matter what the temptation, what the proffered reward may be, Italy will not join in this war on the side of Germany and Austria."

"You are very kind, Comtesse," Norgate said simply, " and I shall respect your confidence."

She rose and laid her fingers upon his arm.

"To people whom I like," she declared, "I speak frankly. I give away no secrets. I say what I belive. And now I must leave you for a much subtler person and a much subtler conversation. Prince Herschfeld is waiting to talk to me. Perhaps he, too, would like to know the answer which will go to his master, but how can I tell? "

The Ambassador had paused before them. The Comtesse rose and accepted his arm.

"I shall take away with me to-night at least two charming memories," she assured him, as she gathered up her skirts. "My two dances, Mr. Norgate, have been delightful. Now I am equally sure of entertainment of another sort from Prince Herschfeld."

The Prince bowed.

"Ah! madame," he sighed, "it is so hard to compete with youth. I fear that the feet of Mr. Norgate will be nimbler than my brain to-night."

She nodded sympathetically.

"You are immersed in affairs, of course," she murmured. "Au revoir, Mr. Norgate! Give my love to Anna. Some day I hope that I shall welcome you both in Rome."

CHAPTER XXXII

Norgate pushed his way through a confused medley of crates which had just been unloaded and made his way up the warehouse to Selingman's office. Selingman was engaged for a few minutes but presently opened the door of his sanctum and called his visitor in.

"Well, my young friend," he exclaimed, "you have brought news? Sit down. This is a busy morning. We have had large shipments from Germany. I have appointments with buyers most of the day, yet I can talk to you for a little time. You were at the ball last night?"

"I was permitted to escort the Baroness von Haase," Norgate replied.

Selingman nodded ponderously.

"I ask you no questions," he said. "The Baroness works on a higher plane. I know more than you would believe, though. I know why the dear lady went to Rome; I know why she was at the ball. I know in what respect you were probably able to help her. But I ask no questions. We work towards a common end, but we work at opposite ends of the pole. Curiosity alone would be gratified if you were to tell me everything that transpired."

"You keep yourself marvellously well-informed as to most things, don't you, Mr. Selingman?" Norgate remarked.

"Platitudes, young man, platitudes," Selingman declared, "words of air. What purpose have they? You know who I am. I hold in my hand a thousand strings. Any one that I pull will bring an answering message to my brain. Come, what is it you wish to say to me?"

"I am doing my work for you," Norgate remarked, "and doing it extraordinarily well. I do not object to a certain amount of surveillance, but I am getting fed up with Boko."

"Who the hell is Boko?" Selingman demanded.

"I must apologise," Norgate replied. "A nickname only. He is a little red-faced man who looks like a children's toy and changes his clothes about seven times a day. He is with me from the moment I rise to the last thing at night. He is getting on my nerves. I am fast drifting into the frame of mind when one looks under the bed before one can sleep."

"Young man," Selingman said, "a month ago you were a person of no importance. To-day, so far as I am concerned, you are a treasure-casket. You hold secrets. You have a great value to us. Every one in your position is watched; it is part of our system. If the man for whom you have found so picturesque a nickname annoys you, he shall be changed. That is the most I can promise you."

"You don't trust me altogether, then?" Norgate observed coolly.

Selingman tapped on the table in front of him with his pudgy forefinger.

"Norgate," he declared solemnly, "trust is a

personal matter. I have no personal feelings. I am a machine. All the work I do is done by machinery, the machinery of thought, the machinery of action. These are the only means by which sentiment can be barred and the curious fluctuations of human temperament guarded against. If you were my son, or if you had dropped straight down from Heaven with a letter of introduction from the proper quarters, you would still be under my surveillance."

"That seems to settle the matter," Norgate confessed, "so I suppose I mustn't grumble. Yours is rather a bloodless philosophy."

"Perhaps," Selingman assented. "You see me as I sit here, a merchant of crockery, and I am a kind person. If I saw suffering, I should pause to ease it. If a wounded insect lay in my path, I should step out of my way to avoid it. But if my dearest friend, my nearest relation, seemed likely to me to do one fraction of harm to the great cause, I should without one second's compunction arrange for their removal as inevitably, and with as little hesitation, as I leave this place at one o'clock for my luncheon."

Norgate shrugged his shoulders.

"One apparently runs risks in serving you," he remarked.

"What risks?" Selingman asked keenly.

"The risk of being misunderstood, of making mistakes."

"Pooh!" Selingman exclaimed. "I do not like the man who talks of risks. Let us dismiss this conversation. I have work for you."

Norgate assumed a more interested attitude.

" I am ready," he said. " Go on, please."

" A movement is on foot," Selingman proceeded, " to establish manufactories in this country for the purpose of producing my crockery. A very large company will be formed, a great part of the money towards which is already subscribed. We have examined several sites' with a view to building factories, but I have not cared at present to open up direct negotiations. A rumour of our enterprise is about, and the price of the land we require would advance considerably if the prospective purchaser were known. The land is situated, half an acre at Willesden, three-quarters of an acre at Golder's Hill, and an acre at Highgate. I wish you to see the agents for the sale of these properties. I have ascertained indirectly the price, which you will find against each lot, with the agent's name," Selingman continued, passing across a folded slip of foolscap. " You will treat in your own name and pay the deposit yourself. Try and secure all three plots to-day, so that the lawyers can prepare the deeds and my builder can make some preparatory plans there during the week."

Norgate accepted the little bundle of papers with some surprise. Enclosed with them was a thick wad of bank-notes.

" There are two thousand pounds there for your deposits," Selingman continued. " If you need more, telephone to me, but understand I want to start to work laying the foundations within the next few days."

" I'll do the best I can," Norgate promised, " but this is rather a change for me, isn't it? Will Boko come along? "

Selingman smiled for a moment, but immediately afterwards his face was almost stern.

" Young man," he said, " from the moment you pledged your brains to my service, every action of your day has been recorded. From one of my pigeon-holes I could draw out a paper and tell you where you lunched yesterday, where you dined the day before, whom you met and with whom you talked, and so it will be until our work is finished.'

" So long as I know," Norgate sighed, rising to his feet, " I'll try to get used to him."

Norgate found no particular difficulty in carrying out the commissions entrusted to him. The sale of land is not an everyday affair, and he found the agents exceedingly polite and prompt. The man with whom he arranged the purchase of about three quarters of an acre of building land at Golder's Green, on the conclusion of the transaction exhibited some little curiosity.

" Queer thing," he remarked, " but I sold half an acre, a month or two ago, to a man who came very much as you come to-day. Might have been a foreigner. Said he was going to put up a factory to make boots and shoes. He is not going to start to build until next year, but he wanted a very solid floor to stand heavy machinery. Look here."

The agent climbed upon a pile of bricks, and Norgate followed his example. There was a boarded space before them, with scaffolding poles all around, but no other signs of building, and the interior consisted merely of a perfectly smooth concrete floor.

"That's the queerest way of setting about building a factory I ever saw," the man pointed out.

Norgate, who was not greatly interested, assented. The agent escorted him back to his taxicab.

"Of course, it's not my business," he admitted, "and you needn't say anything about this to your principals, but I hope they don't stop with laying down concrete floors. Of course, money for the property is the chief thing we want, but we do want factories and the employment of labour, and the sooner the better. This fellow — Reynolds, he said his name was — pays up for the property all right, has that concrete floor prepared, and clears off."

"Raising the money to build, perhaps," Norgate remarked. "I don't think there's any secret about my people's intentions. They are going to build factories for the manufacture of crockery."

The agent brightened up.

"Well, that's a new industry, anyway. Crockery, eh?"

"It's a big German firm in Cannon Street," Norgate explained. "They are going to make the stuff here. That ought to be better for our people."

The young man nodded.

"I expect they're afraid of tariff reform," he suggested. "Those Germans see a long way ahead sometimes."

"I am beginning to believe that they do," Norgate assented, as he stepped into the taxi.

CHAPTER XXXIII

Norgate walked into the club rather late that afternoon. Selingman and Prince Lenemaur were talking together in the little drawing-room. They called him in, and a few minutes later the Prince took his leave.

"Well, that's all arranged," Norgate reported. "I have bought the three sites. There was only one thing the fellow down at Golder's Hill was anxious about."

"And that?"

"He hoped you weren't just going to put down a concrete floor and then shut the place up."

Mr. Selingman's amiable imperturbability was for once disturbed.

"What did the fellow mean?" he enquired.

"Haven't an idea," Norgate replied, "but he made me stand on a pile of bricks and look at a strip of land which some one else had bought upon a hill close by. I suppose they want the factories built as quickly as possible, and work-people around the place."

"I shall have two hundred men at work to-morrow morning," Selingman remarked. "If that agent had not been a very ignorant person, he would have known that a concrete floor is a necessity to any factory where heavy machinery is used."

"Is it?" Norgate asked simply.

"Any other question?" Selingman demanded.

"None at all."

"Then we will go and play bridge."

They cut into the same rubber. Selingman, however, was not at first entirely himself. He played his cards in silence, and he once very nearly revoked. Mrs. Benedek took him to task.

"Dear man," she said, "we rely upon you so much, and to-day you fail to amuse us. What is there upon your mind? Let us console you, if we can."

"Dear lady, it is nothing," Selingman assured her. "My company is planning big developments in connection with our business. The details afford me much food for thought. My attention, I fear, sometimes wanders. Forgive me, I will make amends. When the day comes that my new factories start work, I will give such a party as was never seen. I will invite you all. We will have a celebration that every one shall talk of. And meanwhile, behold! I will wander no longer. I declare no trumps."

Selingman for a time was himself again. When he cut out, however, he fidgeted a little restlessly around the room and watched Norgate share the same fate with an air of relief. He laid his hand upon the latter's arm.

"Come into the other room, Norgate," he invited. "I have something to say to you."

Norgate obeyed at once, but the room was already occupied. A little blond lady was entertaining a soldier friend at tea. She withdrew her head from somewhat suspicious proximity to her companion's at their entrance and greeted Selingman with innocent surprise.

"How queer that you should come in just then, Mr. Selingman!" she exclaimed. "We were talking about Germany, Captain Fielder and I."

Selingman beamed upon them both. He was entirely himself again. He looked as though the one thing in life he had desired was to find Mrs. Barlow and her military companion in possession of the little drawing-room.

"My country is flattered," he declared, "especially," he added, with a twinkle in his eyes, "as the subject seemed to be proving so interesting."

She made a little grimace at him.

"Seriously, Mr. Selingman," she continued, "Captain Fielder and I have been almost quarrelling. He insists upon it that some day or other Germany means to declare war upon us. I have been trying to point out that before many years have passed England and France will have drifted apart. Germany is the nearest to us of the continental nations, isn't she, by relationship and race?"

"Mrs. Barlow," Selingman pronounced, "yours is the most sensible allusion to international politics which I have heard for many years. You are right. If I may be permitted to say so," he added, "Captain Fielder is wrong. Germany has no wish to fight with any one. The last country in the world with whom she would care to cross swords is England."

"If Germany does not wish for war," Captain Fielder persisted, "why does she keep such an

extraordinary army? Why does she continually add
to her navy? Why does she infest our country with
spies and keep all her preparations as secret as possible?"

"Of these things I know little," Selingman confessed, "I am a manufacturer, and I have few friends
among the military party. But this we all believe,
and that is that the German army and navy are our
insurance against trouble from the east. They are
there so that in case of political controversy we shall
have strength at our back when we seek to make
favourable terms. As to using that strength, God
forbid!"

The little lady threw a triumphant glance across
at her companion.

"There, Captain Fielder," she declared, "you have
heard what a typical, well-informed, cultivated German gentleman has to say. I rely much more upon
Mr. Selingman than upon any of the German reviews
or official statements of policy."

Captain Fielder was bluntly unconvinced.

"Mr. Selingman, without doubt," he agreed, "may
represent popular and cultivated German opinion.
The only thing is whether the policy of the country
is dictated by that class. Do you happen to have
seen the afternoon papers?"

"Not yet," Mr. Selingman admitted. "Is there
any news?"

"There is the full text," Captain Fielder continued, "of Austria's demands upon Servia. I may
be wrong, but I say confidently that those demands,
which are impossible of acceptance, which would re-

duce Servia, in fact, to the condition of a mere vassal state, are intended to provoke a state of war."

Mr. Selingman shook his head.

" I have seen the proposals," he remarked. " They were in the second edition of the morning papers. They are onerous, without a doubt, but remember that as you go further east, all diplomacy becomes a matter of barter. They ask for so much first because they are prepared to take a great deal less."

" It is my opinion," Captain Fielder pronounced, " that these demands are couched with the sole idea of inciting Russia's intervention. There is already a report that Servia has appealed to St. Petersburg. It is quite certain that Russia, as the protector of the Slav nations, can never allow Servia to be humbled to this extent."

" Even then," Mr. Selingman protested good-humouredly, " Austria is not Germany."

" There are very few people," Captain Fielder continued, " who do not realise that Austria is acting exactly as she is bidden by Germany. To-morrow you will find that Russia has intervened. If Vienna disregards her, there will be mobilisation along the frontiers. It is my private and very firm impression that Germany is mobilising to-day, and secretly."

Mr. Selingman laughed good-humouredly.

" Well, well," he said, " let us hope it is not quite so bad as that."

" You are frightening me, Captain Fielder," Mrs.

Barlow declared. "I am going to take you off to play bridge."

They left the room. Selingman looked after them a little curiously.

"Your military friend," he remarked, "is rather a pessimist."

"Well, we haven't many of them," Norgate replied. "Nine people out of ten believe that a war is about as likely to come as an earthquake."

Selingman glanced towards the closed door.

"Supposing," he said, dropping his voice a little, "supposing I were to tell you, young man, that I entirely agreed with your friend? Supposing I were to tell you that, possibly by accident, he has stumbled upon the exact truth? What would you say then?"

Norgate shrugged his shoulders.

"Well," he observed, "we've agreed, haven't we, that a little lesson would be good for England? It might as well come now as at any other time."

"It will not come yet," Mr. Selingman went on, "but I will tell you what is going to happen."

His voice had fallen almost to a whisper, his manner had become portentous.

"Within a week or two," he said, "Germany and Austria will have declared war upon Russia and Servia and France. Italy will join the allies — that you yourself know. As for England, her time has not come yet. We shall keep her neutral. All the recent information which we have collected makes it clear that she is not in a position to fight, even if she wished to. Nevertheless, to make a certainty of it, we shall offer her great inducements. We shall be ready to deal with her when Calais, Ostend, Boulogne, and Havre are held by our armies. Now listen, do you flinch?"

The two men were still standing in the middle of the room. Selingman's brows were lowered, his eyes were keen and hard-set. He had gripped Norgate by the left shoulder and held him with his face to the light.

"Speak up," he insisted. "It is now or never, if you mean to go through with this. You're not funking it, eh?"

"Not in the least," Norgate declared.

For the space of almost thirty seconds Selingman did not remove his gaze. All the time his hand was like a vice upon Norgate's shoulder.

"Very well," he said at last, " you represent rather a gamble on my part, but I am not afraid of the throw. Come back to our bridge now. It was just a moment's impulse — I saw something in your face. You realise, I suppose — but there, I won't threaten you. Come back and we'll drink a mixed vermouth together. The next few days are going to be rather a strain."

CHAPTER XXXIV

Norgate's expression was almost one of stupefaction. He looked at the slim young man who had entered his sitting-room a little diffidently and for a moment he was speechless.

"Well, I'm hanged!" he murmured at last. "Hardy, you astonish me!"

"The clothes are a perfect fit, sir," the man observed, "and I think that we are exactly the same height."

Norgate took a cigarette from an open box, tapped it against the table and lit it. He was fascinated, however, by the appearance of the man who stood respectfully in the background.

"Talk about clothes making the man!" he exclaimed. "Why, Hardy, do you realise your possibilities? You could go into my club and dine, order jewels from my jeweller. I am not at all sure that you couldn't take my place at a dinner-party."

The man smiled deprecatingly.

"Not quite that, I am sure, sir. If I may be allowed to say so, though, when you were good enough to give me the blue serge suit a short time ago, and a few of your old straw hats, two or three gentlemen stopped me under the impression that I was you. I should not have mentioned it, sir, but for the present circumstances."

" And no wonder! " Norgate declared. " If this weren't really a serious affair, Hardy, I should be inclined to make a little humorous use of you. That isn't what I want now, though. Listen, Put on one of my black overcoats and a silk hat, get the man to call you a taxi up to the door, and drive to Smith's Hotel. You will enquire for the suite of the Baroness von Haase. The Baroness will allow you to remain in her rooms for half an hour. At the end of that time you will return here, change your clothes, and await any further orders."

" Very good, sir," the man replied.

" Help yourself to cigarettes," Norgate invited, passing the box across. " Do the thing properly. Sit well back in the taxicab, although I'm hanged if I think that my friend Boko stands an earthly. Plenty of money in your pocket? "

" Plenty, thank you, sir."

The man left the room, and Norgate, after a brief delay, followed his example. A glance up and down the courtyard convinced him that Boko had disappeared. He jumped into a taxi, gave an address in Belgrave Square, and within a quarter of an hour was ushered into the presence of Mr. Spencer Wyatt, who was seated at a writing-table covered with papers.

" Mr. Norgate, isn't it? " the latter remarked briskly. " I had Mr. Hebblethwaite's note, and I am very pleased to give you five minutes. Sit down, won't you, and fire away."

" Did Mr. Hebblethwaite give you any idea as to what I wanted? " Norgate asked.

"Better read his note," the other replied, pushing it across the table with a little smile.

Norgate took it up and read: —

"My dear Spencer Wyatt,

"A young friend of mine, Francis Norgate, who has been in the Diplomatic Service for some years and is home just now from Berlin under circumstances which you may remember, has asked me to give him a line of introduction to you which will secure him an interview during to-day. Here is that line. Norgate is a young man for whom I have a great friendship. I consider him possessed of unusual intelligence and many delightful gifts, but, like many others of us, he is a crank. You can listen with interest to anything he may have to say to you, unless he speaks of Germany. That's his weak point. On any other subject he is as sane as the best of us.

"Many thanks. Certainly I am coming to the Review. We are all looking forward to it immensely.

"Ever yours,
"John W. Hebblethwaite."

Norgate set down the letter.

"There are two points of view, Mr. Spencer Wyatt," he said, "as to Germany. Mr. Hebblethwaite believes that I am an alarmist. I know that I am not. This isn't any ordinary visit of mine. I have come to see you on the most urgent matter which any one could possibly conceive. I have come to give you the chance to save our country from the worst disaster that has ever befallen her."

Mr. Spencer Wyatt looked at his visitor steadily.

His eyebrows had drawn a little closer together. He remained silent, however.

"I talk about the things I know of," Norgate continued. "By chance I have been associated during the last few weeks with the head of the German spies who infest this country. I have joined his ranks; I have become a double traitor. I do his work, but every report I hand in is a false one."

"Do you realise quite what you are saying, Mr. Norgate?"

"Realise it?" Norgate repeated. "My God! Do you think I come here to say these things to you for dramatic effect, or from a sense of humour, or as a lunatic? Every word I shall say to you is the truth. At the present moment there isn't a soul who seriously believes that England is going to be drawn into what the papers describe as a little eastern trouble. I want to tell you that that little eastern trouble has been brought about simply with the idea of provoking a European war. Germany is ready to strike at last, and this is her moment. Not a fortnight ago I sat opposite the boy Henriote in a café in Soho. My German friend handed him the money to get back to his country and to buy bombs. It's all part of the plot. Austria's insane demands are part of the plot; they are meant to drag Russia in. Russia must protest; she must mobilise. Germany is secretly mobilising at this moment. She will declare war against Russia, strike at France through Belgium. She will appeal to us for our neutrality."

"These are wonderful things you are saying, Mr. Norgate!"

" I am telling you the simple truth," Norgate went on, " and the history of our country doesn't hold anything more serious or more wonderful. Shall I come straight to the point? I promised to reach it within five minutes."

" Take your own time," the other replied. " My work is unimportant enough by the side of the things you speak of. You honestly believe that Germany is provoking a war against Russia and France? "

" I know it," Norgate went on. " She believes — Germany believes — that Italy will come in. She also believes, from false information that she has gathered in this country, that under no circumstances will England fight. It isn't about that I came to you. We've become a slothful, slack, pleasure-loving people, but I still believe that when the time comes we shall fight. The only thing is that we shall be taken at a big disadvantage. We shall be open to a raid upon our fleet. Do you know that the entire German navy is at Kiel? "

Mr. Wyatt nodded. " Manœuvres," he murmured.

" Their manœuvre," Norgate continued earnestly, " is to strike one great blow at our scattered forces. Mr. Spencer Wyatt, I have come here to warn you. I don't understand the workings of your department. I don't know to whom you are responsible for any step you might take. But I have come to warn you that possibly within a few days, probably within a week, certainly within a fortnight, England will be at war."

Mr. Wyatt glanced down at Hebblethwaite's letter.

"You are rather taking my breath away, Mr. Norgate!"

"I can't help it, sir," Norgate said simply. "I know that what I am telling you must sound like a fairy tale. I beg you to take it from me as the truth."

"But," Mr. Spencer Wyatt remarked, "if you have come into all this information, Mr. Norgate, why didn't you go to your friend Hebblethwaite? Why haven't you communicated with the police and given this German spy of yours into charge?"

"I have been to Hebblethwaite, and I have been to Scotland Yard," Norgate told him firmly, "and all that I have got for my pains has been a snub. They won't believe in German spies. Mr. Wyatt, you are a man of a little different temperament and calibre from those others. I tell you that all of them in the Cabinet have their heads thrust deep down into the sand. They won't listen to me. They wouldn't believe a word of what I am saying to you, but it's true."

Mr. Spencer Wyatt leaned back in his chair. He had folded his arms. He was looking over the top of his desk across the room. His eyebrows were knitted, his thoughts had wandered away. For several moments there was silence. Then at last he rose to his feet, unlocked the safe which stood by his side, and took out a solid chart dotted in many places with little flags, each one of which bore the name of a ship. He looked at it attentively.

"That's the position of every ship we own, at six o'clock this evening," he pointed out. "It's true we are scattered. We are purposely scattered because of the Review. On Monday morning I go down to the Admiralty, and I give the word. Every ship you see represented by those little flags, moves in one direction."

" In other words," Norgate remarked, " it is a mobilisation."

" Exactly ! "

Norgate leaned forward in his chair.

" You're coming to what I want to suggest," he proceeded. " Listen. You can do it, if you like. Go down to the Admiralty to-night. Give that order. Set the wireless going. Mobilise the fleet to-night."

Mr. Wyatt looked steadfastly at his companion. His fingers were restlessly stroking his chin, his eyes seemed to be looking through his visitor.

" But it would be a week too soon," he muttered.

" Risk it," Norgate begged. " You have always the Review to fall back upon. The mobilisation, to be effective, should be unexpected. Mobilise to-morrow. I am telling you the truth, sir, and you'll know it before many days are passed. Even if I have got hold of a mare's nest, you know there's trouble brewing. England will be in none the worse position to intervene for peace, if her fleet is ready to strike."

Mr. Spencer Wyatt rose to his feet. He seemed somehow an altered man.

" Look here," he announced gravely, " I am going for the gamble. If I have been misled, there will probably be an end of my career. I tell you frankly, I believe in you. I believe in the truth of the things you talk about. I risked everything, only a few weeks ago, on my belief. I'll risk my whole career now. Keep your mouth shut; don't say a word. Until to-morrow you will be the only man in England who knows it. I am going to mobilise the fleet to-night. Shake hands, Mr. Norgate. You're either the best friend or the worst foe I've ever had. My coat and hat," he ordered the servant who answered his summons. " Tell your mistress, if she enquires, that I have gone down to the Admiralty on special business."

CHAPTER XXXV

Anna passed her hand through Norgate's arm and led him forcibly away from the shop window before which they had been standing.

"My mind is absolutely made up," she declared firmly. "I adore shopping, I love Bond Street, and I rather like you, but I will have no more trifles, as you call them. If you do not obey, I shall gaze into the next tobacconist's window we pass, and go in and buy you all sorts of unsmokable and unusable things. And, oh, dear, here is the Count! I feel like a child who has played truant from school. What will he do to me, Francis?"

"Don't worry, dear," Norgate laughed. "We're coming to the end of this tutelage, you know."

Count Lanyoki, who had stopped his motor-car, came across the street towards them. He was, as usual, irreproachably attired. He wore white gaiters, patent shoes, and a grey, tall hat. His black hair, a little thin at the forehead, was brushed smoothly back. His moustache, also black but streaked with grey, was twisted upwards. He had, as always, the air of having just left the hands of his valet.

"Dear Baroness," he exclaimed, as he accosted her, "London has been searched for you! At the Embassy my staff are reduced to despair. Tele-

phones, notes, telegrams, and personal calls have
been in vain. Since lunch-time yesterday it seemed
to us that you must have found some other sphere
in which to dwell."

"Perhaps I have," Anna laughed. "I am so
sorry to have given you all this trouble, but yesterday — well, let me introduce, if I may, my husband,
Mr. Francis Norgate. We were married by special
license yesterday afternoon."

The Count's amazement was obvious. Diplomatist
though he was, it was several seconds before he could
collect himself and rise to the situation. He broke
off at last, however, in the midst of a string of inter-
jections and realised his duties.

"My dear Baroness," he said, "my dear lady, let
me wish you every happiness. And you, sir," he
added, turning to Norgate, "you must have, without a doubt, my most hearty congratulations.
There! That is said. And now to more serious
matters. Baroness, have you not always considered
yourself the ward of the Emperor?"

She nodded.

"His Majesty has been very kind to me," she admitted. "At the same time, I feel that I owe more
to myself than I do to him. His first essay at interfering in my affairs was scarcely a happy one, was
it?"

"Perhaps not," the Count replied. "And yet,
think what you have done! You have married an
Englishman!"

"I thought English people were quite popular in
Vienna," Anna reminded him.

The Count hesitated. "That," he declared, "is scarcely the question. What troubles me most is that forty-eight hours ago I brought you a dispatch from the Emperor."

"You brought," Anna pointed out, "what really amounted to an order to return at once to Vienna. Well, you see, I have disobeyed it."

They were standing at the corner of Clifford Street, and the Count, with a little gesture, led the way into the less crowded thoroughfare.

"Dear Baroness," he continued, as they walked slowly along, "I am placed now in a most extraordinary position. The Emperor's telegram was of serious import. It cannot be that you mean to disobey his summons?"

"Well, I really couldn't put off being married, could I," Anna protested, "especially when my husband had just got the special license. Besides, I do not wish to return to Vienna just now."

The Count glanced at Norgate and appeared to deliberate for a moment.

"The state of affairs in the East," he said, "is such that it is certainly wiser for every one just now to be within the borders of their own country."

"You believe that things are serious?" Anna enquired. "You believe, then, that real trouble is at hand?"

"I fear so," the Count acknowledged. "It appears to us that Servia has a secret understanding with Russia, or she would not have ventured upon such an attitude as she is now adopting towards us. If that be so, the possibilities of trouble are immense, almost boundless. That is why, Baroness, the Emperor has sent for you. That is why I think you should not hesitate to at once obey his summons."

Anna looked up at her companion, her eyes wide open, a little smile parting her lips.

"But, Count," she exclaimed, "you seem to forget! A few days ago, all that you say to me was reasonable enough, but to-day there is a great difference, is there not? I have married an Englishman. Henceforth this is my country."

There was a moment's silence. The Count seemed dumbfounded. He stared at Anna as though unable to grasp the meaning of her words.

"Forgive me, Baroness!" he begged. "I cannot for the moment realise the significance of this thing. Do you mean me to understand that you consider yourself now an Englishwoman?"

"I do indeed," she assented. "There are many ties which still bind me to Austria — ties, Count," she proceeded, looking him in the face, "of which I shall be mindful. Yet I am not any longer the Baroness von Haase. I am Mrs. Francis Norgate, and I have promised to obey my husband in all manner of ridiculous things. At the same time, may I add something which will, perhaps, help you to accept the position with more philosophy? My husband is a friend of Herr Selingman's."

The Count glanced quickly towards Norgate. There was some relief in his face — a great deal of distrust, however.

"Baroness," he said, "my advice to you, for your own good entirely, is, with all respect to your husband, that you shorten your honeymoon and pay your respects to the Emperor. I think that you owe it to him. I think that you owe it to your country."

Anna for a moment was grave again.

" Just at present," she pronounced, " I realise one debt only, and that is to my husband. I will come to the Embassy to-morrow and discuss these matters with you, Count, but whether my husband accompanies me or not, I have now no secrets from him."

" The position, then," the Count declared, " is intolerable. May I ask whether you altogether realise, Baroness, what this means? The Emperor is your guardian. All your estates are subject to his jurisdiction. It is his command that you return to Vienna."

Anna laughed again. She passed her fingers through Norgate's arm.

" You see," she explained, as they stood for a moment at the corner of the street, " I have a new emperor now, and he will not let me go."

Selingman frowned a little as he recognised his visitor. Nevertheless, he rose respectfully to his feet and himself placed a chair by the side of his desk.

" My dear Count! " he exclaimed. " I am very glad to see you, but this is an unusual visit. I would have met you somewhere, or come to the Embassy. Have we not agreed that it was well for Herr Selingman, the crockery manufacturer —"

" That is all very well, Selingman," the Count in

terrupted, " but this morning I have had a shock.
It was necessary for me to talk with you at once. In
Bond Street I met the Baroness von Haase. For
twenty-four hours London has been ransacked in
vain for her. This you may not know, but I will
now tell you. She has been our trusted agent, the
trusted agent of the Emperor, in many recent in-
stances. She has carried secrets in her brain, messages to different countries. There is little that she
does not know. The last twenty-four hours, as I
say, I have sought for her. The Emperor requires
her presence in Vienna. I meet her in Bond Street
this morning and she introduces to me her husband,
an English husband, Mr. Francis Norgate!"

He drew back a little, with outstretched hands.
Selingman's face, however, remained expressionless.

" Married already!" he commented. " Well, that
is rather a surprise."

" A surprise? To be frank, it terrifies me!" the
Count cried. " Heaven knows what that woman
could tell an Englishman, if she chose! And her
manner — I did not like it. The only reassuring
thing about it was that she told me that her husband
was one of your men."

" Quite true," Selingman assented. " He is. It
is only recently that he came to us, but I do not
mind telling you that during the last few weeks no
one has done such good work. He is the very man
we needed."

" You have trusted him? "

" I trust or I do not trust," Selingman replied.
" That you know. I have employed this young man

in very useful work. I cannot blindfold him. He knows."

"Then I fear treachery," the Count declared.

"Have you any reason for saying that?" Selingman asked.

The Count lit a cigarette with trembling fingers.

"Listen," he said, "always, my friend, you undervalue a little the English race. You undervalue their intelligence, their patriotism, their poise towards the serious matters of life. I know nothing of Mr. Francis Norgate save what I saw this morning. He is one of that type of Englishmen, clean-bred, wellborn, full of reserve, taciturn, yet, I would swear, honourable. I know the type, and I do not believe in such a man being your servant."

The shadow of anxiety crossed Selingman's face.

"Have you any reason for saying this?" he repeated.

"No reason save the instinct which is above reason," the Count replied quickly. "I know that if the Baroness and he put their heads together, we may be under the shadow of catastrophe."

Selingman sat with folded arms for several moments.

"Count," he said at last, "I appreciate your point of view. You have, I confess, disturbed me. Yet of this young man I have little fear. I did not approach him by any vulgar means. I took, as they say here, the bull by the horns. I appealed to his patriotism."

"To what?" the Count demanded incredulously.

"To his patriotism," Selingman repeated. "I

showed him the decadence of his country, decadence visible through all her institutions, through her political tendencies, through her young men of all classes. I convinced him that what the country needed was a bitter tonic, a kind but chastening hand. I convinced him of this. He believes that he betrays his country for her ultimate good. As I told you before, he has brought me information which is simply invaluable. He has a position and connections which are unique."

The Count drew his chair a little nearer.

" You say that he has done you great service," he said. " Well, you must admit for yourself that the day is too near now for much more to be expected. Could you not somehow guard against his resolution breaking down at the last moment? Think what it may mean to him — the sound of his national anthem at a critical moment, the clash of arms in the distance, the call of France across the Channel. A week — even half a week's extra preparation might make much difference."

Selingman sat for a short time, deep in thought. Then he drew out a box of pale-looking German cigars and lit one.

" Count," he announced solemnly, " I take off my hat to you. Leave the matter in my hands."

CHAPTER XXXVI

Norgate set down the telephone receiver and turned to Anna, who was seated in an easy-chair by his side.

"Selingman is down-stairs," he announced. "I rather expected I should see something of him as I didn't go to the club this afternoon. You won't mind if he comes up?"

"The man is a nuisance," Anna declared, with a little grimace. "I was perfectly happy, Francis, sitting here before the open window and looking out at the lights in that cool, violet gulf of darkness. I believe that in another minute I should have said something to you absolutely ravishing. Then your telephone rings and back one comes to earth again!"

Norgate smiled as he held her hand in his.

"We will get rid of him quickly, dearest," he promised.

There was a knock at the door, and Selingman entered, his face wreathed in smiles. He was wearing a long dinner coat and a flowing black tie. He held out both his hands.

"So this is the great news that has kept you away from us!" he exclaimed. "My congratulations, Norgate. You can never say again that the luck has left you. Baroness, may I take advantage of my slight acquaintance to express my sincere wishes for your happiness?"

They wheeled up a chair for him, and Norgate

produced some cigars. The night was close. They were on the seventh story, overlooking the river, and a pleasant breeze stole every now and then into the room.

"You are well placed here," Selingman declared. "Myself, I too like to be high up."

"These are really just my bachelor rooms," Norgate explained, "but under the circumstances we thought it wiser to wait before we settled down anywhere. Is there any news to-night?"

"There is great news," Selingman announced gravely. "There is news of wonderful import. In a few minutes you will hear the shouting of the boys in the Strand there. You shall hear it first from me. Germany has found herself compelled to declare war against Russia."

They were both speechless. Norgate was carried off his feet. The reality of the thing was stupendous.

"Russia has been mobilising night and day on the frontiers of East Prussia," Selingman continued. "Germany has chosen to strike the first blow. Now listen, both of you. I am going to speak in these few minutes to Norgate here very serious words. I take it that in the matters which lie between him and me, you, Baroness, are as one with him?"

"It is so," Norgate admitted.

"To be frank, then," Selingman went on, "you, Norgate, during these momentous days have been the most useful of all my helpers here. The information which I have dispatched to Berlin, emanating from you, has been more than important — it has been vital. It has been so vital that I have a long dispatch to-night, begging me to reaffirm my absolute conviction as to the truth of the information which I have forwarded. Let us, for a moment, recapitulate. You remember your interview with Mr. Hebblethwaite on the subject of war? "

" Distinctly," Norgate assented.

" It was your impression," Selingman continued, " gathered from that conversation, that under no possible circumstances would Mr. Hebblethwaite himself, or the Cabinet as a whole, go to war with Germany in support of France. Is that correct? "

" It is correct," Norgate admitted.

" Nothing has happened to change your opinion? "

" Nothing."

" To proceed, then," Selingman went on. " Some little time ago you called upon Mr. Bullen at the House of Commons. You promised a large contribution to the funds of the Irish Party, a sum which is to be paid over on the first of next month, on condition that no compromise in the Home Rule question shall be accepted by him, even in case of war. And further, that if England should find herself in a state of war, no Nationalists should volunteer to fight in her ranks. Is this correct? "

" Perfectly," Norgate admitted.

" The information was of great interest in Berlin," Selingman pointed out. " It is realised there that it means of necessity a civil war."

" Without a doubt."

" You believe," Selingman persisted, " that I did not take an exaggerated or distorted view of the situation, as discussed between you and Mr. Bullen, when I reported that civil war in Ireland was inevitable? "

"It is inevitable," Norgate agreed.

Selingman sat for several moments in portentous silence.

"We are on the threshold of great events," he announced. "The Cabinet opinion in Berlin has been swayed by the two factors which we have discussed. It is the wish of Germany, and her policy, to end once and for all the eastern disquiet, to weaken Russia so that she can no longer call herself the champion of the Slav races and uphold their barbarism against our culture. France is to be dealt with only as the ally of Russia. We want little more from her than we have already. But our great desire is that England of necessity and of her own choice, should remain, for the present, neutral. Her time is to come later. Italy, Germany, and Austria can deal with France and Russia to a mathematical certainty. What we desire to avoid are any unforeseen complications. I leave you to-night, and I cable my absolute belief in the statements deduced from your work. You have nothing more to say?"

"Nothing," Norgate replied.

Selingman was apparently relieved. He rose, a little later, to his feet.

"My young friend," he concluded, "in the near future great rewards will find their way to this country. There is no one who has deserved more than you. There is no one who will profit more. That reminds me. There was one little question I had to ask. A friend of mine has seen you on your way back and forth to Camberley three or four times lately. You lunched the other day with the colonel of one of your Lancer regiments. How did you spend your time at Camberley?"

For a moment Norgate made no reply. The moonlight was shining into the room, and Anna had turned out all the lights with the exception of one heavily-shaded lamp. Her eyes were shining as she leaned a little forward in her chair.

"Boko again, I suppose," Norgate grunted.

"Certainly Boko," Selingman acknowledged.

"I was in the Yeomanry when I was younger," Norgate explained slowly. "I had some thought of entering the army before I took up diplomacy. Colonel Chalmers is a friend of mine. I have been down to Camberley to see if I could pick up a little of the new drill."

"For what reason?" Selingman demanded.

"Need I tell you that?" Norgate protested. "Whatever my feeling for England may be at the present moment, however bitterly I may regret the way she has let her opportunities slip, the slovenly political condition of the country, yet I cannot put away from me the fact that I am an Englishman. If trouble should come, even though I may have helped to bring it about, even though I may believe that it is a good thing for the country to have to meet trouble, I should still fight on her side."

"But there will be no war," Selingman reminded him. "You yourself have ascertained that the present Cabinet will decline war at any cost."

"The present Government, without a doubt," Norgate assented. "I am thinking of later on, when your first task is over."

Selingman nodded gravely.

"When that day comes," he said, as he rose and took up his hat, "it will not be a war. If your people resist, it will be a butchery. Better to find yourself in one of the Baroness' castles in Austria when that time comes! It is never worth while to draw a sword in a lost cause. I wish you good night, Baroness. I wish you good night, Norgate."

He shook hands with them both firmly, but there was still something of reserve in his manner. Norgate rang for his servant to show him out. They took their places once more by the window.

"War!" Norgate murmured, his eyes fixed upon the distant lights.

Anna crept a little nearer to him.

"Francis," she whispered, "that man has made me a little uneasy. Supposing they should discover that you have deceived them, before they have been obliged to leave the country!"

"They will be much too busy," Norgate replied, "to think about me."

Anna's face was still troubled. "I did not like that man's look," she persisted, "when he asked you what you were doing at Camberley. Perhaps he still believes that you have told the truth, but he might easily have it in his mind that you knew too many of their secrets to be trusted when the vital moment came."

Norgate leaned over and drew her towards him.

"Selingman has gone," he murmured. "It is only outside that war is throbbing. Dearest, I think that my vital moments are now!"

CHAPTER XXXVII

Mr. Hebblethwaite permitted himself a single moment of abstraction. He sat at the head of the table in his own remarkably well-appointed dining-room. His guests — there were eighteen or twenty of them in all — represented in a single word Success — success social as well as political. His excellently cooked dinner was being served with faultless precision. His epigrams had never been more pungent. The very distinguished peeress who sat upon his right, and whose name was a household word in the enemy's camp, had listened to him with enchained and sympathetic interest. For a single second he permitted his thoughts to travel back to the humble beginnings of his political career. He had a brief, flashlight recollection of the suburban parlour of his early days, the hard fight at first for a living, then for some small place in local politics, and then, larger and more daring schemes as the boundary of his ambitions became each year a little further extended. Beyond him now was only one more step to be taken. The last goal was well within his reach.

The woman at his right recommenced their conversation, which had been for a moment interrupted.

"We were speaking of success," she said. "Success often comes to one covered by the tentacles and parasites of shame, and yet, even in its grosser forms, it has something splendid about it. But success that carries with it no apparent drawback whatever is, of course, the most amazing thing of all. I was reading that wonderful article of Professor Wilson's last month. He quotes you very extensively. His analysis of your character was, in its way, interesting. Directly I had read it, however, I felt that it lacked one thing — simplicity. I made up my mind that the next time we talked intimately, I would ask you to what you yourself attributed your success? "

Hebblethwaite smiled graciously.

" I will not attempt to answer you in epigrams," he replied. " I will pay a passing tribute to a wonderful constitution, an invincible sense of humour, which I think help one to keep one's head up under many trying conditions. But the real and final explanation of my success is that I embraced the popular cause. I came from the people, and when I entered into politics, I told myself and every one else that it was for the people I should work. I have never swerved from that purpose. It is to the people I owe whatever success I am enjoying to-day."

The Duchess nodded thoughtfully.

" Yes," she admitted, " you are right there. Shall I proceed with my own train of thought quite honestly? "

" I shall count it a compliment," he assured her earnestly, " even if your thoughts contain criticisms."

" You occupy so great a position in political life to-day," she continued, " that one is forced to consider you, especially in view of the future, as a politician from every point of view. Now, by your own showing, you have been a specialist. You have taken up the cause of the people against the classes. You have stripped many of us of our possessions — the Duke, you know, hates the sound of your name — and by your legislation you have, without a doubt, improved the welfare of many millions of human beings. But that is not all that a great politician must achieve, is it? There is our Empire across the seas."

"Imperialism," he declared, "has never been in the foreground of my programme, but I call myself an Imperialist. I have done what I could for the colonies. I have even abandoned on their behalf some of my pet principles of absolute freedom in trade."

"You certainly have not been prejudiced," she admitted. "Whether your politics have been those of an Imperialist from the broadest point of view — well, we won't discuss that question just now. We might, perhaps, differ. But there is just one more point. Zealously and during the whole of your career, you have set your face steadfastly against any increase of our military power. They say that it is chiefly due to you and Mr. Busby that our army to-day is weaker in numbers than it has been for years. You have set your face steadily against all schemes for national service. You have taken up the stand that England can afford to remain neutral, whatever combination of Powers on the Continent may fight. Now tell me, do you see any possibility of failure, from the standpoint of a great politician, in your attitude?"

"I do not," he answered. "On the contrary, I

am proud of all that I have done in that direction.
For the reduction of our armaments I accept the full
responsibility. It is true that I have opposed national service. I want to see the people develop commercially. The withdrawing of a million of young
men, even for a month every year, from their regular
tasks, would not only mean a serious loss to the
manufacturing community, but it would be apt to
unsettle and unsteady them. Further, it would
kindle in this country the one thing I am anxious to
avoid — the military spirit. We do not need it,
Duchess. We are a peace-loving nation, civilised out
of the crude lust for conquest founded upon blood-
shed. I do believe that geographically and from
every other point of view, England, with her navy,
can afford to fold her arms, and if other nations
should at any time be foolish enough to imperil their
very existence by fighting for conquest or revenge,
then we, who are strong enough to remain aloof, can
only grow richer and stronger by the disasters which
happen to them."

There was a momentary silence. The Duchess
leaned back in her chair, and Mr. Hebblethwaite, always the courteous host, talked for a while to the
woman on his left. The Duchess, however, reopened
the subject a few minutes later.

" I come, you must remember, Mr. Hebblethwaite,"
she observed, " from long generations of soldiers, and
you, as you have reminded me, from a long race of
yeomen and tradespeople. Therefore, without a
doubt, our point of view must be different. That,
perhaps, is what makes conversation between us so

interesting. To me, a conflict in Europe, sooner or later, appears inevitable. With England preserving a haughty and insular neutrality, which, from her present military condition, would be almost compulsory, the struggle would be between Russia, France, Italy, Germany, and Austria. Russia is an unknown force, but in my mind I see Austria and Italy, with perhaps one German army, holding her back for many months, perhaps indefinitely. On the other hand, I see France overrun by the Germans very much as she was in 1870. I adore the French, and I have little sympathy with the Germans, but as a fighting race I very reluctantly feel that I must admit the superiority of the Germans. Very well, then. With Ostend, Calais, Boulogne, and Havre seized by Germany, as they certainly would be, and turned into naval bases, do you still believe that England's security would be wholly provided for by her fleet? "

Mr. Hebblethwaite smiled.

" Duchess," he said, " sooner or later I felt quite sure that our conversation would draw near to the German bogey. The picture you draw is menacing enough. I look upon its probability as exactly on the same par as the overrunning of Europe by the yellow races."

" You believe in the sincerity of Germany? " she asked.

" I do," he admitted firmly. " There is a military element in Germany which is to be regretted, but the Germans themselves are a splendid, cultured, and peace-loving people, who are seeking their future not at the point of the sword but in the counting-houses of the world. If I fear the Germans, it is commercially, and from no other point of view."

"I wish I could feel your confidence," the Duchess sighed.

"I have myself recently returned from Berlin," Mr. Hebblethwaite continued. "Busby, as you know, has been many times an honoured guest there at their universities and in their great cities. He has had every opportunity of probing the tendencies of the people. His mind is absolutely and finally made up. Not in all history has there ever existed a race freer from the lust of bloodthirsty conquest than the German people of to-day."

Mr. Hebblethwaite concluded his sentence with some emphasis. He felt that his words were carrying conviction. Some of the conversation at their end of the table had been broken off to listen to his pronouncements. At that moment his butler touched him upon the elbow.

"Mr. Bedells has just come up from the War Office, sir," he announced. "He is waiting outside. In the meantime, he desired me to give you this."

The butler, who had served an archbishop, and resented often his own presence in the establishment of a Radical Cabinet Minister, presented a small silver salver on which reposed a hastily twisted up piece of paper. Mr. Hebblethwaite, with a little nod, unrolled it and glanced towards the Duchess, who bowed complacently. With the smile still upon his lips, a confident light in his eyes, Mr. Hebblethwaite held out the crumpled piece of paper before him and read the hurriedly scrawled pencil lines:

> "*Germany has declared war against Russia and presented an ultimatum to France. I have other messages.*"

Mr. Hebblethwaite was a strong man. He was a man of immense self-control. Yet in that moment the arteries of life seemed as though they had ceased to flow. He sat at the head of his table, and his eyes never left those pencilled words. His mind fought with them, discarded them, only to find them still there hammering at his brain, traced in letters of scarlet upon the distant walls. War! The great, unbelievable tragedy, the one thousand-to-one chance in life which he had ever taken! His hand almost fell to his side. There was a queer little silence. No one liked to ask him a question; no one liked to speak. It was the Duchess at last who murmured a few words, when the silence had become intolerable.

"It is bad news?" she whispered.

"It is very bad news indeed," Mr. Hebblethwaite answered, raising his voice a little, so that every one at the table might hear him. "I have just heard from the War Office that Germany has declared war against Russia. You will perhaps, under the circumstances, excuse me."

He rose to his feet. There was a queer singing in his ears. The feast seemed to have turned to a sickly debauch. All that pinnacle of success seemed to have fallen away. The faces of his guests, even, as they looked at him, seemed to his conscience to be expressing one thing, and one thing only — that same horrible conviction which was deadening his own senses. He and the others — could it be true? — had they taken up lightly the charge and care of a mighty empire and dared to gamble upon, instead of providing for, its security? He thrust the thought away; and the natural strength of the man began to reassert itself. If they had done ill, they had done it for the people's sake. The people must rally to them now. He held his head high as he left the room.

CHAPTER XXXVIII

Norgate found himself in an atmosphere of strange excitement during his two hours' waiting at the House of Commons on the following day. He was ushered at last into Mr. Hebblethwaite's private room. Hebblethwaite had just come in from the House and was leaning a little back in his chair, in an attitude of repose. He glanced at Norgate with a faint smile.

" Well, young fellow," he remarked, " come to do the usual ' I told you so ' business, I suppose? "

" Don't be an ass! " Norgate most irreverently replied. " There are one or two things I must tell you and tell you at once. I may have hinted at them before, but you weren't taking things seriously then. First of all, is Mr. Bullen in the House? "

" Of course! "

" Could you send for him here just for a minute? " Norgate pleaded. " I am sure it would make what I am going to say sound more convincing to you."

Hebblethwaite struck a bell by his side and despatched a messenger.

" How are things going? " Norgate asked.

" France is mobilising as fast as she can," Hebblethwaite announced. " We have reports coming in that Germany has been at it for at least a week, secretly. They say that Austrian troops have crossed into Poland. There isn't anything definite yet, but it's war, without a doubt, war just as we'd struck the right note for peace. Russia was firm but splendid. Austria was wavering. Just at the critical moment, like a thunderbolt, came Germany's declaration of war. Here's Mr. Bullen. Now go ahead, Norgate."

Mr. Bullen came into the room, recognised Norgate, and stopped short.

"So you're here again, young man, are you?" he exclaimed. "I don't know why you've sent for me, Hebblethwaite, but if you take my advice, you won't let that young fellow go until you've asked him a few questions."

"Mr. Norgate is a friend of mine," Hebblethwaite said. "I think you will find —"

"Friend or no friend," the Irishman interrupted, "he is a traitor, and I tell you so to his face."

"That is exactly what I wished you to tell Mr. Hebblethwaite," Norgate remarked, nodding pleasantly. "I just want you to recall the circumstances of my first visit here."

"You came and offered me a bribe of a million pounds," Mr. Bullen declared, "if I would provoke a civil war in Ireland in the event of England getting into trouble. I wasn't sure whom you were acting for then, but I am jolly certain now. That young fellow is a German spy, Hebblethwaite."

"Mr. Hebblethwaite knew that quite well," admitted Norgate coolly. "I came and told him so several times. I think that he even encouraged me to do my worst."

"Look here, Norgate," Hebblethwaite intervened,

" I'm certain you are driving at something serious. Let's have it."

" Quite right, I am," Norgate assented. " I just wanted to testify to you that Mr. Bullen's reply to my offer was the patriotic reply of a loyal Irishman. I did offer him that million pounds on behalf of Germany, and he did indignantly refuse it, but the point of the whole thing is — my report to Germany."

" And that? " Mr. Hebblethwaite asked eagerly.

" I reported Mr. Bullen's acceptance of the sum," Norgate told them. " I reported that civil war in Ireland was imminent and inevitable and would come only the sooner for any continental trouble in which England might become engaged."

Mr. Hebblethwaite's face cleared.

" I begin to understand now, Norgate," he muttered. " Good fellow ! "

Mr. Bullen was summoned in hot haste by one of his supporters and hurried out. Norgate drew his chair a little closer to his friend's.

" Look here, Hebblethwaite," he said, " you wouldn't listen to me, you know — I don't blame you — but I knew the truth of what I was saying. I knew what was coming. The only thing I could do to help was to play the double traitor. I did it. My chief, who reported to Berlin that this civil war was inevitable, will get it in the neck, but there's more to follow. The Baroness von Haase and I were associated in an absolutely confidential mission to ascertain the likely position of Italy in the event of this conflict. I know for a fact that Italy will not come in with her allies."

" Do you mean that? " Mr. Hebblethwaite asked eagerly.

" Absolutely certain," Norgate assured him.

Hebblethwaite half rose from his place with excitement.

" I ought to telephone to the War Office," he declared.   " It will alter the whole mobilisation of the French troops."

" France knows," Norgate told him quietly.   " My wife has seen to that.   She passed the information on to them just in time to contract the whole line of mobilisation."

" You've been doing big things, young fellow! " Mr. Hebblethwaite exclaimed excitedly.   " Go on. Tell me at once, what was your report to Germany? "

" I reported that Italy would certainly fulfil the terms of her alliance and fight," Norgate replied. " Furthermore, I have convinced my chief over here that under no possible circumstances would the present Cabinet sanction any war whatsoever.   I have given him plainly to understand that you especially are determined to leave France to her fate if war should come, and to preserve our absolute neutrality at all costs."

" Go on," Hebblethwaite murmured.   " Finish it, anyhow."

" There is very little more," Norgate concluded. " I have a list here of properties in the outskirts of London, all bought by Germans, and all having secret preparations for the mounting of big guns. You might just pass that on to the War Office, and they can destroy the places at their leisure.   There isn't anything else, Hebblethwaite. As I told you, I've played the double traitor. It was the only way I could help. Now, if I were you, I would arrest the master-spy for whom I have been working. Most of the information he has picked up lately has been pretty bad, and I fancy he'll get a warm reception if he does get back to Berlin, but if ever there was a foreigner who abused the hospitality of this country, Selingman's the man."

"We'll see about that presently," Mr. Hebblethwaite declared, leaning back. "Let me think over what you have told me. It comes to this, Norgate. You've practically encouraged Germany to risk affronting us."

"I can't help that," Norgate admitted. "Germany has gone into this war, firmly believing that Italy will be on her side, and that we shall have our hands occupied in civil war, and in any case that we should remain neutral. I am not asking you questions, Hebblethwaite. I don't know what the position of the Government will be if Germany attacks France in the ordinary way. But one thing I do believe, and that is that if Germany breaks Belgian neutrality and invades Belgium, there isn't any English Government which has ever been responsible for the destinies of this country, likely to take it lying down. We are shockingly unprepared, or else, of course, there'd have been no war at all. We shall lose hundreds of thousands of our young men, because they'll have to fight before they are properly trained, but we must fight or perish. And we shall fight — I am sure of that, Hebblethwaite."

"We are all Englishmen," Hebblethwaite answered simply.

The door was suddenly opened. Spencer Wyatt pushed his way past a protesting doorkeeper. Hebblethwaite rose to his feet; he seemed to forget Norgate's presence.

"You've been down to the Admiralty?" he asked quickly. "Do you know?"

Spencer Wyatt pointed to Norgate. His voice shook with emotion.

"I know, Hebblethwaite," he replied, "but there's something that you don't know. We were told to mobilise the fleet an hour ago. My God, what chance should we have had! Germany means scrapping, and look where our ships are, or ought to be."

"I know it," Hebblethwaite groaned.

"Well, they aren't there!" Spencer Wyatt announced triumphantly. "A week ago that young fellow came to me. He told me what was impending. I half believed it before he began. When he told me his story, I gambled upon it. I mistook the date for the Grand Review. I signed the order for mobilisation at the Admiralty, seven days ago. We are safe, Hebblethwaite! I've been getting wireless messages all day yesterday and to-day. We are at Cromarty and Rosyth. Our torpedo squadron is in position, our submarines are off the German coast. It was just the toss of a coin — papers and a country life for me, or our fleet safe and a great start in the war. This is the man who has done it."

"It's the best news I've heard this week," Hebblethwaite declared, with glowing face. "If our fleet is safe, the country is safe for a time. If this thing comes, we've a chance. I'll go through the country. I'll start the day war's declared. I'll talk to the people I've slaved for. They shall come to our help. We'll have the greatest citizen army who ever fought for their native land. I've disbelieved in fighting all my life. If we are driven to it, we'll show the world what peace-loving people can do, if the weapon is forced into their hands. Norgate, the country owes you a great debt. Another time, Wyatt, I'll tell you more than you know now. What can we do for you, young fellow?"

Norgate rose to his feet.

"My work is already chosen, thanks," he said, as he shook hands. "I have been preparing for some time."

CHAPTER XXXIX

The card-rooms at the St. James's Club were crowded, but very few people seemed inclined to play. They were standing or sitting about in little groups. A great many of them were gathered around the corner where Selingman was seated. He was looking somewhat graver than usual, but there was still a confident smile upon his lips.

"My little friend," he said, patting the hand of the fair lady by his side, "reassure yourself. Your husband and your husband's friends are quite safe. For England there will come no fighting. Believe me, that is a true word."

"But the impossible is happening all the time," Mrs. Barlow protested. "Who would have believed that without a single word of warning Germany would have declared war against Russia?"

Mr. Selingman raised his voice a little.

"Let me make the situation clear," he begged. "Listen to me, if you will, because I am a patriotic German but also a lover of England, a sojourner here, and one of her greatest friends. Germany has gone to war against Russia. Why? You will say upon a trifling pretext. My answer to you is this. There is between the Teuton and the Slav an enmity more mighty than anything you can conceive of. It has been at the root of all the unrest in the Balkans.

Many a time Germany has kept the peace at the imminent loss of her own position and prestige. But one knows now that the struggle must come. The Russians are piling up a great army with only one intention. They mean to wrest from her keeping certain provinces of Austria, to reduce Germany's one ally to the condition of a vassal state, to establish the Slav people there and throughout the Balkan States, at the expense of the Teuton. Germany must protect her own. It is a struggle, mind you, which concerns them alone. If only there were common sense in the world, every one else would stand by and let Germany and Austria fight with Russia on the one great issue — Slav or Teuton."

" But there's France," little Mrs. Barlow reminded him. " She can't keep out of it. She is Russia's ally."

" Alas! my dear madam," Selingman continued, " you point out the tragedy of the whole situation. If France could see wisdom, if France could see truth, she would fold her arms with you others, keep her country and her youth and her dignity. But I will be reasonable. She is, as you say, bound — bound by her alliance to Russia, and she will fight. Very well! Germany wants no more from France than what she has. Germany will fight a defensive campaign. She will push France back with one hand, in as friendly a manner as is compatible with the ethics of war. On the east she will move swiftly. She will fight Russia, and, believe me, the issue will not be long doubtful. She will conclude an honourable peace with France at the first opportunity."

" Then you don't think we shall be involved at all? " some one else asked.

" If you are," Selingman declared, " it will be your own doing, and it will simply be the most criminal act of this generation. Germany has nothing but friendship for England. I ask you, what British interests are threatened by this inevitable clash between the Slav and the Teuton? It is miserable enough for France to be dragged in. It would be lunacy for England. Therefore, though it is true that serious matters are pending, though, alas! I must return at once to see what help I can afford my country, never for a moment believe, any of you, that there exists the slightest chance of war between Germany and England."

" Then I don't see," Mrs. Barlow sighed, " why we shouldn't have a rubber of bridge."

" Let us," Selingman assented. " It is a very reasonable suggestion. It will divert our thoughts. Here is the afternoon paper. Let us first see whether there is any further news."

It was Mrs. Paston Benedek who opened it. She stared at the first sheet for a moment with eyes which were almost dilated. Then she looked around. Her voice sounded unnatural.

" Look! " she cried. " Francis Norgate — Mr. Francis Norgate has committed suicide in his rooms! "

" It is not possible! " Selingman exclaimed.

They all crowded around the paper. The announcement was contained in a few lines only. Mr. Francis Norgate had been discovered shot through the heart in his sitting-room at the Milan Court, with a revolver by his side. There was a letter addressed to his wife, who had left the day before for Paris. No further particulars could be given of the tragedy. The little group of men and women all looked at one another in a strange, questioning manner. For a moment the war cloud seemed to have passed even from their memories. It was something newer and in a sense more dramatic, this. Norgate — one of themselves! Norgate, who had played bridge with them day after day, had been married only a week or so ago — dead, under the most horrible of all conditions! And Baring, only a few weeks before! There was an uneasiness about which no one could put into words, vague suspicions, strange imaginings.

" It's only three weeks," some one muttered, " since poor Baring shot himself! What the devil does it mean? Norgate — why, the fellow was full of common sense."

" He was fearfully cut up," some one interposed, " about that Berlin affair."

" But he was just married," Mrs. Paston Benedek reminded them, " married to the most charming woman in Europe,— rich, too, and noble. I saw them only two days ago together. They were the picture of happiness. This is too terrible. I am going into the other room to sit down. Please forgive me. Mr. Selingman, will you give me your arm? "

She passed into the little drawing-room, almost dragging her companion. She closed the door behind them. Her eyes were brilliant. The words came hot and quivering from her lips.

"Listen!" she ordered. "Tell me the truth. Was this suicide or not?"

"Why should it not be?" Selingman asked gravely. "Norgate was an Englishman, after all. He must have felt that he had betrayed his country. He has given us, as you know, very valuable information. The thought must have preyed upon his conscience."

"Don't lie to me!" she interrupted. "Tell me the truth now or never come near me again, never ask me another question, don't be surprised to find the whole circle of your friends here broken up and against you. It's only the truth I ask for. If a thing is necessary, do I not know that it must be done? But I will hear the truth. There was that about Baring's death which I never understood; but this — this shall be explained."

Selingman stood for a moment or two with folded arms.

"Dear lady," he said soothingly, "you are not like the others. You have earned the knowledge of the truth. You shall have it. I did not mistrust Francis Norgate, but I knew very well that when the blow fell, he would waver. These Englishmen are all like that. They can lose patience with their ill-governed country. They can go abroad, write angry letters to *The Times*, declare that they have shaken the dust of their native land from their feet. But when the pinch comes, they fall back. Norgate has served me well, but he knew too much. He is safer where he is."

"He was murdered, then!" she whispered.

Selingman nodded very slightly.

" It is seldom," he declared, " that we go so far. Believe me, it is only because our great Empire is making its move, stretching out for the great world war, that I gave the word. What is one man's life when millions are soon to perish? "

She sank down into an easy-chair and covered her face with her hands.

" I am answered," she murmured, " only I know now I was not made for these things. I love scheming, but I am a woman."

CHAPTER XL

Mr. Selingman's influence over his fellows had never been more marked than on that gloomiest of all afternoons. They gathered around him as he sat on the cushioned fender, a cup of tea in one hand and a plateful of buttered toast by his side.

" To-day," he proclaimed, " I bring good news. Yesterday, I must admit, things looked black, and the tragedy to poor young Norgate made us all miserable."

" 1 should have said things looked worse," one of the men declared, throwing down an afternoon paper. " The Cabinet Council is still sitting, and there are all sorts of rumours in the city."

" I was told by a man in the War Office," Mrs. Barlow announced, " that England would stand by her treaty to Belgium, and that Germany has made all her plans to invade France through Belgium."

" Rumours, of course, there must be," Selingman agreed, " but I bring something more than rumour. I received to-day, by special messenger from Berlin, a dispatch of the utmost importance. Germany is determined to show her entire friendliness towards England. She recognises the difficulties of your situation. She is going to make a splendid bid for your neutrality. Much as I would like to, I cannot tell you more. This, however, I know to be the basis of her offer. You in England could help in the fight solely by means of your fleet. It is Germany's suggestion that, in return for your neutrality, she should withdraw her fleet from action and leave the French northern towns unbombarded. You will then be in a position to fulfil your obligations to France, whatever they may be, without moving a stroke or spending a penny. It is a triumph of diplomacy, that — a veritable triumph."

"It does sound all right," Mrs. Barlow admitted.

"It has relieved my mind of a mighty burden," Selingman continued, setting down his empty plate and brushing the crumbs from his waistcoat. "I feel now that we can look on at this world drama with sorrowing eyes, indeed, but free from feelings of hatred and animosity. I have had a trying day. I should like a little bridge. Let us —"

Selingman did not finish his sentence. The whole room, for a moment, seemed to become a study in still life. A woman who had been crossing the floor stood there as though transfixed. A man who was dealing paused with an outstretched card in his hand. Every eye was turned on the threshold. It was Norgate who stood there, Norgate metamorphosed, in khaki uniform — an amazing spectacle! Mrs. Barlow was the first to break the silence with a piercing shriek. Then the whole room seemed to be in a turmoil. Selingman alone sat quite still. There was a grey shade upon his face, and the veins were standing out at the back of his hands.

"So sorry to startle you all," Norgate said apologetically. "Of course, you haven't seen the afternoon papers. It was my valet who was found dead in my rooms — a most mysterious affair," he added, his eyes meeting Selingman's. "The inquest is to be this afternoon."

"Your valet!" Selingman muttered.

"A very useful fellow," Norgate continued, strolling to the fireplace and standing there, "but with a very bad habit of wearing my clothes when I am away. I was down in Camberley for three days and left him in charge."

They showered congratulations upon him, but in the midst of them the strangeness of his appearance provoked their comment.

"What does it mean?" Mrs. Benedek asked, patting his arm. "Have you turned soldier?"

"In a sense I have," Norgate admitted, "but only in the sense that every able-bodied Englishman will have to do, in the course of the next few months. Directly I saw this coming, I arranged for a commission."

"But there is to be no war!" Mrs. Barlow exclaimed. "Mr. Selingman has been explaining to us this afternoon what wonderful offers Germany is making, so that we shall be able to remain neutral and yet keep our pledges."

"Mr. Selingman," Norgate said quietly, "is under a delusion. Germany, it is true, has offered us a shameless bribe. I am glad to be able to tell you all that our Ministry, whatever their politics may be, have shown themselves men. An English ultimatum is now on its way to Berlin. War will be declared before midnight."

Selingman rose slowly to his feet. His face was

black with passion. He pushed a man away who stood between them. He was face to face with Norgate.

"So you," he thundered, suddenly reckless of the bystanders, "are a double traitor! You have taken pay from Germany and deceived her! You knew, after all, that your Government would make war when the time came. Is that so?"

"I was always convinced of it," Norgate replied calmly. "I also had the honour of deceiving you in the matter of Mr. Bullen. I have been the means, owing to your kind and thoughtful information, of having the fleet mobilised and ready to strike at the present moment, and there are various little pieces of property I know about, Mr. Selingman, around London, where we have taken the liberty of blowing up your foundations. There may be a little disappointment for you, too, in the matter of Italy. The money you were good enough to pay me for my doubtful services, has gone towards the establishment of a Red Cross hospital. As for you, Selingman, I denounce you now as one of those who worked in this country for her ill, one of those pests of the world, working always in the background, dishonourably and selfishly, against the country whose hospitality you have abused. If I have met you on your own ground, well, I am proud of it. You are a German spy, Selingman."

Selingman's hand fumbled in his pocket. Scarcely a soul was surprised when Norgate gripped him by the wrist, and they saw the little shining revolver fall down towards the fender.

" You shall suffer for these words," Selingman thundered. " You young fool, you shall bite the dust, you and hundreds of thousands of your cowardly fellows, when the German flag flies from Buckingham Palace."

Norgate held up his hand and turned towards the door. Two men in plain clothes entered.

" That may be a sight," Norgate said calmly, " which you, at any rate, will not be permitted to see. I have had some trouble in arranging for your arrest, as we are not yet under martial law, but I think you will find your way to the Tower of London before long, and I hope it will be with your back to the light and a dozen rifles pointing to your heart."

A third man had come into the room. He tapped Selingman on the shoulder and whispered in his ear.

" I demand to see your warrant!" the latter exclaimed.

The officer produced it. Selingman threw it on the floor and spat upon it. He looked around the room, in the further corner of which two men and a woman were standing upon chairs to look over the heads of the little crowd.

" Take me where you will," he snarled. " You are a rotten, treacherous, cowardly race, you English, and I hate you all. You can kill me first, if you will, but in two months' time you shall learn what it is like to wait hand and foot upon your conquerors."

He strode out of the room, a guard on either side of him and the door closed. One woman had fainted.

Mrs. Paston Benedek was swaying back and forth upon the cushioned fender, sobbing hysterically. Norgate stood by her side.

"I have forgotten the names," he announced pointedly, "of many of that fellow's dupes. I am content to forget them. I am off now," he went on, his tone becoming a little kinder. "I am telling you the truth. It's war. You men had better look up any of the forces that suit you and get to work. We shall all be needed. There is work, too, for the women, any quantity of it. My wife will be leaving again for France next week with the first Red Cross Ambulance Corps. I dare say she will be glad to hear from any one who wants to help."

"I shall be a nurse," Mrs. Paston Benedek decided. "I am sick of bridge and amusing myself."

"The costume is quite becoming," Mrs. Barlow murmured, glancing at herself in the looking-glass, "and I adore those poor dear soldiers."

"Well, I'll leave you to it," Norgate declared. "Good luck to you all!"

They crowded around him, shaking him by the hand, still besieging him with questions about Selingman. He shook his head good-humouredly and made his way towards the door.

"There's nothing more to tell you," he concluded. "Selingman is just one of the most dangerous spies who has ever worked in this country, but the war itself was inevitable. We've known that for years, only we wouldn't believe it. We'll all meet again, perhaps, in the work later on."

Late that night, Norgate stood hand in hand with Anna at the window of their little sitting-room. Down in the Strand, the newsboys were shouting the ominous words. The whole of London was stunned. The great war had come!

"It's wonderful, dear," Anna whispered, "that we should have had these few days of so great happiness. I feel brave and strong now for our task."

Norgate held her closely to him.

"We've been in luck," he said simply. "We were able to do something pretty soon. I have had the greatest happiness in life a man can have. Now I am going to offer my life to my country and pray that it may be spared for you. But above all, whatever happens," he added, leaning a little further from the window towards where the curving lights gleamed across the black waters of the Thames, "above all, whatever may happen to us, we are face to face with one splendid thing — a great country to fight for, and a just cause. I saw Hebblethwaite as I came in. He is a changed man. Talks about raising an immense citizen army in six months. Both his boys have taken up commissions. Hebblethwaite himself is going around the country, recruiting. They are his people, after all. He has given them their prosperity at the expense, alas! of our safety. It's up to them now to prove whether the old spirit is there or not. We shall need two million men. Hebblethwaite believes we shall get them long before the camps are ready to receive them. If we do, it will be his justification."

"And if we don't?" Anna murmured.

Norgate threw his head a little further back.

"Most pictures," he said, "have two sides, but we need only look at one. I am going to believe that we shall get them. I am going to remember the only true thing that fellow Selingman ever said: that our lesson had come before it is too late. I am going to believe that the heart and conscience of the nation is still a live thing. If it is, dear, the end is certain. And I am going to believe that it is!"

THE END